Worthy

Worthy

Catherine Ryan Hyde

LAKE UNION
PUBLISHING

Published by Lake Union Publishing, Seattle

www.apub.com

Amazon, the Amazon logo, and Lake Union Publishing are trademarks of Amazon.com, Inc., or its affiliates.

ISBN-13: 9781477830130
ISBN-10: 1477830138

Cover design by Shasti O'Leary-Soudant / SOS CREATIVE LLC

Library of Congress Control Number: 2014921962

Printed in the United States of America

The Railroad Bridge

Nineteen Years Ago

Chapter One: Buddy

"You ready, Buddy?" his dad asked.

Buddy turned away from the window to see his dad in front of the mirror, straightening his red tie. Buddy didn't think his dad should wear a tie to the diner, because nobody else there wore a tie. But he wasn't sure this was one of those moments when his opinion fit.

"Yes," he said. "Ready."

But he wasn't, really. Because part of what they were about to do was scary.

They walked away from the house together, Dad holding Buddy's hand.

A forest of trees rustled over their heads, and Buddy liked that. He also liked the way their house was so close to the mountains—in the foothills, his dad said—that he had to tip his head back to see their tops. It was the other part, the railroad bridge part, that he didn't like.

Buddy could hear his sneakers and his dad's best suede shoes crunching on the gravel of their path. Their Queensland heeler, Sheila, trotted along behind them, mouth gaping open, panting.

It looked like a toothy smile. The stump of her docked tail wagged continuously as they walked toward the road together.

Sheila loved it when they walked places. Buddy did not.

It was a hot summer afternoon, hot enough that Dad would bring Sheila water once they got to the diner. Virginia the waitress always filled one of those Styrofoam to-go containers with water for Sheila if it was warm outside, and it was. Warmer than Buddy liked, in fact. He liked it when it was just hot enough that you didn't need to wear your sweater, but not so much that it made your shirt collar wet with sweat.

He glanced over his shoulder at his dad's motorcycle, leaning on its kickstand in the driveway. It was red, and fast. Buddy used to love riding on it, squeezed in between Dad's thighs, feeling the wind push his little helmet back on his head. Feeling the vibrations come up through the gas tank where he rested his legs.

It was scary fun, but fun all the same, in what seemed to be exactly the same measure. But it's different when you're scared with your dad wrapped around you. Buddy sought out that scary fun every time.

"Why can't we take the motorcycle?" he asked his dad.

"Buddy . . ."

"What?"

"You're always doing that."

"Doing what?"

"Asking questions I know you know the answer to. You know why I don't take you on the bike now."

"Grampa says not to. He says I'm too little and it's not safe. But Grampa moved away. He and Gramma live in Florida now. How would he even know?"

"Because he knows everybody around here and they know him. I'm not taking any chances. We've been through *that* before, too."

They walked a couple of dozen steps in silence. Buddy looked back at the motorcycle again. Wistfully.

Dad stopped in his tracks, and Buddy didn't notice at first, because his neck was craned back toward home. He walked to the end of Dad's reach, and then his grip on Dad's hand stopped him. He bounced back a step.

Dad said, "Are you actually trying to say, 'I wish we could'?"

"Yes," Buddy said. "That. Then we could go on the road. And then we wouldn't have to go over the railroad bridge."

"Then just say that. Just say, 'I wish we could take the motorcycle, Dad.'"

"I wish we could take the motorcycle, Dad."

"You and me both, kid. Life was a lot easier when we could. But you know how it is when your grampa goes on the warpath. Even from Florida." They walked in silence for a minute or two. And it seemed like a minute or two, which wasn't always true with time. Buddy thought it felt a proper minute or two long. Then Dad said, "We couldn't take Sheila along if we went on the bike."

"She just has to sit outside the door of the diner anyway. She can't come in and eat."

"True. But she likes it."

"She likes sitting outside?"

"Well, I don't know about that. But she likes getting to go. And we always save her something from our plates."

"Yeah," Buddy said. He looked up at his dad towering over him. Past Dad's head he saw thousands of green leaves. They shifted in the breeze, and the sun behind them created a sparkly effect as it appeared and disappeared. Sheila walked alongside him, and he placed his free hand on her back. "Dad?"

"Yeah, Buddy?"

"Why are you wearing a tie?"

"Just to look nice."

"But nobody at the diner wears a tie."

Dad stopped suddenly. Buddy looked up at him, and at the leaves, and the sparkling. And waited for trouble. He thought his dad might lose his temper over too many questions.

"You know," Dad said, "that's a good point. You think the tie is too much?"

"I think so," Buddy said.

He wasn't really sure what "too much" meant in this case, but it sounded like it meant maybe Dad shouldn't wear it. And Buddy definitely thought he shouldn't wear it.

"I think you're right," Dad said. "I'm trying too hard."

He pulled the knot loose on the tie, then pulled until it came off from around his neck and dangled in his hand. He unbuttoned the top two buttons of his good shirt.

Buddy waited, partly impatient to move again, partly happy to not be any closer to the railroad bridge. It would be nice if they never got there, but if they really weren't going to turn around and walk home, which Buddy figured they weren't, it would almost be better to get it over with.

He watched his dad feel around for a shirt or pants pocket that would hold the tie. But from the frown on his dad's face, Buddy figured none of them would.

After a time his dad took the tie over to an evergreen tree and hung it on the stump of a broken-off low branch. He snugged up the Windsor knot, like he was adjusting the tie on the neck of a real person. He had to bend down to reach the branch, and the tie hung down nearly to the ground.

"We'll pick it up on the way back," his dad said.

Buddy thought that was funny. A tree wearing a necktie. Even though none of the other trees did. Trying to stand out, like his dad trying to stand out at the diner so Virginia would notice him. When it was pretty obvious she already did.

They walked again in silence for a time.

Then Buddy looked up and saw the railroad bridge, and stopped.

He had been wrong about the minutes. They were not proper minutes. They had compressed themselves somehow. Squeezed down. And now Buddy and his dad and Sheila were close enough to see the railroad bridge.

"Can we go the long way?" Buddy asked.

"We tried that last time. And you got tired, and I had to carry you half the way there and all the way home. You're a big boy these days, Buddy. It's not so easy to carry you like when you were a baby. You're not even a toddler anymore. You're heavy. But I'll carry you on my shoulders over the railroad bridge if you want."

"No," Buddy said. "That's okay."

They walked again.

They'd tried that once, and it had only made things worse. Because not only had the river been far, far below the railroad ties, but the railroad ties had been far, far below Buddy. He felt better with the solid bridge under his feet.

All he had to do was not look down. And yet he always looked down. Every time. The more he told himself not to look down, the more he looked. It was a key example of life running frustratingly out of his control. Even Buddy seemed to be outside Buddy's sphere of influence.

And now they were much closer to the bridge. Almost ready to step out.

Dad stopped and put his ear down to the track. That way, he always said, he would know if there was a train coming. He said you could hear—and also sort of feel—a buzzing in the rails even if the train was much too far away to see.

Then they had to hurry.

It was Buddy's least favorite part of anything they did together. It was worse than being left at day care. It was worse than when they got to the diner and Dad started paying attention to Virginia and forgot to pay attention to him. It might even have been worse than going to the dentist to get his teeth checked, although Buddy allowed for the possibility that it might have been a tie in that case.

The bridge wasn't very long, but it seemed long, because Buddy's fear played a trick with the minutes. Dad said it took only a minute or two to walk over it, but that minute or two was as long as minutes ever got.

The bridge had a truss. Or at least that's what Dad called it. A tall structure of silvery steel beams that curved up into an open framework over their heads. Buddy thought that made it look like it was more important for the bridge to be strong up there in the air. That made no sense to Buddy, who thought all the steel should be under their feet so the bridge could never break. Every twenty feet or so there was a beam going up to that truss, but in between beams there was nothing to stop you from falling. But Dad said, "If you don't walk too close to the edge, you won't fall." Still, if you ever did . . .

The railroad ties had spaces in between, so if you looked down you saw the river as much as you saw the wood and steel, which Buddy found terrifying. It looked as if you'd walked right off a cliff and there was nothing holding you up at all. But if you walked to one side or the other of the rails, the steel structure was solid underneath the ties. Still, there was no special safe spot for people to walk, because people were never intended to walk there. The bridge was no wider than the train that might come if you didn't listen, or didn't hurry.

They always walked beside the rails, not right in the middle. Otherwise Buddy would freeze up and not move at all. Dad always walked on the outside, near the edge. He called Buddy's side "the safe side." He'd always say, "You be on the safe side, Buddy." He must have just enjoyed saying it, because Buddy was always on the inside already.

Buddy could feel beads of sweat break out on his forehead as they stepped out onto the bridge. He could feel the hair that fell forward onto his face sticking to his skin because of sweat.

"Can I close my eyes?" he asked, holding Dad's hand tightly with both of his own smaller ones.

"Try it. See if it helps."

Buddy squeezed his eyes closed. The first step or two was okay, but then he imagined a big, gaping hole in the bridge in front of his feet, making him think his next step would be into nothing. Into thin air.

He gasped, feeling a jolt to his body as if he really were falling. His eyes flew open. As soon as they did, he saw the river. Saw it over the edge of the bridge on one side of them and through the rails on the other.

He stopped dead, frozen.

The tracks began to buzz lightly.

Buddy's dad picked him up. Just hoisted Buddy to his waist and carried him under one arm, sideways, his top half drooping. Dad jogged a big handful of steps. Forward, not back the way they had come. Half-upside-down, Buddy saw Sheila loping ahead at a crazy and dizzying angle.

Then they were on solid ground again.

Dad jogged about ten steps away from the tracks before he set Buddy down. The train still had not come.

"See, Buddy? See what I always tell you? Even if we can feel a train coming while we're on the bridge, we still have tons of time to get off before it comes. Wait till you see how long it is before that train actually gets here."

They waited, Buddy's arms wrapped around one of his dad's thighs. What seemed like a minute passed, but he still couldn't hear a train. Just birdsongs, and Sheila panting behind him.

"Maybe something else made the train tracks buzz," Buddy said, craning his neck to see his dad's face.

"Just wait."

A train whistle sounded, but way off in the distance.

"See how much time we have?" Dad asked.

It sounded like clattering now. Like the tracks clattered instead of buzzed. The clattering got louder and louder. Then the whistle blew again and it was so close it made Buddy jump.

His dad laughed. "And we still can't see the train yet. See? I told you it's safer than you think."

Buddy wanted to say something, but the train was so loud now he knew he wouldn't be heard. Besides, he really didn't know what to say. He wanted to explain that a scared part of him was still scared. That no matter how many times Dad explained that Buddy was safe, the scared part of him never heard, or never believed. But he had no idea how to frame such a thought with words.

The train came into view from behind a stand of trees, and Buddy let go of his dad's leg to press the heels of both hands over his ears.

When the last train car had crossed the bridge and disappeared around a bend, Buddy let his hands fall again.

"See, Buddy?" Dad said. "I wouldn't steer you wrong. Now come on. Let's go see Virginia."

Chapter Two: Virginia

When Virginia stepped out of her car at the diner, ready to start her shift, she saw it. It was pretty damned hard to miss.

Right outside the diner's front porch a thick post had been driven into the hard, dry soil. On it hung a sign printed in the bright red, white, and blue logo of Wagner's Realty.

"For Sale," the sign said.

"Shit," Virginia muttered under her breath.

She teetered there for a moment, trying to decide whether to send her imagination down the road to all the aspects of her life that were about to change. Then she shook her head, deciding against it. For the moment, at least. She had a Saturday lunch rush to worry about.

She jingled her way through the front door.

Fern, that day's second lunch waitress, looked up from behind the counter. Looked right into Virginia's eyes and then looked away. Fern had been on shift since before breakfast, and she already looked sweaty, harried, and in need of a cigarette break.

Virginia walked around behind the counter and took down a starched white apron. She kept looking at Fern, hoping for some sort of comment. Some sort of commiseration. Fern continued to avoid her eyes.

Virginia could hear Dave, the owner, rattling around in the walk-in freezer off the kitchen.

She moved closer to Fern, to avoid being overheard.

"Well?"

"Well what?" Fern asked, still not looking up.

"Well what do you think? Did you not see it?"

"I saw it. Couldn't very well miss it."

"And you got nothing to say?"

"This day sucks. Is that as good a thing as any?"

"Suppose so," Virginia said.

Then she sighed, and started in on her side work. She filled salt and pepper shakers, ketchup and mustard squeeze bottles. Washed and filled syrup pourers. They might be used again soon, because the diner served breakfast all day.

Washing the stickiness off her hands at the big double kitchen sink, she thought about Aaron. Wondered if he would come in that day.

At first it was a pleasant thought. If he did, and she saw him, things would be better.

Then it struck her: if she lost this job, he would have no way to casually stop in and visit her. Unless she could find an opening at the general store, or the pharmacy. But there would be four out-of-work waitresses all vying for that same opening. If there even was an opening.

Then she remembered the two cooks and the dishwasher.

Maybe she would have to leave town to find work.

It struck her hard in the gut, a sort of sickening depression mixed together with muted panic. If he didn't ask her out soon . . .

Fern appeared at the sink to wash off the base of a ketchup squeeze bottle. It apparently had been set down in the leftovers of somebody's fried eggs.

"Just when I find a job I can really live with," Virginia said. Quietly, so Dave would not overhear.

She couldn't hear Dave anymore and didn't know where he was, but she could hear his two kids playing in the dirt lot behind the diner. She could recognize their aggressive gun noises. Making their voices into automatic weapons to mow each other down.

"Yeah, and don't think we'll find anything else in a town this small. Not all of us, anyway. Somebody's going to end up moving away."

Virginia thought of Aaron again, and she felt a tightness threaten to close up her throat. "Maybe somebody'll buy it and keep it as a diner."

"Or turn it into a hardware store or a convenience market."

"Well. They'll still need people to work, won't they?"

"I suppose," Fern said. But she didn't sound optimistic. Then again, when did Fern ever sound optimistic?

———

When the lunch rush was good and over, and Fern had gone home, Virginia stepped out back to have a smoke behind the Dumpster.

She drew almost aggressively on the cigarette, watching the burning tip turn long and glowing. She had switched to a lower-tar brand, because it was supposed to be slightly better for her lungs. But try as she might, she could never seem to get all she needed from one.

The real plan had been to quit, not switch brands. But she was postponing the inevitable. And today's news didn't make her feel any more likely to choose this as quitting day.

A sound like a gunshot made Virginia jump. Literally jump. She dropped her cigarette and accidentally stepped on the filter as she spun around to see. It sounded for all the world as though someone had taken a shot at her, and she was halfway inclined to feel all around her torso to be sure she hadn't been hit.

Behind her she saw Patty and Jimmie, Dave's two difficult kids, laughing. They'd set off a firecracker, she now realized, one that did nothing but make a single big bang. She put a hand to her chest, calming her heart. They continued to laugh and lit the fuse on another bit of pyrotechnical madness, using a bright yellow disposable lighter.

Who gives a disposable lighter to a ten- and twelve-year-old? Virginia wondered. Or maybe they just stole what they wanted.

The new firecracker didn't go bang. Instead it let off a fountain of white fire and crackling sounds against the late-afternoon sky.

"You kids better get away from here with those. I'm telling your daddy."

"He went home," Patty said.

"Why didn't he take you?"

"We can walk," Jimmie added.

"Well, then walk. Walk away from here with that crap before you scare somebody to death. And another thing. You see all these dry weeds around here? It's summer, as if you need me to tell you that. As if you don't have brains in your heads. It hasn't rained or snowed in months, and this is not the time you come out here and set off fireworks. You send one in just the wrong direction, you could burn the diner down. Hell, you could burn the whole town down. And don't think I won't tell the police who started the fire."

Finally, on that last note, the little brats stopped grinning.

"You won't tell," Patty said.

"Hell I won't!"

"My daddy would fire you if you got us in trouble."

"Well, just in case you're as blind as you are careless, Patty, let me tell you a thing or two. Your daddy just put the place up for sale. He as good as fired me the minute that real estate agent's signpost got pounded into the ground. I just don't know yet when my last day is. But it'll come soon enough. And now I've got nothing to lose. So I'm telling you again. You go take those illegal fireworks home, or at least off somewhere where there's nothing to set on fire and nobody to scare to death. And if I hear them again, I'm calling your daddy. I have his home number for emergencies. And I'm telling him what you're up to."

The two kids looked at each other, then down at the ground. Then they shuffled away, kicking at the dry weeds.

Virginia watched them until they were out of sight. She lit another cigarette, hoping it would calm her nerves.

Aaron hadn't come in for lunch. It was high time to process her disappointment over that. Then again, there was still dinner. He had one more chance for the day.

———

When Virginia got back inside, Ruth, one of the three other waitresses, had shown up for the dinner shift.

"Well, isn't *this* just something?" Ruth asked Virginia without ever meeting her eyes. "Where's Dave? I'm halfway tempted to give him a piece of my mind. I'm serious. Let me at him."

"He went home. Anyway, what good would that do?"

"I don't know. But if he hadn't gone home, the coward, I'd do it anyway. We can mouth off to him now. What have we got to lose? The thing that burns me is that he didn't even tell us before he listed it for sale. He let the sign do his dirty work for him. The little weasel."

Virginia tossed her gaze over her shoulder toward the kitchen, warning Ruth without words that the dinner cook and the dishwasher could hear her.

"Well, what the hell do I care, Ginnie? It's over now anyway. Hey, Roddy! Hey, Miguel! You hear what I just said? Dave Kingsbury is a rotten, cowardly little weasel!"

A light, wheezy laugh from the kitchen, but no words.

Then Ruth sidled closer to Virginia. As though there were some words that really should not be overheard. "So. Aaron come in for lunch?"

"No," Virginia said, cutting her gaze away. She grabbed up a rag and began to wipe an already-clean counter.

"Think he'll come in for dinner?"

"Now how would I know that?" Virginia thought she could feel her own face flushing. "Why're you asking me about Aaron, anyway?"

"Oh, come on, Ginnie. You think we're all stupid? We see the way you two look at each other. Why he didn't ask you out months ago, I'll never know. You're blushing, Ginnie. You know that, right?"

Virginia turned her back to Ruth and looked out the window. In the distance she saw two figures. A man and a boy. Her heart jumped, then pounded. They were much too far away to know for sure. But the boy was barely waist-high to the man. So her chances were good.

"He's a widower," she said, her heart still pounding. Her eyes still fixed on the distant figures. "He hasn't been seeing anybody since his wife died. These things take time, you know."

Then Virginia saw the distant silhouette of the dog loping up from behind them, and she knew. Her heart hammered harder, and she felt dizzy, as if she might pass out on the spot.

"His wife died two and a half years ago, Ginnie." Ruth's voice came to her as if from far away, filtering through more important thoughts and feelings. "I don't know how long you think it's supposed to take."

"It just takes some people longer than others is all."

"And how do you know he hasn't seen anybody since?"

"Well. You know. It's a small town. You hear things."

She wished Ruth would stop talking to her. So she could just watch them approach.

"You mean you asked around."

"Would you get off my case about this, Ruth? So what if I like him? Would that be such a bad thing?"

"Oh, I think you passed *like* a very long time ago, Ginnie. And also I think if he hasn't asked you out by now, there's something holding him back. I think if he was gonna do, it he would have done it months ago."

If she hadn't been watching Aaron and Buddy and Sheila out the window, Virginia definitely would have told Ruth to shut her mouth. Maybe even never to speak to her on the subject again. But the three figures walking in her direction were more important than Ruth.

They were more important than anything.

She was vaguely aware of hearing Ruth sigh and then walk away, but Virginia never looked around. She just took a step closer to the window. Put her fingers on the glass. Even though she was the one who would have to wipe off the prints later. She knew that, but did it anyway.

Then Aaron looked up, looked toward the diner. And he must have seen her in the window, because he stopped in his tracks.

Her heart jumped again. You have to like someone a lot to stop in your tracks when you see them.

He raised his hand to wave to her. She raised her hand to wave back.

"You are so hopeless when you're in love," Ruth said from somewhere in the vicinity of table three.

"Oh, shut up, Ruth," she said, without ever turning around.

Chapter Three: Buddy

_____

"Wait right here," Dad said.

They had been walking across a field behind some houses, and Dad had stopped suddenly. It took Buddy a minute to notice.

"Where are you going?"

"Not far. I'm just going to go over and pick some of those miniature roses."

"What roses? I don't see them."

"Over there." His dad pointed. "On that vine."

"But the vine is on somebody's fence. Doesn't that mean the roses belong to them?"

"The vine started on their fence, but now it's growing out into the bushes in that field. So they don't own the ones that are off their property."

"Oh," Buddy said, still wishing his dad wouldn't go.

"I'll be right where you can see me," Dad said.

Then he left Buddy standing in the dirt with Sheila and walked away. Buddy put one hand on the dog's back and watched him for a long time. Watched him look at a lot of tiny roses on a lot of different bushes, but not pick any.

When he looked around, those two kids were there. It made his belly cold to see them. He didn't know their names, but they were bigger than Buddy. Much bigger. They hung around the diner most days. A boy and a girl. And they teased him. Mostly about his name, but really about anything. They teased him because they didn't like his shorts, or because his hair was too neatly combed. They just looked at him and used whatever they could find.

They walked right up to him. Closer than he wished anybody— at least, anybody who wasn't his dad—ever would.

Buddy looked away because he didn't like the smiles on their faces. They weren't good smiles. Not the kind that meant they were happy and you could be, too. These were the kind of smiles people smile when they're about to pick on you.

"*Jo*-dee," the girl said, in a mean voice. She almost sang it, like a song. But somehow it was clear that it was hurled as an insult, even though it was really just his own first name.

Buddy continued to look away. Down at the dirt. In his peripheral vision, he could see that their pockets were strangely stuffed and lumpy, but he didn't want to look directly. He just wanted his dad to be back.

"Don't you talk, *Jo*-dee?" the boy asked.

Then he stepped in quickly, his hand reaching for Buddy's shoulder to give him a shove. The boy was fast, but Sheila was faster. She appeared quickly between the mean boy and Buddy's shoulder, facing the boy. Then she lowered her head and growled, deep in her throat. It was not a big, loud growl. But it was not a growl you would ignore, either.

The boy stepped back and dropped his hand, his face whitening.

Buddy felt his dad's big hand on his shoulder. The two kids looked up. Over Buddy's head. Their faces whitened further.

"Sorry, Mr. Albanese," the girl said.

"Yeah. Sorry," the boy added.

They ran a wide circle around Buddy and his dad and Sheila, and they kept running.

Buddy looked up into his dad's face.

"What was that about, Buddy?" his dad asked.

"Nothing," Buddy said.

"But they were picking on you, right?"

"They always do."

Dad sighed. They began to walk again.

Buddy looked at both of his dad's hands. They were empty.

"You didn't pick any roses."

"No. They didn't look too good. They were past their prime."

"I don't know what that means."

"It's summer. And they bloom in the spring. So now they're old. Not pretty enough to give to Virginia."

"Oh," Buddy said. It made his stomach a little sad to know they would have been for Virginia if they'd been pretty. But he wasn't sure exactly why.

They walked a few moments in silence.

Then Buddy said, "Jody's not a girl's name, is it?"

Dad sighed. "We've talked about this a lot, Buddy Boy."

"It's not," Buddy said. It was not a question. It was a recitation of the answer he always got.

"No."

"It's both. It can be for girls or boys."

"Right."

"Why didn't Mom give me a name that's only for boys?"

"You know that, too. It's because it was her grandfather's name. So you know it's a boy's name. Because a grandfather is a boy."

"Oh," Buddy said.

"Did those kids say it was a girl's name?"

"No. Not exactly. They just say it like they think it is. Like it's not a good name to have. Is that why everybody calls me Buddy? Because Jody's not a good name to have?"

But his dad never answered. He had stopped in his tracks again. And he was looking at the diner. There was someone in the window, a lady in a waitress uniform. Buddy figured it must be Virginia, even though she was too far away to know for sure. She had one hand raised, waving at them. Well . . . waving at Dad.

Jody looked up to see his dad waving back.

"Dad?" he asked.

But it was too late. He would not have his dad's full attention until they'd left the diner again. Until the walk home.

———

"Oh, no," his dad said.

It made Buddy's heart do a little flip. Because even though Dad had a lot of moods and made a lot of comments, Buddy didn't often hear him sound so sad and disappointed.

They stood, hand in hand, in the dirt parking lot in front of the diner.

"What?" Buddy asked, when the possibility of hearing what was so bad began to hurt less than not knowing.

"They're selling the place."

"Oh," Buddy said, hoping he didn't sound too eager. But he had been worried it was something terrible, and this didn't sound even a little bit bad. In fact, it sounded fine.

Virginia stepped out onto the porch in her white waitress uniform and white apron. She looked at Buddy's dad and Buddy's dad looked at her. They did that a lot. But this time it was different.

"I know," she said, without making it even slightly clear—at least to Buddy—what she knew.

"How long have you known?" Dad asked.

"I found out the same way you did, Aaron. I came in to work today and saw the sign."

"Well, that bites."

"Tell me about it."

She held the door open, and Buddy and his dad walked inside. Sheila had to wait on the porch. But Virginia gave her a pat between the ears, and Sheila smiled that way she did. And she seemed content enough just to settle.

"We're not quite ready to serve dinner yet," Virginia said, letting the door drift closed.

"Good," Buddy's dad said. "You can come sit down and talk to me. Unless you have work to do."

"I do," she said, and Buddy could tell how badly she wished she could say she didn't. "But . . . I'm almost done anyway. Two minutes. Grab a table and give me two minutes and then I'll be there."

Dad walked around a couple of tables until he found the one that gave them the best view of Virginia working in the kitchen. Even though she would be there in two minutes anyway.

"That's such a shame," his dad said, more or less to no one. He sat down.

"What's a shame?" Buddy asked, sitting next to him. He really needed a booster seat, but he wouldn't ask for one, because he had decided they were for babies and he had grown beyond them.

"That they're selling the diner."

"Why is it a shame?"

"Because poor Virginia has to find a new job. And now we won't be able to come eat here. And visit her. And we like that. Right?"

"I don't know," Buddy said. "I guess."

Then she was back, and it hadn't even been two minutes.

"Sorry," she said. She was acting in that silly way grown-ups sometimes did, seeming embarrassed and shy when there was no reason to be acting weird at all.

"No," his dad said. "Don't be." And he was acting the same way.

"You should just buy it," Buddy said.

His dad paid no attention at all. It was Virginia who looked at him and noticed he had spoken. It just took a weird amount of time. Like she was listening too slowly.

"Were you talking to me?" she asked Buddy.

It made his face feel a little hot, the way she stared at him and smiled.

"Yes," he said.

"What should I buy?"

"The diner." She laughed, and so did Dad. It made Buddy feel a little bruised inside. "Why's that funny? Then you could still work here. Because if you own it, then you can work here as long as you say you can."

"A business costs a lot of money, Buddy," his dad said. "It's not like a soda or a pack of gum. I doubt Virginia has tens of thousands of dollars in her pocket."

"You got that right," she said.

Buddy wrinkled up his forehead, like a frown, but higher up. "You bought the motorcycle shop," he said to his dad. "And you didn't have all that in your pocket."

"Well, yeah." Dad seemed impatient, as if he wanted to talk about something else. Buddy had gotten his dad's attention, but his dad seemed to want it back again. "But that was different. I had to go to the Small Business Administration. Apply for a loan."

"Couldn't she . . . do that thing? What you just said?"

But just then the other waitress, whose name Buddy didn't know, stuck her head out of the kitchen. "Ginnie—" she said. She stopped dead when she saw the three of them sitting together talking. "Oops," she said. "Never mind. Didn't mean to interrupt anything important."

Her head disappeared again. And Virginia's face got red. And Buddy lost the attention battle again.

"Everybody calls you Ginnie but me," Dad said.

"I know," she said, still blushing.

"What do you like to be called?"

"Virginia."

"Then why doesn't anybody call you that?"

"Damn good question," she said. "I always introduce myself as Virginia, but then they'll hear someone else call me Ginnie. It's contagious. Like the flu or something. People act like Ginnie is just so much easier. But really . . . it's one more syllable. I mean, how much time is that really going to take out of their day?"

"Can I have a cheeseburger for dinner?" Buddy asked.

But no one was listening.

Chapter Four: Virginia

Aaron hung around all the way through the dinner hour, which was wonderful. But it caused Virginia to miss all the usual cigarette breaks she might have caught on the fly.

Now she and Ruth were cleaning up after the last customer, and Aaron and Buddy were still there.

It made her almost dizzily happy. But she needed that smoke break.

Finally she just tied up a bag of garbage, stuck her head out of the kitchen to signal Aaron that she'd be right back, and ducked through the kitchen door to the Dumpster.

She leaned on the cool metal of its side and lit a cigarette. She sighed deeply as she drew the smoke down into her lungs. Even though her lungs still missed all that extra tar.

She looked off in the direction of the railroad bridge. She could just barely see it off in the distance. The sun had begun to set behind its steel frame. It got dusky fast up here in the foothills, because the sun went down behind the mountains far sooner than it would disappear beneath a flat horizon.

She worried about Aaron and Buddy and their good dog walking home in the dark. But she knew she wouldn't say anything about it. Because she didn't want them to leave.

She thought again about Dave's little brats and their fireworks. Well, maybe not *thought* exactly. It was more as if her very cells remembered being startled in this same location earlier, and warned her to look out for more. She looked all around herself, just to be sure she was safe this time. Three hundred and sixty degrees.

As her eyes came around to the back of the diner, she saw Aaron. He was walking around the outside of the building to join her.

She quickly dropped her cigarette and stepped on it, leaving her foot in place to cover the mildly shameful secret.

He raised one hand in a wave and headed straight for her.

Her heart hammered again, because she knew this was it. This was that rare chance for a private talk, and he had sought it out. Either he'd ask her out, or she'd know, right there and then, that Ruth was right. That something was holding him back.

"Where's Buddy?" she called out as soon as he was close enough to hear.

Aaron walked a few more steps. "I gave the cook five bucks to sit with him on the front porch. They're feeding Sheila the last of Buddy's cheeseburger."

Virginia's heart pounded harder. This was it, all right.

"I don't think I've ever seen you without Buddy."

He walked right up to her, until they were face-to-face. He wasn't a very big man, and they were almost the same height. His eye level was a perfect match for hers. And his eyes were huge and dark, like someplace you could get lost forever and not even mind. Though she wanted to focus on happier thoughts, Virginia wondered if he could smell the tobacco smoke on her breath from where he stood.

"I didn't know you smoked," he said. "But it's okay," he added quickly.

"It's not, though. It's not okay at all. I'm just about to quit. I swear I am. I know everybody says that, but I really mean it. I already switched to one of those low-tar brands that are hardly like smoking at all."

"That's a good way to go about it."

"It is?"

"Sure. Isn't that why you did it? To sort of taper off?"

"Oh. Yeah. I guess. Actually, I was going to just flat-out quit, but at the last minute I turned chicken." Then she cursed herself, silently. Wished she could grab that last sentence back.

"It's hard to quit," he said. He was still very close. Closer than he had ever been to her before. "Believe me, I know. But it's okay. You don't have to be ashamed of it. Not around me, anyway."

"It's just disgusting, though," she said, knowing as she said it that shutting up would have been better. But the knowledge of it embarrassed her, so rather than shutting up a sentence too late, she doubled down on the error. "I mean, it makes your clothes smell bad and everything. And people can smell it in your hair. And on your breath. I mean, who wants to get close to someone whose breath smells like a cigarette?"

Aaron took a step closer. Then his face moved alarmingly in the direction of hers.

It brought an instinctive reaction, but not the one she expected. It was a reaction much the opposite of what her heart had always wanted. In other words, she almost flinched away. Because she was embarrassed about her breath. Thank God she was too frozen to actually move.

"*I* would," he said.

His lips touched hers. Lightly at first. Almost tentatively.

Because he was not a big brute of a man like Virginia's ex, his lips felt light and almost soft. Like they could play a game or do a dance with her own lips, rather than knowing only how to crush them into submission.

Then she relaxed a little, and his kiss grew more intense. His lips never parted. It wasn't that kind of kiss. He just made his point more earnestly.

"Oops," somebody said.

But it could not possibly have been either one of them. That's all Virginia knew for sure. She looked up to see Ruth hurrying back into the diner through the kitchen door.

It broke the moment, though. And the kiss never resumed. On the one hand, Virginia regretted that. On the other hand, ignoble a thought as she knew it was, she was happy to have had a witness.

That should shut Ruth up but good.

They just stood and looked at each other, their eyes only inches apart. Virginia felt pleasantly numb, as if she hadn't quite registered what had just happened to her.

Aaron spoke first. "So . . . I'd have to find a babysitter, but . . . if I can, maybe we could go out. To . . . I don't know. Something. Anything. I don't care what, just . . . out. Dinner and a movie?"

"Or if you can't get a babysitter, that's okay." Virginia's head felt cottony and spinny, but she was pretty sure that's what she'd said.

He laughed, but just a little. "How could that be okay? Buddy's quite a heavy third wheel. You know. On a date, I mean."

"But if you can't find someone to watch him, we could all go on a picnic or something."

His eyes softened. She could see that in the dusky light. She'd said the right thing.

"So give me your number," he said. "I'll call you."

She took the order pad out of her apron pocket. Tore off a sheet. Wrote her home phone number on the back. Her hands shook slightly. At first she hoped he wouldn't notice. Then she wondered why she would want to hide the truth: that this meant a lot to her.

"Maybe next weekend," he said. "Or do you always work the dinner shift on weekends?"

"I'll trade with Fern."

"Okay. We'll work it out."

He smiled at her. With his eyes as well as his mouth. She looked into those eyes and saw all of him. The fear. The joy. The absolute skinless lack of emotional armor.

God help me, she thought. *I'm already head over heels in love. And we haven't even been on our first date.*

She thought of what Ruth had said earlier. That Virginia had passed *like* a long time ago. Virginia briefly wished she could be a woman with a poker face—that she didn't have to wear her secrets for everyone to see. But what's the point of wishing you're someone else entirely, when you know you never can or will be?

He turned and began to walk away, looking over his shoulder once to smile at her. She thought the smile looked a little sad. Along with every other way it looked. Then he turned away again.

"Aaron," she said.

He stopped. Turned back. Waited.

But Virginia had no idea what to say.

She knew what she *wanted* to say. But she also knew better than to say it. If she could have spoken purely unfiltered words, she would have said, "I can be trusted to be a mother to that little boy. I'll learn to love him. I won't be one of those ridiculous stepparents who are jealous of their mate's child. I wouldn't stoop to that. I can raise him, and you won't be sorry you gave me a chance to try."

But what kind of thing is that to say to a guy who just finally asked for your phone number for the first time?

"What is it?" he asked, when she had kept him waiting too long.

"I like Buddy," she said.

He was too far away for Virginia to see well, so she never knew if his eyes changed. Softened, or whatever. She tried to imagine that they did.

"He's been having a hard time since his mom died. You know. He's kind of clingy. And spooky. Seems like everything scares him. Or maybe he was always that way. It's hard to know, because he was only nineteen months. Barely toddling. Hard to know what he would have been if his mom hadn't gotten cancer. But anyway, I'm glad you like him."

"I don't think he likes me, though."

"He'll come around. Give him time. He doesn't really know you yet. When he gets to know you, he'll like you as much as I do. You'll see."

And with that he was gone.

Chapter Five: Buddy

————

"I think it's too dark," Buddy said.

"We have time to get home before it's pitch dark."

"But the bridge . . ."

"We're almost there. It'll be fine, Buddy Boy."

But it didn't seem fine. Buddy tried on a lot of different ways to say so. Well, that's not quite accurate. He tried to find a way to say it—any way, any words—and from a lot of different angles. But he never found a single word, or set of words, to fit the moment.

So he just stopped in his tracks.

He could see it off in the distance, the steel beams of its truss looking black against the faded orangey sky. They weren't black, those beams. They were silver, like most steel. But it was getting close to dark, and they looked black and hulking in silhouette.

"Better if we go fast, Buddy."

"I don't want to."

"We have to get home. We don't have any other choice."

"We shouldn't have stayed so long."

"Water under the bridge, Buddy Boy."

Buddy wondered why his father would bring up anything as scary as the river flowing under the railroad bridge. Especially at a time like this.

"Maybe the lady'll give us a ride home," Buddy said.

"Oh. Yeah. Now I wish I'd asked her. But anyway, I didn't. It's a long walk back there, Buddy. And she might've gone home already. Come on. We'll just go fast. It'll be fine."

He tugged on Buddy's hand, and they moved forward. But Buddy was not so much walking voluntarily as allowing himself to be towed.

Time got tricky again, and then the next thing Buddy knew they stepped out onto the darkened bridge.

He held tightly to his dad's hand.

It wasn't bad. Not even as bad as usual. Because Buddy could barely see the water below. When he looked down—which he still couldn't stop himself from doing—everything beneath him looked mostly dark.

"Are you going to get married to her?" Buddy asked his dad.

He spoke to ease his nerves. Because talking about something else distracted him from what they were doing. But then he immediately wished he'd found something different to distract himself. Because talking about *that* situation gave him the same funny feeling as walking over the railroad bridge.

"That's a weird question, Buddy Boy."

"Why is it weird?"

"Because people usually know each other a lot better before they get married."

"Why?"

"So they have a better idea whether it'll work out."

"How do you know if it'll work out?"

"Well . . . you don't."

"Then why do people wait?"

"Holy crap, Buddy. You ask the hardest questions."

"I'm sorry."

Dad sighed. "You never really know for sure if marrying some-body will work out. But sometimes, while you're getting to know them, stuff happens that makes you pretty sure it won't. Work out, I mean. And then you know not to get married. But if nothing goes wrong, and you decide to get married, you still don't know for sure that it'll work out."

"I don't understand that," Buddy said.

"Nobody really does," his dad said in reply.

They walked in silence for about ten steps.

Buddy wanted to talk more about the getting married thing. But they never did. Because a big noise and a flash of light filled up his world, and then Buddy's hand somehow came free of his dad's hand and he landed on his chest on the ends of two wooden railroad ties, bruising his ribs badly. His heart pounded so hard Buddy felt like it might break right out of his rib cage, and then he would be dead.

The bridge in front of him was lit up like daylight—an intense white light, a white fire, with huge sounds. The bridge—the whole world, maybe—had gone crazy with white fire and explosive noise.

Shocked into absolute stillness, Buddy watched the trails and arrows of white fire shoot in every direction, tailing out and falling onto the rails, or through the rails toward the river below.

An occasional hiss as fire touched water.

Then it was dark again. And quiet.

Buddy thought he heard footsteps ahead of him on the bridge. More than one person's worth of footsteps, running away.

He heard Sheila barking wildly.

He looked around for his dad. His dad was nowhere. He was not on the bridge at all. Not in any direction.

"Dad!" Buddy screamed, and pulled himself to his knees. His ribs hurt when he moved, but he had to. "Dad!"

He expected his dad to come walking onto the bridge, out of the darkness, from one direction or the other. He never did. The only sound was Sheila's wild barking.

Buddy rose unsteadily to his feet, thinking he would fall, or maybe even faint. He was alone on the bridge except for Sheila. She was crouched at the very edge of the bridge structure, front end down, the backs of her front legs pressed to the steel, paws dangling over the edge, rear end and stump tail in the air. Barking. And barking. And barking.

Buddy walked closer, to be able to see her better in the dim light.

Before he could reach her, she pushed off. Hard. And fast.

"Sheila!" Buddy screamed. "No!"

It was too late. She stretched out in midair, her body arcing away from the bridge, her movement all sideways and not down. At least, for a long, tricky second.

Then she fell, disappearing into darkness.

Buddy heard the splash when she hit the water.

He ran to the spot where he'd last seen her. Got down on his belly and hung his head over the bridge, which was dizzying, and terrifying. His eyes were adjusting to the lack of light again, but the crazy white fire seemed to have burned his eyes, creating streaks and spots in his vision that wouldn't go away.

Then he saw her head break the surface of the river.

He hadn't bothered to notice it before, but the moon was up. It cast one wavering strip of light on the otherwise dark water. It was within that strip that Sheila appeared. She swam in a crazy arc, barking. Buddy could see the way she paddled forward while the pull of the river carried her sideways and almost backward.

In a few paddles she swam out of the moonlit strip and was swallowed by the darkness again. But Buddy could still hear her frenzied barking.

"Dad!" he screamed again.

Nothing.

A deep chill ran down Buddy, along his spine, through his gut, at the base of his neck. He felt tears streaming down his cheeks. They had probably been streaming for a long time without his feeling them. He was alone.

And the tracks were buzzing.

They hadn't just started to buzz, either. Buddy knew that. They were buzzing too hard for that. They were buzzing just at the edge of clattering.

But he didn't want to run off the bridge without his dad. He didn't want to do anything without his dad. Not even stand up.

Buddy squeezed his eyes shut, hard, harder than he ever had before, and wished to be transported. He willed himself to be lifted straight up and taken away from here. He could still hear Sheila's frantic barking.

He opened his eyes and saw the edge of the bridge under his chin. His wish had been denied.

The tracks were rattling hard now, as if the train were almost upon him. It hurt his ribs, the way they jostled him up and down.

"Dad!" he screamed again.

Feeling numb, as if he weren't inside his body at all, Buddy scrambled to his feet. The train whistle jolted him, made him jump a mile. He looked back in the direction they had come, and he saw the light on the front of the train.

And the light must have seen him, too. Because the whistle sounded again, and this time it didn't stop. It was so loud that he couldn't tell if Sheila was still barking. It was so loud that he couldn't think, almost couldn't live.

Buddy pressed both hands over his ears and ran. He ran in the direction of the sudden burst of fire that had caused all this. Which was like running toward the end of the world. What would happen when he reached that spot? What would the demon do with him once it got hold of him? But he did it because he had to do it. Because he was being chased by a train. And the train was winning.

His foot wedged beneath a railroad tie, and he hit the end of that tether with force. It stopped him cold, but not before painfully wrenching his foot and stretching the muscles and tendons in that seized leg.

Buddy cried out in pain.

The world had suddenly morphed into a monster. There was nothing else to think. First it put crazy danger ahead of him. Then it put more crazy danger behind him. Then it took his dad. Then their dog. Then it grabbed him and held him so he couldn't run away and be saved.

He reached down with both hands to try to pull the foot free. It wouldn't budge. The world had gone white again, the light of the train igniting everything, forcing Buddy to squeeze his eyes closed so he would not go blind. But even through his eyelids, the world was on fire.

Buddy knew he must have broken through the crust of the earth into some kind of hell.

His ears uncovered now, he heard the constant, earsplitting, head-destroying whistle of the train. But another sound, too. Now the train was shrieking at him. A horrible sound, like metal shearing. Like the bridge were being ripped apart with a screaming power saw as big as the world. It made Buddy cry harder, because it hurt his ears so much.

He tried again to pull the foot free. He wanted to pull his foot out of the sneaker and leave the sneaker behind, but it was impossible. Not only was the sneaker wedged, but the foot was wedged inside it.

There was nothing more he could do.

Buddy covered his ears again and waited for the end. Waited for everything to be over. He felt a warm wetness seep down his thigh.

The train whistle disappeared. And something happened to the shrieking. It got higher. More shrill. Even more excruciating, if such a thing were possible. And then, just like that, it wrapped itself up. Wound down to nothing.

Even the engine that powered the train shut down.

Absolute silence.

Sheila was no longer barking. The train was completely silent and still. Everything was completely silent and still. All Buddy heard was the desperate pant of his own breathing.

He wasn't dead. At least, he didn't think he was. But he wasn't sure of anything, because he had no idea how it felt to be dead.

He couldn't open his eyes because the light was still trying to blind him, even through his closed lids.

Someone stepped down out of the train. Buddy couldn't see that happen, but he could hear it. He could hear someone coming.

A big hand reached down and held his ankle, then twisted his foot, wrenching it free. Buddy cried out.

The hand was shaking. It was the hand of a big, giant man, but it was trembling out of control. That shook Buddy more than anything else in this new hell. Because everything scared Buddy. Everything always had. But when a big, giant stranger couldn't keep his hands from shaking . . .

Buddy felt his legs turn to melted butter. He didn't fall so much as he swooned.

He dissolved into the arms of the trembling man.

Chapter Six: Virginia

When Virginia arrived at work the following morning, Fern was leaning hard on the counter with both elbows, reading the morning paper. A mug of coffee steamed near her left hand.

She looked up, her gaze searing into Virginia's face, as if to find something there to criticize.

"What're you so happy about?" she asked.

It struck Virginia as a strange thing to find wrong.

"Happy?" She certainly was, there was no doubting that. She just hadn't known she was wearing it so visibly. But maybe she should have known. Since she had never been one to hide what she was feeling. Not successfully, anyway.

"You look like you just swallowed the world's biggest canary. Which leads me to believe you must've gotten a jump on that employment situation. You found yourself another job, huh? Where?"

"I didn't," Virginia said, tying on a fresh apron. "It's not a thing like that."

"What's it a thing like?" Virginia didn't answer, so Fern looked up into her face again. "Oh. Wait. Don't tell me. He finally asked?"

"He did!" Virginia said, her voice coming out as an embarrassing squeal.

"Well, I'm happy for you. I am. 'Bout time."

It seemed so like Fern, to throw in that one little takeaway at the end.

"I feel like dancing," Virginia said, giddy and buoyant with the feelings she had unleashed.

She ran to Fern, grabbed her, and tried to pull her out into the middle of the dining area. Fern dug her feet in, but Virginia was bigger and stronger. It was a little like towing a mule once he's planted his hooves into a stubborn stance, but she just kept towing. Then she grabbed Fern's arms and tried to waltz her around the room between tables. But the only one who moved was Virginia. You can hold on to anything you please when you're dancing, but if what you're holding won't dance, then you're in it alone.

"Have you lost your mind?" Fern shrieked. She yanked her arms out of Virginia's grasp and straightened her hair, even though the horseplay really hadn't mussed it.

"If I had, do you think I would care?"

"Girl, you are a piece of work when you fall for somebody. Shouldn't fall so deep in love before you ever even go out on a date. It's not safe. It's not smart."

With that, Fern walked back behind the counter and leaned over her paper again.

Virginia sighed.

"You are such a stick-in-the-mud, Fern. Thirty-eight years old and you act like you're seventy."

Fern offered no reply.

Virginia walked back behind the counter and poured herself a mug of the freshly brewed coffee. She breathed in the smell, realizing it pleased her more than it ever had before. Everything did.

"We should buy this place," Virginia said.

Fern glanced briefly over her shoulder. "Nice to know your loss of sanity is complete, at least."

"No, I'm serious."

"And crazy."

"Why is it crazy?"

Fern grabbed her purse from its cubby underneath the counter. Dug out a smaller change purse and emptied it onto the counter. There were a few bills in there, and she separated them out among the quarters and dimes, pointing at each bill as she silently counted, her lips moving.

"There you go. Forty-two dollars and change. Dig out whatever you got and pool it all together, and then take it to Dave and see if he accepts our offer."

She swept the money off into her hand with one big motion and began to stuff it back into the change purse.

"I'm not suggesting we try it with just what we've got. We could go to the Small Business Administration down in the valley and see if they'd give us a loan."

Fern looked into her face for a long moment. Long enough to make Virginia squirm. "Exactly who or what put this idea into your head?"

"Actually," Virginia said, straightening her apron slightly, "it was Buddy's idea."

"Buddy."

"Yeah."

"That spooky little kid who's scared to death of his own shadow."

"Yeah."

"You just seriously presented me with a business plan you got from a four-year-old."

"Well . . . yeah."

"I got news for you. It shows. It sounds like something a four-year-old would dream up. That part makes sense. What I don't get is why you're repeating it to me."

Virginia shook her head and wandered off in the direction of the kitchen, still holding and smelling that great mug of coffee.

"Ginnie," she heard Fern say.

She turned around. Walked back a few steps. Waited.

"You asked any of the other waitresses about this? About going in with you?"

"No. And I wouldn't. You're the only one I'd trust to do it right."

"Speaking of doing it right . . . it's pretty clear to me why Dave can't make a go of this place. You got thoughts on that as well?"

Virginia leaned in the kitchen doorway. Took a deep gulp of the hot coffee and sighed, because it was that good. She hadn't ever thought about the question Fern had just proposed. But as soon as she did, it seemed pretty clear.

"I think he's a fool to serve dinner," she said. "This place should be breakfast and lunch only. It would cut down on employees and their shifts more than it would take away from income. Because people don't come to a place like this for dinner. They go somewhere nicer. This is a place people come for breakfast any old day of the week, or for lunch on weekdays, because they only have just so much time off from work for lunch. But if they're going to go out to dinner, they stay in town."

"Right," Fern said.

"So why do *you* think he can't make a go of it?"

"Exactly what you just said, Ginnie."

Virginia waited. Sipped. But Fern didn't seem inclined to say more.

"Does this mean you're actually thinking about it?"

"I wouldn't go that far," Fern said, eyes still down on her paper.

But Virginia could hear the difference in her tone, as if she were already lost in thought.

Virginia wandered over to the window, vaguely remembering seeing Aaron and Buddy and Sheila walking in her direction, from the same window, the day before. But there was no one out there. Way off in the distance, she could see two emergency vehicles of some sort parked by the railroad bridge. They were too far away to know anything more about them, but she could see the light bars flashing on their roofs.

Maybe Dave's kids were playing on the bridge and fell in, she thought. Without a great deal of regret. But then she felt a pang of guilt for not wanting everybody's kids to be okay, even Dave's two spoiled monsters. So she turned back away from the window and didn't think about it again.

———

The deputy sheriff came in well before the breakfast rush started. It was Fred Cooper, the oldest guy in the department. The guy everybody figured would have retired about five years ago.

Fern was back in the kitchen, or the freezer, or out behind the place, or somewhere that wasn't the seating area of the diner. So Virginia set a mug of coffee on the counter and wordlessly indicated that he should sit.

"Coffee, Fred? We're not really serving breakfast yet."

"I'm not here for breakfast," he said. "This is official business. But I'll take a cup of coffee, yeah. Thanks."

It set off a note of alarm in Virginia's belly as she fetched the coffeepot. *Funny how we're all afraid of the law,* she thought. She knew damn well she hadn't done anything wrong. But it was a knee-jerk reaction. Then she decided it was probably Dave he'd come to discuss, not her. Maybe there was a reason he was selling the place all of a sudden. Something bigger than a weak dinner crowd. Maybe he needed to get out of town fast.

She poured Fred a full mug, careful to look only at the mug and not at the deputy.

"You take cream? I haven't filled the cream pitchers yet, but I'll get you one."

"No. Just black. You know Aaron Albanese?"

Virginia's whole body turned to ice. Tingling, buzzing ice.

"Well . . . yeah. I do. Why? He didn't do something wrong, did he?"

"We're not sure. Is he the kind of guy who'd leave that little bit of a boy untended, d'you think? You know him well enough to know?"

"No. He wouldn't. I'm sure he wouldn't."

"So you knew him pretty well."

"Knew?"

"Know, I mean. You know him well enough to know he wouldn't."

"Absolutely. Why, just yesterday he was in here—"

"Yeah, that's what the boy said. That's why I'm here. But— sorry. Didn't mean to interrupt. Go on."

But Virginia couldn't remember how to go on. She couldn't think where she'd just been, or where she'd been going. "What was I saying?" she asked through the buzzing ice.

"You were telling me why you were so sure he wouldn't leave the boy untended."

"Oh. Right. Just yesterday he wanted to come talk to me. You know. Sort of . . . just the two of us. And he wouldn't even leave Buddy that long. Not even right in the diner. He tipped the cook to sit out on the porch with him. What's this all about, Fred? Did something happen to Buddy?"

The deputy just stared into his coffee mug for a minute. Well, probably not a minute. Probably a second or two. But it stretched out into something so long and unbearable in Virginia's gut that she thought a scream of frustration would burst out of her if he didn't speak soon.

"We're not sure yet what happened, Ginnie. We're trying to piece it all together. Only thing we know for sure is this: a train engineer picked up that little boy on the railroad bridge last night. Almost had to pick him up the hard way. It's not easy to brake a train that size. They don't exactly stop on a dime. He really thought he was going to hit the poor kid. He swears he stopped with less than twenty feet to spare."

"Well, where was Aaron during all this?" she almost shrieked. She didn't mean it to come out as a shriek, but it seemed the only tone available to her.

"That's the part we don't know."

Virginia looked around for someplace to sit. Which was foolish, she realized, because there was no place like that behind the counter. She leaned the backs of her forearms on the counter to steady herself. Then, slowly, she made her way around the counter and sank onto a stool.

"Fred. You trying to tell me you have no idea where Aaron is?"

"Right. We don't. He's officially a missing person at this point. Only options we can think of are that he purposely abandoned that child on the bridge . . . which would be something like murdering him . . . which nobody thinks he would do . . ."

"He wouldn't," Virginia said, her voice trembling. Her voice seemed to know now. The seriousness of the situation was still a secret kept from her brain and her heart, but her voice knew. "He loves that boy. He would never do a thing like that."

"Which means Aaron went into the river."

Virginia swallowed hard. If those were the two options, then Aaron went into the river. Every part of her knew that. Not just her voice.

"But . . . why? *Why*, Fred? I know you're not supposed to short-cut across the bridge, even though we all know lots of people do. I know it's not safe. But why would somebody be walking on it and just fall off?" To her embarrassment, on the last couple of words, Virginia began to cry quietly.

The deputy reached out and briefly put one of his big, rough hands on hers. "It's still something of a mystery," he said. "The little boy's pretty traumatized. He doesn't remember much. By the time we got to the hospital—"

"Hospital? You said he didn't get hit!"

"He didn't. But he tore some ligaments in his leg. His foot got stuck under a tie. Would have been easy enough to get unstuck, according to the engineer. All he really had to do was pull backward instead of forward. But the kid's four. And I guess it's hard to go any way but forward when you're about to be hit by a train. So he had some possible tendon damage that needed to be checked, and of course they're sedating him. He was in shock. Probably still is. Anyway, when we got there, he didn't remember a damn thing except the dog jumping off the bridge. He thinks the dog went in to rescue his father. But he doesn't know anymore what happened. He was conscious for a minute or two with the engineer. While they were waiting for an ambulance to show up. He said the kid tried to tell him the story. But it wasn't a very clear explanation. He said he and his dad were walking home from the diner. That's why I came in here to check his story. I guess he didn't know what happened on the bridge, just what it looked like. From the description it sounded like maybe an electrical transformer exploding, except there aren't any on the bridge. Or maybe a comet, but I can't imagine a comet startling somebody that much unless it whizzed by about an inch from their ear. There's really nothing else we can think of that would match his description."

Virginia sat quietly for a moment. She realized her mouth was hanging open, but she didn't bother to close it. She could feel tears running on either side of her open mouth, but she didn't care. The buzzing was no longer buzzing and the tingling was no longer tingling. But her body still felt cold. It felt as though the numbness was beginning to wear off. She couldn't even bring herself to think about what that might mean. What might lie ahead.

She looked up to see Fern standing in the kitchen doorway, staring at her. Fern's face was a mirror. Virginia had no idea how long Fern had been standing there, or how much she'd heard. But it was clear by her eyes that she knew something had happened. Something very bad. And by looking into Fern's eyes, Virginia found herself faced with how bad it really was.

The coldness left, replaced by nothing. Virginia felt nothing.

"Fireworks," she said.

"Yeah," Fred said. "Could have been fireworks, I guess. Not sure why somebody would be out on the railroad bridge with fireworks, though."

"So they wouldn't start a fire in the dry weeds." Her voice sounded like someone else, somewhere else. Sounded and felt detached from her.

"Well, anything's possible I suppose, but I'm not sure why you'd guess—"

"I'm not guessing," her detached voice said. "I know. I know what happened. And I know who's responsible."

———

The hospital was down in the valley, a good half-hour drive. Virginia watched her hands as she drove, only peripherally aware of the road outside her windshield. She noticed that they gripped and released on the steering wheel, gripped and released. Over and over she watched her knuckles whiten, then return to normal color again.

Her brain was not speaking to her. Or maybe it was the other way around. But she could feel the disconnect—a no-man's-land of blankness, like a moat hastily dug to foil an advancing enemy.

And she didn't question that, or try to change it. When the news is that bad, she figured, you stop listening to the person trying to deliver it.

Even if that person is you.

———

"I'm here to see Buddy," she told the nurse.

The woman didn't look up from her charts at first. Then, when she did, she had an exaggerated look of confusion on her face. As if Virginia were speaking in some made-up, make-believe language and the nurse wanted to be clear that she objected to such foolishness.

She was blonder than Virginia, and thinner, and younger. It made Virginia feel as if they had just played a game or fought a battle and Virginia had lost miserably.

"Buddy?"

"The little four-year-old boy. Everybody calls him Buddy. I don't know his real first name, but his last name is Albanese."

"Oh," the nurse said. "Right." The look on her face changed entirely. Now instead of mocking Virginia for being too vague, it drew her close in a shared act of pity. "That's a sad thing. Hard to remember when something that bad even happened around here."

But Virginia had no more patience for this new attitude than she'd had for the one before it.

"Can I see him?"

"Are you immediate family?"

"Well . . . no."

"I'm sorry, then. Immediate family only."

"But he doesn't even have any!" Virginia nearly shrieked the words.

The nurse winced. Virginia winced. They both looked around to see whom they might have disturbed. But all the doors—at least, the doors that could be seen from that nurses' station on that floor—were closed. The halls were empty.

"Sorry," Virginia said in a quieter tone. "I'm a little bit upset."

As she said it, she felt a stirring from the land on the other side of the moat. She knew the phrase "a little bit" had set off a flurry of emotion, a strong claim that she was compressing the enormity of something. But she hadn't taken a good look at that something yet, and she wasn't about to start now in the company of this young, thin blonde nurse. Or anybody else, for that matter. Herself included.

"I can imagine," the nurse said. "Did you know the father?"

"Yes. I did. He was my . . . boyfriend."

"Oh. I'm sorry."

"I don't understand why I can't see him. How is anybody going to see him if you limit it to family? What family do you think he has left?"

"His grandparents are coming to get him."

"Grandparents?" Virginia asked as if through a sudden haze. A fog had set in, and Virginia immediately felt lost in it. The world had turned flat white. Visibility was gone, leaving her feeling emotionally blind and without landmarks.

"Yes, his grandparents are flying in from Florida. And when the doctor clears him to leave, they're going to take him back with them."

The fog thickened. Virginia reached a hand out to steady herself on the counter of the nurses' station.

"They're taking him away to Florida?"

"That's what I hear, yes. He's lucky he has somebody."

He has me, Virginia screamed silently inside her head. But she knew better than to say it out loud. She barely knew Buddy and he barely knew her. The thread between them was more than tenuous. It was invisible. Something no one but Virginia would even see. Why had she thought she was not about to lose Buddy as well?

Or maybe she hadn't thought that. Maybe she knew damn well he was just as gone from her life as Aaron had suddenly become. Maybe the simple truth of it had been right there all along. Right on the other side of the gap.

"When are they coming?" she heard herself ask. It surprised her, because her own voice sounded calm and reasonably composed.

"Tomorrow, I think. If you came in when they were here, and they gave their permission for you to go in with them and see him, then we could allow it."

"Oh," Virginia said, lost in the fog again. "When tomorrow are they coming?"

"I have no idea," the nurse said.

———

It was after six when the hard knock sounded on Virginia's door. It hit her like an ice-water bath, because it was that scary, official kind of knock.

But when she opened the door, it was only Fern.

"Oh," Virginia said. "It's you. I didn't even know you knew where I live."

"It's a small town," Fern said.

Fern was holding a brown paper grocery sack. Its contents clinked as she shifted it from two arms to only one. She reached in and pulled out a bottle. White frosted glass. Obviously liquor, though Virginia wasn't close enough to read what its label said.

"I'm here to get you drunk," Fern said. "I brought all the ingredients for my world-famous vodka martinis."

Virginia felt her brow furrow. "I'm a lightweight," she said. "It won't take all that."

"Well, whatever it takes, what say we get at it?"

Virginia stepped out of the doorway and let her by.

———

"How'd it go at the hospital?" Fern called in from the kitchen.

"They wouldn't let me see him."

"Oh. That's too bad."

Fern emerged from the kitchen holding two perfect martinis. They were in just the glasses a nice bar would use to serve them, even though Virginia didn't have martini glasses. They each had two olives on a red toothpick. Virginia didn't have red toothpicks, either.

"You even brought martini glasses?" Virginia asked, taking the drink Fern held out to her.

"If you're going to do something, you ought to do it right. That's how I look at things, anyway."

Fern settled beside her on the couch. They stared at the glasses for a long time. Or it seemed long, anyway. The drinks were so perfect, so visually artistic. Virginia could honestly believe she would find her salvation in one.

She took a long swallow. It kicked hard. It was unexpectedly strong. It burned at the back of her throat, but in a way that made her wish to be burned again. And again.

Fern still hadn't said a word since sitting down.

"Nice of you to come by," Virginia said. "Especially seeing as we were never friends outside work or anything."

"First time for everything," Fern said.

And with that they fell into another long silence.

In time Fern pulled a pack of cigarettes out of her purse. She tapped the pack against her hand until a few filters protruded, then held it out to Virginia.

Virginia shook her head. "I quit," she said firmly.

"Since when?" Fern asked, indicating the ashtray full of low-tar butts on the coffee table.

"Since today."

"Today of all days? Who quits smoking on a day like this?"

"I told Aaron I was going to quit. And I'm not going to make a liar of myself."

"Oh. You want me to hold off, then? Or take it outside?"

"No. Go ahead. I don't even care."

Fern sighed. Shrugged. Lit one for herself. Smoked in silence for a good half a cigarette.

A creeping sense of something—something unidentified, something bad—made its way from Fern's side of the couch to Virginia's mind. Fern seemed weighted down by something she had not yet said.

"Penny for your thoughts," Virginia said when she couldn't stand not knowing for another minute.

"Trying to decide if I should tell you they dragged that river today."

Virginia squeezed her eyes closed. Took another long drink.

"No," she said.

"No, I shouldn't tell you?"

"No, you shouldn't tell me."

How much time went by after that, Virginia could not have said. A second or two. Ten minutes. Twenty. Probably closer to a second or two.

"Okay, I guess I have to know. If there's still any hope at all, tell me. If they didn't find him, and he's still just missing, and if we still think it's the worst but we don't really one hundred percent know how this ends, then say so real quick."

A long, stunning silence.

Virginia picked up her drink again and upended it into her mouth, finishing off the last of it in one huge gulp. She held the toothpick against the side of the glass so she wouldn't accidentally swallow it.

She held the glass out to Fern without looking in her direction.

"Hit me again," she said.

———

"So what about Dave's brats?" Virginia asked.

She was lying on her back on her own carpet, the last few drops of her third martini still in the glass in her hand. She could feel the thin, fancy stem between her fingers. She wanted to drink the last of it, but she would have had to sit up to do that. So instead she just stared at the patterned plaster of her own ceiling and measured whether she was about to be sick.

"Not sure how that'll go," Fern said. "It was them all right. They're not trying to pretend otherwise. Fred said they cracked like a couple of walnuts when he showed up at their door. Cried and cried and cried. They didn't do it on purpose, you know. They didn't know there was anybody on the bridge. They were just trying to go off somewhere they wouldn't start a fire. I don't know if they'll have to pay a price for it or not. They might just rule it accidental. But they're awful young to be out by themselves after dark. I think if anything Fred'll go after Dave for letting them run wild like that."

"That's who I blame," Virginia said. Then a wave of nausea washed over her, and she waited to see if it would pass. Just as it was fading, it hit her that it might not have been the alcohol. Not that time. "And myself."

"*You?* What the hell did *you* do?" Fern's voice was disembodied, drifting over to her from somewhere in the direction of the couch. It was a land Virginia would have had to move her head to see, and so would remain blindly uncharted.

"It was all my fault, Fern."

"You've had too many of those. You're right. You *are* a lightweight."

"It's true."

"How do you figure?"

"Dave's kids were shooting off those illegal fireworks behind the diner. I chased them off."

"So? Who wouldn't have?"

"I told them they were going to burn down the diner. Maybe the whole town. You know. Setting off fireworks around all those dry weeds."

"Sounds like good enough advice to me. I still don't get—"

"They took those fireworks out on the bridge because of what I said."

A long silence. Virginia could smell the smoke of a fresh cigarette drift across her patch of carpet. It made her want one. Desperately want one. But she wouldn't have one. She would never have one again.

"Well, you're just exactly wrong," Fern said. "That doesn't make it your fault."

"If I had called their dad and told him what they were doing, it never would've happened."

"Maybe. Or maybe Dave wouldn't have cared, and wouldn't have come and gotten them, and it would have gone just the same. Look. Ginnie. I totally get how bad you wish you had that moment to do over again. We've all got something like that in our past. Something we want to go back and redo, because we know now what we didn't know then. But we can't. And if we were doing our best with what we had in the moment, then it's not our fault. And we shouldn't beat ourselves up for it."

"But we always do," Virginia said.

She heard a sound from Fern that could have been a rueful wheeze of a laugh, or it could have been a sigh.

"Okay," Fern said. "I'll grant you that."

"I have to go meet his grandparents tomorrow."

"Why?"

"So I can find out where they're taking him."

"Why?"

"So I can keep in touch with him as he grows up, and I swear to God, Fern, if you say 'why' one more time . . ."

"Ginnie," she said, and it sounded bad. It was the way somebody speaks your name right before they say something you won't like one bit. "I know this is not what you want to hear. Might even sound mean. But it's the truth, and I think you need to hear it. I honestly think you don't mean as much to that little boy as he means to you. I've watched you two together. He hasn't accepted you at all. You had this image in your head of how you'd all three be this nice family. He didn't. Or if he did, he didn't like the image."

"How do you know what he does or doesn't like?"

"You ever met a kid who liked the idea of his dad getting with somebody new after his mom dies?"

Virginia sat up, fairly sure she would need to get herself to the bathroom soon. She placed one hand on her roiling stomach.

"So what are you saying, Fern? That I should just let him go?"

"It's what I would do."

"Well, it's not what *I'm* going to do. I'm going to get to the hospital first thing in the morning and stay all day, until I meet them. You can just tell Dave I'm sick. Which I'm sure I will be, but I'm going to the hospital anyway. And I'm going to get his new address, so I can write him letters all his life. Because he won't be a kid forever, Fern. And when he grows up, he'll see it differently. He'll understand why his dad moved on after a couple of years. And he'll want to know somebody who knew his father. Somebody who loved his father."

"Okay," Fern said. "You do what you need to do, I guess."

Virginia teetered to her feet, fast, and stumbled to the bathroom, where she lost the scant contents of her stomach—mostly martinis—into the toilet. She flushed, and then rinsed and wiped her mouth. Then she held still, realizing she felt a bit better.

She made her way out to the living room again, picked up her glass, and downed the dregs of her third martini.

"Hit me again," she told Fern.

By the time the light woke her, light was a very bad thing. Very painful and unwanted.

Virginia opened her eyes, which immediately struck her as a mistake. She winced and covered them with one hand. Her head felt as though someone were pounding an iron stake into it, one vicious blow at a time.

She was on the couch, she saw, having never made it to bed. She sat up carefully.

"Fern?" she called.

She walked to the window and pulled back the curtain with a wince. Fern's car was gone.

She teetered her way into the kitchen, where the clock on the stove informed her it was after ten thirty.

"Oh, crap!" she said, out loud, to no one. "I have to get to the hospital. I have to get to the hospital right now."

But after racing into the bathroom and looking at herself in the mirror, she knew it was not a "right now" proposition. She had to clean herself, do something with her hair. Change her clothes. Drink enough coffee to be fit to drive. Or maybe she could just take the coffee with her.

But before meeting the grandparents and identifying herself as Aaron's new love interest, she had to make something decent of herself. And considering that she would have to throw up at least three more times before getting out the door, that wasn't going to happen in an instant.

The same nurse manned the station, though there was another nurse sitting behind her this time. A bigger, horsier woman, older than Virginia, who did not intimidate her as much. But the thin blonde nurse knew her story, and Virginia felt unable to start from the beginning.

Both nurses looked up, and Virginia could see a great deal in their faces. Too much. She had not done as good a job as she'd thought making herself presentable. They were shocked at the visible aspects of her condition.

Imagine if they could see inside, she thought.

But she had no time to worry about any of that.

"Are they here?" she asked the blonde nurse.

"Come and gone," the nurse said.

Virginia leaned on the counter. Felt all the energy drain from her body. As though it had been nothing but adrenaline all along.

"They took him?"

"Checked out an hour ago," she said.

"Do you have an address for them?"

The nurse gave her that look again. As though she were speaking words that made no sense. "Why would we have their address?"

"Don't you have to bill them for his care?"

"Nope. They paid the bill by credit card and now they're gone."

Chapter Seven: Buddy

When he woke up, he was in a car. But it wasn't a car he knew. And it wasn't a waking up he knew, either. It was not a clean and sudden journey from asleep to awake.

It felt as though he were trying to surface through a mental sludge as thick as wet concrete. And even when he got up above it, his face barely out into fresh air, it was still trying to pull him back down.

He drew his knees to his chest and hugged around them with both arms, even though the seat belt made that hard to do. Even though his ribs and his leg hurt a lot, and he had to move carefully and slowly, and even then it still hurt.

He could hear Gramma and Grampa arguing in the front seat. They must not have known he was awake.

It made him edgy, the way any kind of anger always did. Always had. But the mental sludge made it hard to feel that edginess. It made it hard to feel anything. In a way, Buddy liked that. That artificial calm. In another way it frightened him. If he couldn't feel the sharpness of his fear, maybe that just made him a sitting duck, like in those dreams where the monster is chasing you, but your legs feel like lead and you can't run away fast enough no matter how hard you try. It felt like a handicap, preventing him from knowing what could hurt him.

Maybe he needed his fear more than ever now.

"So much is changing for him," Gramma said. "And all at once, too. It's going to be overwhelming for the poor little guy no matter what we do. I think you should at least leave him his name."

"Which one?" Grampa asked, not raising his voice, but clearly irritated.

"Well, both. At least at the beginning."

"No. Not a chance in hell, Margaret. She gave him the name Jody, and it's just plain offensive for her husband to bury it in a silly little nickname like it's something to be ashamed of. It's a good name. Maybe if it was your relative instead of mine he was named after, you'd feel differently."

"Not at all," Gramma said. "It has nothing to do with who named him. Or who they named him for. He's a little boy, and he's leaving behind everything he's ever known, and now you're about to tell him he doesn't even know his own name. That he was Buddy Albanese for the four years he's been alive, but he's all of a sudden somebody different now."

"Who am I now?" Buddy asked. It sounded thin and weak, like there was more sludge to speak through than he'd realized.

Grampa and Gramma exchanged a look, but stayed silent for a moment. Maybe even more silent than most times when nobody is talking, though Buddy would have been the first to admit that he had no idea how a thing like that would work.

"We didn't know you were awake, pumpkin," Gramma said.

"Who am I now?" Buddy asked again. A little stronger this time.

"You're just who you always were," Grampa said in his big, booming voice. It startled Buddy, but the wet concrete of sleepiness muted the feeling. "You know your name is Jody."

A silence.

"Right, son? You know your first name."

"Yes, sir," Buddy said.

He always called Grampa "sir." He couldn't remember if he'd been carefully taught to do so, or if it was just something Grampa inspired. If he was just the "sir" type.

"So the only difference is that you'll have our last name. Schilling."

"Why?"

"Because you're going to be ours now."

"Oh," Buddy said.

He wanted to say much more. He started to.

He even opened his mouth to ask after Dad. To ask where he was. But something pulled the words back down again. There was something bad down there, like a monster under the bed. He needed to stay clear of the monster more than he needed to ask questions.

Plus, part of him already knew. Or at least the monster knew. Was the monster part of him? That was a tricky thing to even think about. Especially now, with his brain moving so slowly.

"I still think it's appropriate for him to have his father's name," Gramma said quietly in the front seat.

"I'm his father now."

"No, you're not, Ed. You're still his grandfather."

"Well, I'm his guardian."

"We, Ed. *We're* his guardians."

"And our name's not Albanese."

Then the car fell silent for a time.

Buddy thought the sludge of sleepiness was going to pull him under again, but he fought it. Fought hard.

He sat up straighter and turned halfway around to look out the back window. He thought he'd see the town where he lived. See it stretched out behind them. But there was nothing familiar back there. They weren't even in the foothills of the mountains anymore. Everything he saw looked dusty and flat. He had never seen the earth look dusty and flat.

"Where are we going?" he asked.

"Florida," Grampa said.

"Why?"

"Because we live in Florida, and you're coming to live with us now."

"But you used to live where Dad and I live. Why did you move?"

"You know that, Jody," Grampa said, sounding impatient. Though, truth be told, not much more so than usual.

"I do?"

"Yes. You do. We told you why we were moving when we moved."

"I don't remember."

"You could if you tried," Grampa said.

Gramma reached over and punched her husband on the arm. Hard, from the look of it. It surprised Buddy. But again, the feeling was so muted as to nearly be lost to him.

"He's still on that sedative," Gramma said. "Leave the boy alone." Then, turning to Buddy and switching tones, she said, "We moved to Florida because it gets so darned cold up there in the mountains. Your grampa doesn't mind it. But I mind."

"But I don't know anybody in Florida."

"You will," she said, her voice seeming cheerful. Yet Buddy was convinced it was not genuine cheer, but something plastered on over the same sadness and dread he himself felt.

"Everybody I know is at home. Won't we ever go back home?"

"Florida will be your new home," Grampa said.

Buddy didn't think it was a very good answer.

"We still have that vacation home," Gramma said. "So we can come back for a visit sometimes, but it has to be in the summer. That is, if you want me to come along."

"What's a vacation home?"

"That little cabin by the lake," she said.

"Oh. The cabin." He wanted to add, "Why didn't you just say so?" Started to. Then he caught himself, thinking it might be rude. Instead he asked, "How far is it to Florida?"

"Very far," Grampa said.

"How long does it take to drive?"

"Days. But we're not driving. We're just driving to the airport and then we'll fly home."

Another jolt of strangely dulled panic. Jody had never been on a plane. But he'd seen them. And, worse yet, he'd heard them. They were terrifying and deafening.

But he didn't say that, because Grampa wasn't very patient with fear.

Instead he just said, "What do we do with the car, then?"

Grampa only sighed.

Gramma said, "It's not our car. We just rented it. We'll turn it back in when we get to the airport."

"Oh," Buddy said. "I thought it didn't look like your car. Your car is so big. And this is so small. Why didn't you rent a big one?"

He watched them exchange a look with each other. No one said a word. Which seemed odd to Buddy. It felt like a perfectly reasonable question.

In that silence, he closed his eyes.

He heard Gramma say, "You forgot how many questions kids ask, didn't you?"

"Valerie never asked this many questions. None of our girls did."

It was a sweet sting in Buddy's midsection, to hear his mother's name spoken out loud. All he really knew of her now was her name. Her photos had faded to flat images, too often seen, and he had no personal memories of her to fall back on anymore.

"Oh, yes they did. You were at work, and I had to answer them."

"Well, you may have to answer these, too. I'm not as young as I used to be."

"You're also not off at work all day like you used to be. So get used to it."

Buddy chose not to let on that he was awake.

A moment later he wasn't awake. At least, not completely. In that thin moment between conscious and unconscious, he thought of Sheila. Somehow his mind dared to go to Sheila but did not dare imagine his dad. He saw the perfectly replayed image of her leaping from the bridge. It brought a sense of alarm, but, like everything else, whatever they gave him at that hospital made it hard to register the feeling.

Relatively safe in that thick blanket of dulled senses, he poked around to feel if there was anything else he might remember.

Nothing else. Everything else just felt gone.

The Conundrum
and the Ice Storm

Present Day

Chapter Eight: Virginia

When she unlocked the diner's front doors on that icy winter morning, the sting of cold metal on her bare hands felt almost like a burn. She should have worn her mittens. She'd argued with herself about it before leaving the house. But she'd wanted to look at the new ring throughout the ten-minute drive.

The strip of holiday-style jingle bells tinkled as she pushed her way inside. They were supposed to sound merry, and maybe once upon a time they had, even to her. Now they just sounded like work.

She knew it was silly, but once inside she stopped, still wrapped in her coat and scarf, and looked around the place. Just to see if anything looked different. Nothing did. The hats on the ceiling beams still looked dusty. They'd already looked dusty enough when she and Fern bought the diner almost nineteen years earlier. And let's face it, as the years go by, things get more dusty. Never less. The ticking of the solidly filled wall of twenty-seven wood-slab clocks, each with an image lacquered to its face, still sounded loud, off rhythm, and annoying. The clock with the mallard duck had stopped running again, and the one with the face of Jesus had lost two minutes in the night, as it always did. Virginia sighed and manually pulled the clock's long minute hand forward to the proper time.

She could feel, without exactly being able to capture the sensation in words, that she had expected more from this day.

That's what expectations will do, she thought. *It's always a setup.*

She started a pot of coffee and plunked into a sit while it brewed.

———

Locked into their morning ritual of choreographed preparations for opening, Fern darted to the left and right of Virginia, setting flatware at each place on the counter. Virginia arranged freshly filled salt and pepper shakers and bright red and yellow condiment squeeze bottles. But there was something *too* crisp in Fern's movements. Fern was silent that morning. Then again, Fern was silent most mornings. She didn't schmooze naturally; it tired her. So she held on to the blessed silence as long as possible.

But Virginia couldn't shake the feeling that Fern was more silent than usual, if such a thing were possible. Or maybe more *deliberately* silent.

Comfortable silence was one thing, but Virginia hated a forced silence more than just about anything. So she broke it. Decisively. Maybe even bordering on harshly. "Guess I'll have to ask you straight out, then," she said.

Fern stopped moving. Just for a beat. Then the practiced daily routines continued as though nothing had happened.

But something had.

Fern glanced briefly at Virginia's left hand, her gaze scarcely pausing. "I noticed it," she said after a time.

"And you got nothing more to say?"

Fern took down one of the freshly starched white aprons off the hook on the wall and sighed. She was a full head shorter than Virginia. About the same age, meaning she was also no spring chicken. Yet she managed to stay thin. Maybe because she smoked. And because she rarely stopped moving. "You know that old joke?" Virginia knew that, whichever old joke it turned out to be, she wouldn't like it. "The one where you thank somebody for some little thing, something that was much less than they ought to have done, and they say it was the least they could do? And you say, 'Yeah. That really *was* the least you could do.'" She tied the apron on and tucked a fresh order pad into one pocket of it. The right one, because she was left-handed, and so she held the pencil with her left. Then she set off into the kitchen.

"That's just plain mean," Virginia called after her. "So it's not a big diamond. That's not the important thing. Right?"

Fern appeared again, with a half-gallon carton of coffee creamer in her left hand. "No, it's not," she said. "The important thing is finding a guy who treats you right."

Virginia looked down at her hands, then found herself averting her eyes from the ring. It was a very small diamond. There was no arguing that.

"Let's not get into it over Lloyd again."

"You asked," Fern said flatly.

"That's true. I did. Look, Fern—"

"Thought you didn't want to get into it."

They fell into a stilted silence that lasted until the first of the regulars came jingling through the door.

———

After the breakfast rush, Virginia bagged up the trash and headed through the kitchen for the Dumpster. Technically, according to the guy from the county health department, you weren't supposed to take bagged trash through the kitchen. But that seemed absurd to Virginia. After all, it's sealed up in plastic. Besides, he wasn't around. She generally obeyed the basic decency of health codes even when no one was looking, but this one was just plain silly.

And Petey, the breakfast cook, would never say a word about it.

He was scraping down the griddle surface, and he glanced over at her as she scooted by. "What's that I see on your left hand, Ginnie?"

She stopped in her tracks. "None of the regulars noticed."

"Didn't notice or didn't say." His gaze returned to his scraping. "So old Lloyd is making an honest woman out of you."

"That's not a very nice saying, Petey. I'm not a dishonest woman now."

"No offense intended," Petey said.

"Okay," she said, and sighed. "None taken, I suppose."

She hurried out the back door into the stinging cold. Fern was leaning on the Dumpster, taking a cigarette break. In just her apron and short-sleeved uniform. A light snow was falling, building up on branches of the tall pines overhead, then letting go and flurrying down around them.

"Aren't you freezing, Fern? Why didn't you put on your coat?"

Fern nodded in Virginia's direction with her chin. "Why didn't *you*?"

"Because I'm not staying out here long."

"Look, Ginnie," Fern said, and it was clear that their talk had just taken a serious turn. The small talk was about to get big. "If I'm wrong, and he turns out to be a good husband for you, and you're happy, then I'm really happy for you."

"Thank you," Virginia said. Her cold, numbing lips resisted forming the words. "What's so terrible about him anyway?"

"Not terrible. Just not good enough for my best friend."

"Just 'cause he flirts doesn't mean he really does anything about it."

Fern blew a blast of smoke into the biting air. It didn't look much different from the frozen clouds they both exhaled on each breath. "Hope you're right. But that's not the main thing, anyway. It's how you work longer and harder than him every day, but he sits in front of the TV waiting on you to cook dinner. And how—"

"He's old-fashioned like that." Virginia had to work to form words now, because her teeth wanted to chatter. She was still holding the bagged garbage and standing her ground. As if afraid to approach her oldest friend. Fern had always been one to speak her mind. Not mince words. But in the past those words had been comfortably directed elsewhere.

"Is that a nice expression for lazy?"

"Oh, come on. You want me to be alone all my life because the guy likes dinner on the table? That's not much to fault a guy for. I'm not like you, Fern. I can't be happy with just five cats and all that silence. I'm fifty-six years old. I might not get another chance."

"Or you might get a better one. Who knows? The dinner isn't the thing, either. It's that I don't trust a man who's jealous of his girlfriend's dog. It's petty. You know? It shows how insecure he is."

"Well, maybe I can make him more secure," Virginia said, desperately wishing she was back inside where it was warm.

"Right. The battle cry of the lonely woman. 'My love will fix him!'"

"You're crossing the line into too mean now, Fern, and I don't appreciate it."

"Sorry," Fern said. "I got your best interests at heart."

"It'll work out between him and the dog. T-Rex likes Lloyd."

Fern laughed out another huge cloud of smoke, her head dropping back to keep it away from Virginia's face. "T-Rex likes everybody," she said. "That big, sweet, dumb dog never met a man, woman, or child he didn't like. Why, I once saw that silly mutt wag his tail at the wooden Indian in front of the discount tobacco store."

Virginia smiled, remembering. It felt good to smile. And different. As though she could not remember when she last had.

Fern bent down and crushed the burning tip of her cigarette butt under the toe of one sensible white waitress shoe. Then she examined it for remaining embers. Finding none, she tossed the butt over her shoulder into the Dumpster. She pulled her tiny breath-spray dispenser from her apron pocket and pumped three short blasts onto her tongue. As always.

She squeezed Virginia's arm on the way by. Virginia wondered how a hand could be so cold as to feel colder, in contrast, than her own half-frozen arm.

"Hope I'm wrong," Fern said. "It's happened before."

Then she hurried back inside.

Chapter Nine: Jody

"I'm going out to shovel, Grampa!" he shouted. Jody didn't like to shout. It fed back to his ears like anger, and anger was sandpaper on his nerves. But Grampa was hard of hearing, and besides, he had the TV up loud.

"What?"

Grampa sat in front of the TV, the volume cranked up to blaring. It hurt Jody's ears and wore on his peace and balance. He walked over close to Grampa's chair, leaned one hand on the armrest, and said it again directly into the ear of the frail old man.

"I'm going out to shovel!"

Grampa looked up into Jody's eyes, his own eyes watery, red, and confused. "Shovel what?"

Jody knew, just from the look on the old man's face, that he not only didn't know what Jody was offering to shovel, he likely didn't know who Jody was. Yesterday he had. But maybe not today. Maybe later, when Jody got back inside and knocked the snow off his boots, Grampa would know more.

"Doesn't matter," he said. "I'll be back."

He zipped up his down parka and stepped out into the silent, brilliant morning. He could still hear a trace of the TV, so he moved farther from the house, where he could not. If indeed "house" was even the right way to say it. It was more of a cabin perched on a hill over the lake.

The sun was high, nearly overhead, and it shone on the tops of the evergreen trees and their white coating of snow. Here and there it would melt a clump just enough to cause it to let go, releasing a powdery flurry near where Jody stood.

He watched a bright-orange snowplow wind its way along the narrow two-lane Highway 22. The highway was a good distance down from the cabin, but nobody had plowed their little road yet, and it could easily be a day or more until anybody did.

Jody set to work shoveling the driveway all the same. He had no car, and neither did Grampa. He'd never learned to drive in those teen years when most kids did. Partly because he had no car. Partly because Jody viewed driving as an adventure for those with steadier nerves. Still he kept the driveway clear, because Grampa had a bad heart, and a bad tendency to wander off and get lost. Jody never knew when he might need to call a cab. Or the police. Or an ambulance.

He shoveled until his heart pounded and his breath came in gasps, disappointed to have to mar the perfect white blanket of winter. There was something peaceful about an untouched fall of snow. Like being in another world, where nothing can go wrong. Because nothing can find you.

He leaned on the shovel, catching up with his own breathing.

He looked out over the disturbed snow at his feet to the undisturbed lake. The plow had rounded a bend out of sight. The sky was cloudless, but not blue. That winter color, like steel. Hardly different from the white horizon. He pretended for a moment that he couldn't see where one left off and the other began. He had to squint to make that image work.

Nothing and nobody moved.

And then something did.

A red pickup truck inched its way along the freshly plowed Highway 22, half-obscured behind the walls of snow formed by the plow. Jody watched with some interest. He'd never seen the truck in this neighborhood before. And whoever was driving it seemed unsure where he was going. Either that or not anxious to get there very fast.

Just where the narrow highway edged up to the shore of the lake, the truck stopped right in the middle of its lane. Where else could it stop, really? There was no place to pull over. And it didn't matter anyway, because no one else was fool enough to be out here on these tricky roads on a day like this.

A man stepped out.

He didn't seem dressed for the weather. He wore a light jacket, but it could not have been enough. It was the kind of jacket you'd wear on a slightly cool summer night. He was completely bald, his head shaved clean, but he had a bushy gray beard. It was an odd look, because his sideburns rose up from the beard and then just ended. They were trimmed off flat on the top, not on the bottom. He wore no gloves.

He was old. But not Grampa old.

As he moved around the side of his truck, the man glanced around as if to convince himself that no one was watching. But Jody was watching. The man never saw him, though, because Jody was up on the hill, and the man looked in every direction but up.

Then Jody saw the dog. He was in the bed of the truck, but not tied down in any way. Which was illegal in this county. And also not very nice. He was a big dog, maybe sixty or seventy pounds, and the color of a golden Labrador, but he had ears that stood up big and straight like a German shepherd. He wagged furiously as the man moved back to the tailgate of the truck. He tried to lick the man's bearded face, but was only roughly pushed away.

Jody bit down harder on his own molars. The cold stung his fingertips right through his gloves, but he focused off it again.

The man let down the tailgate and took the dog by the collar, pulling him hard, so he had to jump down onto the road. Once the dog was down on the frozen tarmac, the man yanked off his collar. Just pulled hard, and pulled it off right over the dog's head. It looked like it had been on a bit loosely, but not loosely enough to be taken off like that, and Jody heard the dog yip in pain. Then he wagged again. Wagged at the person who had just hurt him.

The man wound up like a pitcher on a mound and hurled the collar into the lake. Well. *Onto* the lake. Had this guy really been thoughtless enough not to understand that the lake would be frozen? It seemed like a simple enough concept. The collar skidded a few feet across the ice.

Jody laughed out loud. Of course, he was too far away to be heard.

"Now how stupid do you have to be not to see that one coming?" he asked, of no one in particular.

The man scrambled over the snowbank left by the plow and set off to the edge of the lake to retrieve the collar. He tested the ice before putting his full weight on it. Then he stepped out cautiously, and Jody briefly wished for him to fall through. He'd go rescue him, of course. But the ice-water bath would serve him right.

The man did not fall through. He did, however, slip. His arms windmilled comically, his feet came forward, and he landed hard on his ass.

Jody laughed again.

The dog, maybe due to not knowing what was expected of him, jumped back up into the bed of the pickup.

The man carefully retrieved the collar, then hauled the dog roughly out of the truck bed again. This time he put the tailgate back up. He wound up to pitch again, hurling the collar into the soft, untouched snow at the edge of the lake.

He jumped back into the truck, made a clumsy three-point turn in the narrow road, and drove back the way he'd come. The dog ran after him until it was clear he would never keep up. Then he sat down on the centerline of the highway, still wagging.

"You son of a bitch," Jody quietly told the retreating truck.

He threw the shovel aside and walked downhill to the highway. It wasn't easy. The snow was as high as his thighs in some places, and he had to post-hole his way along at a snail's pace. His boots filled with snow, and the effort made his legs tired.

About halfway down his unplowed road to the highway, the dog noticed him. He stood, ears tuned in Jody's direction, and wagged his tail. Every few seconds he would look back in the direction the truck had taken. As if it might appear again. Or maybe to communicate to Jody that he was concerned about having missed his ride.

It felt good to burst out of the thigh-high snow and onto the plowed road. The dog met him halfway, and licked his hands, even though Jody still had his gloves on.

"Now what are we gonna do with *you*?" Jody asked him.

The dog cocked his head and wagged harder.

"Well, you got a nice disposition. But I think you're not smart enough to figure out what a mess you're in. What's your name, boy?"

Then his face burned red, because it had been a stupid question. A hopeless thing to say. Even reminding himself that no one but a dog could hear him didn't ease his shame.

"Let's go see where that collar went off to," he said.

The dog eagerly followed him over the snowbank. Well, half over and half through. Jody tracked back and forth in the snow, sorting a careful grid across the area where he was sure he'd seen it come down. But in that blanket of untouched white, every place looked a lot like every place else.

A good ten minutes went by without results. Jody wasn't sure whether to recheck the same grid or accept the fact that he was looking in the wrong location.

Then he looked up. In the snow, maybe six feet away, he saw a ring-shaped disturbance in the powdery surface. If the light hadn't hit it just right, he might never have seen it at all.

Crouching, he dug around close to the frozen ground, snow working its way under the wrists of his gloves, which were quickly soaking through. Then he wrapped his hand around the collar and pulled it free. Held it up in front of his face. The dog walked up and sat beside him, head raised, as if assuming that Jody would—or suggesting that he should—put it back on.

It was bright green, made of nylon webbing. It had a shiny stainless-steel buckle. On the steel ring were three tags, a dog license and rabies tag, both metal, and a red plastic identification tag. It was etched with only the dog's name, and a phone number.

"T-Rex," Jody read, and the dog wagged harder. "That's a stupid name. I don't like it. If you were my dog, I'd give you a better name than that. Something more like what you deserve. Then again, if you were my dog, I wouldn't haul you out into the woods by the lake on one of the coldest days of the year, and then treat you like you're not even worth the ride home. Now what am I supposed to do with you? Grampa won't allow a dog. And I've got no car to drive you to the pound. Maybe if I called Animal Services they'd drive their truck out here and get you."

Jody stood up. Sighed.

Then he began the long trudge back up to the cabin.

He looked over his shoulder, expecting to see the dog right at his heels. The dog wasn't following. He was waiting in the road, right where he'd been dumped. As if he'd been charged with some sacred pact to stay put.

It's heartbreaking, really, Jody thought, *the things you can do to a good dog.*

"Well, don't just sit there!" he called.

The dog turned his head to look at Jody. Then he looked back down the road again.

"He's not coming back for you. I'm sorry. He's an idiot, but he doesn't want you. He should. But he doesn't. He made that real clear. Now, come on. You'll freeze out here."

He waited, but the dog didn't move.

"Come!" he called.

Apparently unaccustomed to disobeying a direct order, the dog followed him back up the road to the cabin, bounding to keep his head up out of the snow.

Chapter Ten: Virginia

She had to park on the street, the passenger side of her car scraping into a snowbank left by the plow, because Lloyd had not shoveled the driveway. He had promised to do so if it snowed all day, erasing her hard-won morning shoveling job. She felt slightly vexed by his broken promise, but not particularly surprised, which sharpened the sense of irritation.

She stumbled up the driveway, lifting her legs extra high to try to keep them clear of the snow on each step. Then she noticed two tracks where the collected drifts were shallower. Lloyd had taken his truck out today.

She unlocked the front door, the knob and keys hurting her hands with their coldness. Lloyd was on the couch, in sweatpants and a bathrobe, watching TV. He had the volume up too loud.

She locked the door behind her and flopped onto the couch beside him, rubbing the top of his smooth scalp.

He recoiled, pulling his head away. "Hey! Your hand is cold!"

He hadn't shaved it recently, his head. She could tell. He had five-o'clock shadow around the edges—that ring over his ears where he would have had hair if he'd allowed hair.

"Mind if I turn this down?" She didn't wait for him to answer. She picked up the remote and notched the volume down with four clicks. "What are you watching?"

"A man's remote is sacred. You know that, Ginnie."

"Except it's my remote. My house, my TV, my remote."

"Whatever happened to 'what's mine is yours and what's yours is mine'?"

"Well, that's a good point," she said.

He lifted her left hand to his face, as though he couldn't wait to see the ring again. But he looked at it from too close-up, and she realized he wasn't wearing his glasses. Maybe he'd lost them. He lost them a good three times a week. He held the hand so close that his beard tickled her knuckles.

"What did Fern say about the ring?" he asked, sounding eager, and more like a boy than a nearly retired man.

She took the hand back. Averted her gaze. "Well, you know how Fern is."

Then, to change the subject utterly, she tried to move over onto his lap. But he bellowed out a big sound to stop her, and she plunked into a sit beside him again.

"Sorry, but don't, Ginnie. I hurt my hip."

"What happened?"

"Oh, nothing. Just slipped on the ice. Landed harder on my left sitting bone than my right, and it hurts."

"Should you get that x-rayed?"

"It's just bruised up is all."

"Never hurts to be sure."

"Until we're married, I'm not on your insurance."

"Oh," she said. "That's right." Even on low volume, the sound of the TV made it hard for her to talk. Even to think. He was watching some kind of sports roundup. One of those programs that show all the best plays of the week. Except he wasn't watching.

He was talking to her. So she picked up the remote and clicked it off. Surprisingly, he offered no comment. "You go out today?"

"No. I been in all day."

"Thought you were gonna go put a bid on that drywall job."

"Vick Gleeson already got it."

"Oh."

Virginia remembered the tracks in the driveway. The ones that indicated he'd pulled his truck out as the snow collected. But she couldn't get a bead on what that meant, and didn't want to question him on it, so she filed it away in her brain.

Then it hit her. It should have hit her sooner, she realized. Six years she'd had that dog, since he was barely old enough to eat solid food. And not one day had he failed to greet her at the door.

"Where's T-Rex?"

"Don't know, hon," he said, and clicked the TV back on.

"Well, he couldn't have gotten out unless you let him. Did you let him out?"

"Of course I let him out. He has to piss, right?"

"Since when does he not come back about six seconds later, though? He hates the cold. He doesn't like the way the snow balls up between the pads of his feet."

"I wouldn't know nothing about that, hon."

"So you're saying you let him out to pee and he just never came back?"

"I don't know, Ginnie. I don't remember. I was watching TV."

"Do you stand at the door and wait for him?"

"No, I don't stand there and wait. Why would I? I can't see what he's doing unless I leave the door open, and it's too cold for that. If he wants to get back in, he'll scratch at the door."

"And he never came back and scratched, and you never noticed?"

"You're making too big a deal of this, hon. You always make too big a deal about that dog. He's a dog. He's out doing dog things. Chasing squirrels. Exploring."

She rocked her head back, as if to look at him from a greater distance. Gain more perspective. "Have you ever *met* T-Rex?"

Lloyd never answered.

Virginia let herself out through first the front and then the back door, and called for T-Rex as loud as she could. Loud enough and long enough that her neighbor, Leona, pulled back the curtains to look out and see what all the fuss was about. It was just her style, Leona, that brand of veiled complaint.

T-Rex was nowhere within the sound of her voice. And the sun would be going down soon.

———

"Maybe he got picked up by the animal regulation people," Fern said.

They stood together at the side of Highway 22, both leaning on Fern's car. Fern was taking a smoke break. They'd been driving around looking for almost three hours.

"I called," Virginia said. "I caught 'em just at closing time. They only picked up two dogs today. A Chihuahua and a pit bull mix."

"Well, I just don't know then," Fern said on a huge exhale of smoke.

Virginia caught a blast of that smoke smell. Usually she hated that; it smelled nasty to her. Right at that moment though, it smelled good. Like she wished she could hold that cigarette in her own hand. Take a deep draw to numb everything down. It had been so many years since she'd quit. But there it was again.

"I'm just beside myself, Fern."

"I don't blame you."

"It's supposed to go to seven degrees tonight."

"Not much warmer than that now."

"If we don't find him, he'll die. He won't survive one night out here."

"I know it," Fern said. "And I swear I feel just as sick about it as you do. Or pretty damn close anyway. But I just don't know what else we can do. We've looked and called in every direction . . . farther than he could walk in one day anyway. I hate like hell to say it, but if he's not coming to the sound of your voice, something must've happened to him."

"Coyote pack? Is that what you're thinking? But it was broad daylight when he disappeared."

"I was thinking maybe he walked out into the road and got hit."

"Then we'd have found him in the road," Virginia said, wincing at the mental image. She realized that she'd been braced for just such a find as long as they'd been driving around. And acknowledging so out loud made her feel like she might be about to burst into tears. But she held it inside.

"Maybe the person who hit him took him to a vet," Fern said.

"He had a collar on. Tags. Someone would have called."

And yet Virginia liked the idea. And part of her continued to cling to it. Because it was that rare scenario in which her dog was still alive.

"You could call both vets' offices," Fern said.

"In the morning I could. Nobody'll be open now." They stood in silence a moment, Virginia hugging her coat more tightly around the solid bulk of herself. "Maybe somebody took him in so he wouldn't freeze."

"That could be," Fern said, sounding optimistic. Or sounding like she was trying to be, anyway. "In the morning before work you could put up some signs."

"But his phone number was right on his collar."

"Unless he got it off somehow."

"I guess," Virginia said. "He never did before. In six years."

Fern sighed.

It dawned on Virginia, an ugly realization: they were done for the night, because there was nothing more they could do. She would have to give up and go home without T-Rex.

As if overhearing her thoughts, Fern said, "Well. We got work in the morning."

"Yeah. Go home, Fern. Get some sleep. I'm gonna drive around a little bit more. But thanks for helping me look. I know I complain about you sometimes, but you're always right there when the chips are down. I appreciate that."

Fern gave Virginia's heavily coated upper arm a squeeze and then did exactly what Virginia was hoping she would not do. She gave up and went home.

———

It was after 1:00 a.m. when she climbed into bed beside Lloyd. It was warm under the covers. It was so different climbing into a bed with somebody else's body heat. Such a luxury.

Until he spoke.

"Hard to believe," he said. She could tell he was wide awake, and had been for a while.

"What's hard to believe? That he never turned up?"

"That you spent our first night engaged looking for him. You always put that dog over me."

A chill formed in her gut and spread out along her arms and legs, a sickening, clammy feeling.

"I don't *put him over you*. He's out in the freezing cold alone. If you were out in the freezing cold alone, I'd be looking for you. And it's not our first night engaged. You gave me the ring at dinner yesterday. We were engaged last night."

"First full day, then."

"Oh, what the hell difference does it make? T-Rex is gone!" She was surprised to hear the rise in her voice. She never raised her voice to Lloyd. She rarely raised her voice to anyone.

"He's a dog."

"Yeah, I'm clear on that part, Lloyd. I never thought otherwise."

"I'm your husband."

"Husband-to-be, and one has nothing to do with the other. He's in trouble and you're not. And I'm beginning to gather that you're not the least bit worried about him."

"He's a dog," Lloyd said.

Virginia said no more. Because what she was thinking, she was not yet ready to say. It wasn't cowardice. Not this time. It was just a big thing to form into words. And big things needed consideration. Especially the kinds of things you could never entirely take back once they'd been said.

She was thinking that maybe this future with Lloyd, the one she'd really only clutched in her hand for a little over a day, was not going to come to pass after all.

Chapter Eleven: Jody

When Jody rolled over in the night, he was alarmed at a constriction on the lower half of his body, as if he couldn't move his legs. As if someone or something had him pinned.

He turned on the light and sat up as best he could, his heart drumming.

The dog tapped his tail hard on the bedspread and leaned over to lick Jody's face, managing only to lick the air in his general direction. He was curled up against Jody's legs in such a way as to tightly pin the covers down.

Jody sighed. "I don't recall inviting you up here," he said.

The dog tapped harder at the sound of his voice.

Jody reached out to the dog's collar and held the three tags in his fingers, looking at them in the soft light of his bedside lamp. He wondered who would do all that for a dog—keep his rabies vaccine up to date, pay for a license, keep an ID tag on him so he couldn't get lost—and then purposely lose him.

He was seized with a strong feeling that he wanted the tags off the dog's collar. He sat up straighter, and leaned in. The tags were on a split ring, like the kind you use for your house keys. He pried the ring layers apart with his thumbnail and twisted until the whole thing came free. The ring and all three tags.

"I need to give you another name," he said. The dog gazed into his face calmly. "A better one. One that makes you sound more deserving. That let's everybody know you're worth better than this. You know?" He looked into the dog's eyes, then averted his gaze. "Then again, I'd best not name you if I'm not going to keep you. I would keep you. It's not me. I love dogs. It's Grampa." He turned the tags in his fingers for a minute. "Then again, Grampa's so bad off these days. Mentally, I mean. Maybe I could just say, 'What dog?' He doesn't exactly know what's real and what's not anyway." He braved a look at the dog's face. "Is that mean? That might be mean. I sure would like to keep you, though. My dad had a dog. She was such a good dog. Sheila, her name was. She was a Queensland heeler. Not to make you feel bad. Mutts are good dogs, too. But she was great. I was little, but I sure remember her. She gave up her life trying to save him. She didn't. Save him, I mean. But she sure tried. He was in the water, and she went in after him and just swam around and around looking for him until she couldn't swim anymore. All she had to do was pull herself out onto the riverbank. But she never did."

Jody looked at the tags again. The area code on the phone number was local. The same area code as his. So the dog couldn't be too far from home. Then again, that area code was two and a half counties long. They weren't very heavily populated counties, so that code cut a wide swath.

Maybe if Jody took the dog to the pound, he'd die there. Maybe nobody would adopt him. He wasn't all that young. And he wasn't the prettiest dog in the world. But he had a nice temperament.

"I could take you in and leave you for two weeks," he told the dog, "and I could call every day. And if nobody takes you, I could come rescue you. Only . . . would they charge me an adoption fee?

They would, I bet. And those are expensive. I don't have that kind of money lying around."

Then it hit him. If he took the dog to the pound, his owner might go in and get him back. The guy might feel guilty, or have a change of heart. Maybe the dog did something wrong—chewed up his favorite shoes or peed on the rug—and maybe the guy had a hair-trigger temper. Later, after he'd bought new shoes or rented a carpet cleaner, he might calm down and miss his old friend.

"No," Jody said sharply. The dog laid his ears out sideways. As if he'd done something wrong. "No, not you. I'm not saying no to you. I'm saying no to him. He doesn't deserve you back. And he's not getting you back. Unless it's over my dead body."

He opened the drawer of his bedside table and tossed the tags in. Slid the drawer closed.

The dog whimpered, a thin sound.

"What? You need to go out?" No reaction. "You're still hungry, aren't you? I didn't give you enough to eat."

Apparently "eat" was a magic word, and well within the dog's vocabulary. He pulled to his feet and leaned over Jody, wagging furiously and breathing that nasty dog breath into his face.

"I don't know what I'm supposed to give you," Jody said. "But come on in the kitchen, and we'll see what's what."

———

"Dog food," he said. Grimly, as if he were discussing the inevitability of death. He opened the refrigerator and peered in. Opened a cupboard. Closed it again. "How am I supposed to get dog food? Or the money for dog food? I'll have to take a bus all the way out to the mall. That'll take half the day. You can't go on the bus. And I'm not sure about leaving you alone here with Grampa. And it's too cold to leave you outside. And I bet you eat a lot, too. You're big. Shoot. What am I getting myself into?"

He plunked hard onto a kitchen chair. The dog padded up to him and set his head down on one of Jody's thighs. Gazed up into his face.

"Don't do that to me," he said. "It's not fair."

A movement caught his attention, and he looked up to see Grampa wander into the kitchen. He looked more asleep than awake. He shuffled so weakly that his bedroom slippers barely lifted off the linoleum on each step.

Jody's heart leaped up into his throat.

"What are you doing up, Grampa?" He tried not to sound panicky. He sounded pretty panicky. At least to himself.

"Heartburn," Grampa said.

"I'll make a bicarbonate of soda and bring it in to you."

Grampa turned his full gaze to Jody for the first time. Jody waited for him to say something about the dog. The dog wagged his tail hard, hitting the table leg with a solid thunk on every wag. Jody held his collar so he couldn't go introduce himself to Grampa, which he seemed inclined to do.

"Okay," Grampa said. He shuffled out of the kitchen again.

Jody looked down into the dog's face. The dog looked back.

"Let me go take care of this," he said.

He heated half a glass of water in the microwave. Just twenty seconds. Warm but not hot. Then he stirred in half a teaspoon of baking soda. He set the spoon in the sink and carried the glass into Grampa's room.

The old man was sitting up in bed, the quilt pulled up to his armpits. Just waiting. Staring into space.

Jody wrapped Grampa's hand around the glass. Made sure Grampa really had it before letting go. He sat on the edge of the bed and waited. At first he thought Grampa might have fallen back asleep with his eyes open. He did that sometimes. Then the old man took a sip. Carefully, as if it might be too hot. But Jody never made it too hot. Then Grampa drank the whole thing in one long gulp.

He handed the glass back to Jody. "What was that?" he asked.

"What was what, Grampa?"

"In the kitchen. That dog."

"Dog?"

"In the kitchen."

"I don't know what you mean, Grampa."

"Oh."

"Maybe you weren't quite awake yet."

"Oh."

Jody let himself out, closing Grampa's door behind him.

The dog was right where Jody had left him.

"That didn't feel good," he told the dog. "I still don't know if that's mean. Then again, I tell him all day long that he's wrong about things. And it isn't mean, it's just true."

He opened the pantry.

"I guess I'll have to make you some pasta," he said. "Not that dogs eat pasta much. Or that it's all that good for you. But I guess it'll tide you over until I can get some dog food. However I'm supposed to do that. I need to sleep before I figure out stuff like that."

He took down a pot and ran water into it, and set it on the stove to boil.

While he waited, he sat down on the kitchen chair again. Again the dog set his head on Jody's lap. This time Jody leaned forward and held the dog, his arms wrapping around his big, soft middle.

"I could put some milk on it. Your pasta. But right now that's really all I've got. It's the best I can do." The dog thumped his tail predictably. "I guess you're mine now. Good, bad, or whatever. I might as well admit it. I think it's too late now and you're just mine."

Chapter Twelve: Virginia

The first people to roll in for breakfast were the phone company guys and the guys who cut and cleared trees for the county. Quite a few trees had come down in the wind, and under the weight of the snow. Not here so much, and not much in town, but up by the lake, which was higher up into the mountains. The snow had been deeper and the wind had blown harder up there.

The diner sat more or less in the middle of nowhere, at least by road, marking the intersection between the 132 into town and the 22 out to the lake. Remote a spot as it was, that location made the diner popular for workmen moving back and forth. In the summer, guys went up there to man shops and tend yards and deliver supplies for the part-time residents, which was more or less all of them. So far as Virginia knew, nobody lived up there year-round. In the winter, it was mostly about keeping roads clear. Or pulling pine trees off power lines. And houses.

And everybody wanted a good breakfast on their way up.

Two of the phone company linemen were new. Guys Virginia hadn't seen before. Maybe Rick was training them.

Rick stepped up to her counter, unzipping his thick parka and blowing warm breath into his hands. She poured him a mug of coffee without having to be asked.

"Shame about your dog, Ginnie," he said. He never quite looked her in the eye. Apparently her situation was too sad for that. "I was pretty shocked when I saw your sign about him on that phone pole."

"Oh. Was I not supposed to tack it to a phone pole?"

"I don't care," he said, scratching his unshaved chin. "What difference does that make? I'm just sorry your dog's gone. We'll keep our eyes peeled when we're out and around today."

"Thanks," Virginia said. Then she felt that sinking in her gut. "But . . ."

"Yeah, I know. Not good. His chances aren't so great. But even if he didn't make it . . . it's still better if we tell you what we see, right? I mean, you'd still want to know."

"I think I would. Yeah."

Fern popped out of the kitchen and Rick slipped off his ski cap, as if to salute her out of respect. Then Virginia wondered why he hadn't taken his cap off for *her*. Why she didn't seem to command that same brand of respect.

"Morning, Fern," he said, pointing at one of the fresh jelly doughnuts on its covered pedestal stand. "I'll have that one right there."

"I could have gotten you a doughnut, Rick," Virginia said, trying to keep her voice light.

"Oh. Hell. Sorry, Ginnie. I know. I just got distracted about the dog. Anyway, we'll let the county guys and the contractors know. Everybody we bump into who drives all over the area. If he's around, we'll find him."

But Virginia could tell just by the way he said it that T-Rex still being around was a depressingly remote possibility.

———

When the lunch rush was over, and the diner had been cleaned up and put to bed for the day, Virginia asked Fern something. Spit out some words she'd been holding just at the base of her throat all day long.

"You want to go out and get a beer with me?"

Fern looked at her for a long time. As though the source of Virginia's insanity might jump up to be identified. "It's three thirty in the afternoon."

"So? We start work early, and it's the end of our day."

Fern examined her for a while longer, and it was all Virginia could do not to squirm. "I'm surprised you're not in a hurry to get home to your new fiancé."

Virginia did not answer, and she carefully avoided Fern's eyes.

"Ah," Fern said. "So it's like that. Well, then I'd say we best go get a beer or two and you can tell me all about it."

———

"I might not marry him," she said. She said it quietly so John, the tavern's owner and bartender, would not hear. And she kept her eyes down. She ran her thumb along the edge of the wet label of her beer bottle, and she watched the thumb carefully.

"Is this about what I said?"

"No," Virginia said quickly. "Well. Maybe a little. Maybe just the part about T-Rex."

She heard Fern suck in her breath, and it frightened Virginia, even though she had no idea why. It settled into a place in her stomach that had been rocky anyway, and set the demons loose again.

"So you think so, too," Fern said, her voice low with gravity.

"Think what?"

"Oh. Never mind."

"Think what, Fern?"

"I guess we weren't on the same page with that like I thought."

"Well, you know I have to hear it now, though."

"Why don't you start by telling me exactly what's making you maybe not want to marry him? And then we'll go on from there."

Virginia sighed and removed her thumb from the beer bottle. She took a sip from her glass. Looked at herself in the mirror behind the bar. Then she cut her eyes away again, as if ashamed. Well, not even so much "as if." She was ashamed. She just couldn't put her finger on why.

"He's just not very unhappy about T-Rex being gone. When I got back from looking last night, he was mad. Because it was our first full day as an engaged couple, and I spent it looking for the dog. He said I always put the dog first. Which is ridiculous, because T-Rex was in trouble and Lloyd wasn't. If they'd both been drowning and I'd saved T-Rex first, then I might say he had a point. But this was just silly. I know he's not much of a dog person, so I'm not insisting he should be personally heartbroken. But you'd think at least he'd see it's a hard thing for me. I mean, I didn't need someone jumping down my throat last night. I needed some support. Still do."

Fern placed a hand on Virginia's sleeve and gave her forearm a squeeze. Virginia smiled at the hand. She still couldn't bring herself to look up. Just for a minute she felt better. Then the demons set up a fuss in her gut again. Reminded her what she was forgetting.

"What were you going to say about it?"

"Oh, crap," Fern said, and sighed. "I really went and stuck my foot in it."

"Maybe. But you have to tell me now."

Fern lit up a cigarette, as if to buy time. John brushed by and left an ashtray on the bar in front of her. He seemed to know a serious discussion when he saw one, and he was staying respectfully away.

"It just seems like a big coincidence. You know? You get engaged to this guy who doesn't like your dog, and has kind of a chip on his shoulder against him. And not twenty-four hours later, the dog is nowhere to be found."

"You're saying you think he did something to T-Rex?"

"It crossed my mind. Yeah."

The fluttering in Virginia's belly stopped. The whole area turned to sickening concrete. It turned out she'd been fluttering between half-okay and not okay. And now she'd landed solidly on not. In a weird way, it was almost a relief. Given a choice between "maybe all is lost" and "all is lost," there seemed to be some comfort in just getting it over with.

"Like what?"

"Now how would I know that, Ginnie?"

"You think he took him out in the woods and shot him?" she asked, forcing out the words without pausing to absorb their gravity.

"He got a gun?"

"He hunts deer, yeah."

"Why am I not surprised?"

"He wouldn't do that, Fern. I mean, I just can't believe he would. I know you're no fan of Lloyd. And in some ways I don't blame you. But I just can't believe . . . okay, he can be a little childish. I'll give you that. But what you're talking about would be plain evil. He's not evil. Besides, he said he never left the house yesterday."

And, on those words, the filing cabinet in her brain opened up and showed her what she'd tucked away. Tire tracks. There had been partly covered tracks in the snow on the day he'd said he hadn't taken the truck out. Something like static jarred her torso. She wanted to say something, but didn't know what it was, and couldn't pull herself together to speak anyway.

She heard Fern say, "You got the guts to ask him straight out if he hurt that dog?"

Virginia looked up. Looked Fern right in the eye. It surprised her. It surprised both of them, apparently. "Yes," she said.

"Good."

Virginia sighed. Opened her mouth to speak. Closed it again. Then she pushed harder. "It just makes me wish . . ."

"This sentence better not end with Aaron."

Fern glanced up at Virginia's face. Virginia knew she must look stung. How could she help it? She couldn't force out a reply, so Fern went on.

"Oh, I'm sorry. I know it sounds terrible, and so I really try not to say it every time it comes up. But Ginnie. Honey. It's been nineteen years. *Nineteen years.* Sooner or later you got to get beyond the 'what ifs.' I know you loved him; I don't doubt that for a minute. But you didn't really know him yet. So you really don't know what your life with him would have been. And since you'll never know, it's easy to make it all idyllic. This is why I hated *The Bridges of Madison County.* Hated it. Here these two had an affair for a couple of weeks, and then for the rest of forever they're all 'He was the one' or 'She was the love of my life.' But that's too easy. Wait till you have to get right down to who's gonna take out the trash on a night when the mercury dips into single digits. Once you get that worked out, I'll believe you. I really tried to stay off your back about it before this. You were grieving and I didn't blame you. But now . . . I don't quite know how to say this, but I swear it's true. I'm really saying all this out of some sort of kindness to you. My problem is not that I don't believe the two of you would've lived happily ever after—"

"The three of us," Virginia added.

"Right. Three. But it's not about whether it would've worked out. It's more that it seems like a cruel trick to play on yourself, to be so sure he was the one. You don't exactly know how much you lost, but you've built it up into the biggest loss imaginable. Doesn't seem like the best way to go."

Virginia breathed as steadily as possible for a minute before answering.

"I never knew you felt this way."

"Nobody wants to speak ill of the dead. Not that I would have been exactly, but you know. But now . . . now I feel like it's just making this thing with Lloyd even harder than it needs to be. Just leave the past out of the picture for now, Ginnie. Ask him straight out about the dog."

"But if he denies it, I'll never know what's true."

"Maybe not, but it's a start."

"Part of me just wants to give him his ring back. But it's hard. What if I'm wrong?"

"You're not wrong about the fact that he couldn't even show you any sympathy about it."

"Well . . . yeah. But that might be a onetime thing."

"Nothing's a onetime thing," Fern said. "Not in relationships. Everything is the tip of the iceberg. Everything points to something much bigger floating down where you can't see. If you see something rear its head once, expect to see it again. It's like if you see a cockroach in your kitchen. And you don't call the exterminator 'cause you figure it's just that one, and how long can it live? Yeah, good luck with that."

"You're a big know-it-all. You know that, Fern?"

Fern laughed too loudly. "Let me think whether anybody ever pointed that out before."

"Besides. That sounds so pessimistic."

"Not at all," Fern said, tapping her cigarette almost aggressively against the ashtray. Much harder than could ever be needed to knock ashes off the tip. "It's realistic. *You* see something come up and you put it away again. Like maybe it hardly happened at all. *I* see something come up and I believe it. I take it into account."

They sipped for a few minutes in silence. Virginia finished her beer and signaled John to bring another. She rarely drank two beers in a row. But today she liked the feeling she got from it. Or maybe the lack of feeling would describe it better. She had begun to feel mildly numb.

"I don't know what to do," she said after a time.

"Nobody ever does," Fern said. Virginia's head snapped up, and she looked at her friend in surprise. Fern laughed again. "What? You think the rest of us have a crystal ball or something? When you marry somebody, or even just throw your lot in with him, you don't really know what you're getting into. We all just take our best shot. What does your gut say?"

"That he's probably my last chance."

"That's not what I mean. What does your gut say about whether you're better off with a rotten guy or no guy at all?"

"I don't know," Virginia said.

But really she did.

Chapter Thirteen: Jody

Jody got the bank teller he liked best. Vicky. She was only a few years older than he was, and he liked the way she smiled. Not like something she'd pasted on from the outside. Not a mouth-only smile. A big from-the-inside-out kind of smile.

"Hi, Jody," she said, and turned his withdrawal slip around to face her. "Haven't seen you for a while."

"Oh," he said. His face reddened. He didn't have a crush on her or anything. It was nothing like that. It just embarrassed him to talk to people, because he so seldom did anymore. "I try not to dip into the college fund. You know."

He opened his passbook again and frowned. He closed it fast, so she wouldn't see how little he had left. Then he realized how silly that was. She was probably looking at his balance on her computer screen.

"Not much of a college fund anymore," he said, which he realized was a dramatic understatement of the truth. He sighed. "Oh, what does it matter anyway, right? I'm never going to go to college."

She looked up and smiled at him, but this time it was more of a troubled smile. She was wearing her hair in a ponytail. It made her seem younger. "You could go to college."

"With what?"

"You could go to the community college. Or get a scholarship. Or something like that."

He pursed his lips as though tasting something sour, then shook his head. "I might as well face it. I'm twenty-three. That's the age people get *out* of college, not go into it."

"That's not always true. I had an aunt who went back to school when she was seventy-two."

"But I have to take care of my grandfather and all. Anyway, I can't really think about that right now. My dog needs some dog food, and that's more important."

"That sounds pretty important," she said.

He thought about the dog. For the fiftieth time at least, he worried whether he'd be okay at home. Jody had left him in the garage, on a pad made of three folded blankets, and with a space heater blowing in his direction. His brain kept playing images of bad things, like the old wiring shorting out, or the dog tipping over the heater so its hot coils touched the blankets.

It made him feel like he needed to hurry.

"I have to go," he said.

He swept his money off the counter and hurried back out into the cold. But he needn't have bothered rushing. Because it was thirty-five freezing minutes before the next bus came.

———

The mall had one of those big chain pet stores that let you bring your dog right inside to shop with you. It made Jody wish he could have brought his dog along.

They were holding some kind of adoption event in the heated entryway, which made the place extra crowded.

Jody raced up to the engraving machine at the front of the store. It loudly advertised that you could pick out a size and color of tag and it would put your name and address and phone number on it while you waited. He could see that a family of three, a mom and dad with a girl of about seven, was headed in that direction with their new dog. He could tell that the dog—who looked like a cross between a Lhasa apso and a poodle—was new because he still wore the bandanna that said, "Adopt Me."

Any hint of a line forming made Jody feel competitive, so he beat them there without letting on that he was trying.

He chose a tag in blue, then realized he didn't know what he wanted the dog's name to be. He leaned on the machine and thought a minute, but he was aware of the family waiting behind him. The more he let himself be influenced by that pressure, the less he could think.

The father leaned in and spoke over his shoulder. "Dog's name," he said.

"What?"

"The first line that you haven't filled out yet. That's for the dog's name."

"Right," Jody said. "I know."

"If you don't know your dog's name, can we go first?"

"But I already started. I picked the medium blue tag and all."

He heard the man sigh sharply. Almost more like a huffing sound. "We've only had this dog for five minutes, and we already know his name. You shouldn't step up to the machine if you haven't decided yet."

"It's Max!" the little girl said.

Jody fought to stay balanced, but his sense of panic was growing fast. Soon it would be bigger than he was. "I know my dog's name," he said.

The mom spoke up for the first time. She had a nice voice. Sweet and pleasant, like everything she said was meant to put somebody at ease. "Honey, go take the dog out to pee, okay? The man just needs a little more time."

The father huffed again, but then he pulled the dog outside.

Jody looked over his shoulder at the woman. She had pretty blue eyes. She smiled reassuringly.

"Sorry," she said.

"I lied. I totally don't know my dog's name."

"You can use the name Max," the little girl said. "We don't mind sharing."

Jody smiled in spite of his tension. "Max is a nice name," he said. "But I was looking for something different. This dog needs a name that's really special. I want people to hear it and know he's deserving. You know what I mean? I want something that makes him sound worthy."

"Well," the woman said, "let's see. 'Deserving' is a terrible name for a dog, but what about 'Worthy'?"

"Worthy," Jody said. Then, without any more thought on the matter, he typed the letters into the machine. W-O-R-T-H-Y. Worthy. "That's perfect," he said. "Thanks. I have no idea why I didn't think of it."

"Worthy," the little girl repeated as he typed in his phone number. "Worthy, Worthy, Worthy. I don't want to name our dog Max anymore. I want to name him Worthy."

"But, honey," her mom said, "we can't use that name. That's this man's name for *his* dog."

"But I was willing to share Max with him."

"That's true," Jody said, just as his tag dropped out of the machine. "I don't mind sharing."

"Well, that's very sweet of you," the mom said. "But I have a strong feeling her dad'll want to stick with Max."

As he stepped into the checkout line, the tag clutched in his fingers and a fifty-pound sack of kibble on his shoulder, he saw it. It was on a bulletin board behind the checker's head. A notice on regular typing paper, printed right off somebody's computer.

It said, "Lost dog. Answers to T-Rex. Six years old, golden retriever/German shepherd mix. Owner heartbroken. Please help." Under that it had a phone number, in much bigger font. It was the same number as on the tag he'd hidden in his drawer.

The bulk of the paper was taken up with a big picture of the dog. His dog. Worthy. Jody noted that the bright green of the dog's collar was plainly visible in the photo.

"Excuse me," he said to the woman in line behind him. "I forgot something."

She moved aside right away, but her enormous wolfhound did not. And it was hard for Jody to get around him. When he eventually did, he walked down the collar and leash aisle, still hauling the heavy bag on his shoulder, and picked out the least expensive nylon collar he could find. He chose blue.

Then he stood in line again, his eyes darting back and forth to the notice on the board.

Heartbroken my ass, he thought to himself. *I don't even believe he has a heart to break. He must just feel guilty, that man. Well, he should. He deserves to feel guilty. And now he's using this "heartbroken" thing to manipulate everybody who sees the sign into helping him get his dog back. But he isn't getting his dog back. Because what if he just changes his mind again? What if the dog does some other little thing to piss him off? And what if next time the guy drops him where there's nobody around to save him?*

Then, just for a moment, Jody wavered. Maybe it wasn't right to take somebody else's dog. Maybe it wasn't a fair choice to make.

He closed his eyes and felt around for guidance. Sometimes when he wasn't sure what to do, he asked his father in his head.

He wasn't entirely sure he believed his late father could hear him, or could provide counsel. But just asking that way seemed to help.

No, he decided. *That dog is my responsibility now, and so now it's my job to keep him safe. And he's obviously not safe at his old home, so—*

"Sir?"

It was the checker, wanting him to step up and put his purchases on the belt. Which he was not doing, being so lost in thought.

"Oh," he said. "Sorry."

He set the massive sack of food down for her to scan, and his body felt so light he thought he might float away. He counted out the money from the bank, and was left with just about the change he needed to get home on the bus and not much more.

———

On the way to the bus stop, he encountered two more of the signs. He wondered why he hadn't noticed them on the walk from the bus to the store.

He tore them both down, crushed them into a ball, and stuffed them in his jeans pocket.

———

"Here, boy," he said. "Have yourself a decent meal."

He set the mixing bowl of kibble on the kitchen floor, and the dog dove right in. Ate like he hadn't eaten in days. But he was slightly overweight, big and soft in the middle, so Jody couldn't imagine he'd missed many meals. Just an enthusiastic eater, most likely.

"I shouldn't call you 'boy' anymore. You have a new name now. A good one. Your name is Worthy. Hear that, boy? Worthy. That's you."

The dog's head did not come up. Nor did his ears twitch. And he didn't wag his tail any harder than he'd been wagging at the food all along.

"You'll get used to it in time," Jody said.

———

About an hour after dinner Jody left the dog in his bedroom with the door closed and went to check on Grampa.

He found him in the kitchen.

Grampa had opened the pantry door, as if looking for something. He had unrolled the top of the huge sack of kibble and was running his fingers over and among the little pellets of food.

His eyes came up immediately, and he looked into Jody's face.

"Jody Boy," he said.

It filled Jody's heart with a lightness, almost an elation. It had been days. Grampa always called him Jody Boy, because the kids at school had teased Jody over what they perceived to be a girl's name. Then again, Grampa only called him Jody Boy when he remembered who Jody was.

"Good to see you, Grampa. Welcome back."

Grampa's eyes looked deep and sad. He was wearing his old, faded robe over pajamas, his spine bent forward, chest sunken in. The more time went by, the shorter he became.

"There really is a dog, isn't there?"

"Yes, sir."

"But you know I don't like dogs."

"Yes, sir. But I'll be honest. More than I've ever been with you. I never thought that was fair. You knew how much I loved them. And how much I missed Sheila. And it just didn't seem like you could dislike them so much that it outweighed how much I liked them. I needed another friend. I didn't have much. But you were the one who took care of me, so there was nothing I could do. Now I'm the one taking care of you. I'll keep him away from you if you want. But he needs me, this dog. He would've died without me. So he's going to be around now, yes."

The rate of Jody's beating heart had ratcheted up with each sentence. Now, waiting for Grampa to answer, it pounded so hard that he had to steady himself with one hand against the kitchen table.

"I'd like to go back to bed," Grampa said. "Will you help me get back to bed?"

"Sure, Grampa. But . . . you came out here for something. You needed something from the pantry. Right? What did you need?"

Grampa's eyes came up to meet his again, their helplessness breaking his heart. It struck Jody that his heart had been broken multiple times a day for as many years as he could remember. Struck him hard.

"I don't know anymore."

"Okay, Grampa. It's okay. If it's important, it'll come to you again. Let's get you back to bed."

Chapter Fourteen: Virginia

Virginia pulled her car up to the curb in front of her home. The bank of snow at the edge of her street had grown dirtier, more pebbly in appearance. It also blocked her view of the driveway.

She stepped out, careful not to slip on the icy tarmac. When she'd made the ten or so steps to the bottom of her driveway, she was surprised to see it had been shoveled. Lloyd had cleared the driveway while she was away at the diner and having those beers with Fern. It struck her as sad that she hadn't even thought to look.

She carefully picked her way back to the car and started it up again. As she pulled into the driveway, she wrestled with a nagging feeling in her gut. At first she assumed it was the pressure of the difficult talk they were about to have. But as she watched the automatic garage door rolling up, she realized it was more complicated than that. She was slightly miffed that Lloyd had gone and done something thoughtful, because it took the edge off her anger. And right when she needed her anger most.

She drove in next to his red pickup. Turned off the engine. She sat a minute, forehead resting on the steering wheel. Then she looked at her bare left hand.

She took a huge, slightly shaky breath and made her way inside.

Lloyd was standing in the kitchen, looking eager for her to come through the door. He was all dressed up, wearing his gray suit with a red tie. His head was freshly shaved and his beard trimmed.

It made her forget what she'd been about to say.

"What are you all fancied up for, Lloyd?"

"Been waiting for you to get home. What took you so long? Change your clothes, and put on something special. A nice dress or something. I'm taking you out."

"Out?" she asked, as if none of the words he'd spoken had any meaning to her.

"Yeah, out. You remember out. We're going to the Steak 'n' Bake, and then I thought maybe even a little dancing."

"What's got into you, Lloyd?"

His eyes softened. Just for a flash, Virginia thought she saw something desperately sad there. But he quickly covered it over again.

"I just want things to be good between us, Ginnie. I'm sorry if you were upset last night and I was no help. I just want us to be okay again." His eyes flickered down to her hands, and the wounded look flashed across his face again. "Where's your ring?"

"Oh. I forgot it."

"How can you forget it?" he whined, sounding a little like a hurt child.

"I was just doing some dishes last night and I forgot to put it back on."

"Well, go put it on and change. I'm taking my baby to town."

He looked into her eyes and smiled in a way that was not only plainly sincere, but a little vulnerable and scared in the mix. He knew she'd been wavering, because people know. Whether they admit it to you, whether they admit it to themselves, people know where they stand with each other.

Virginia reached inside for the anger she had brought home with her, but it had completely dissolved. Dissipated like water vapor. She could not have pulled it back down into her heart if she'd tried.

———

"Well if you aren't just the most handsome couple in town," Darlene said. She was a waitress at the Mountview Inn and Suites Cocktail Lounge. But Virginia mostly knew her from the diner, because they had never—before tonight—come out for drinks and dancing at the lounge. It was too fancy and too expensive, and not really much her style anyway.

"The handsomest couple in town will have champagne," Lloyd said grandly.

The minute Darlene left their table, he leaped to his feet and tried to pull Virginia out onto the dance floor.

"Wait, wait," she said, laughing. "Not quite so soon. I'm too full of all that dinner you just fed me. Let's let it set a bit first."

He sat back down, looking disappointed. Then he reached out and took her left hand and held it, his big, rough fingers running over the tiny diamond in her ring. She felt an instinctive desire to pull her hand away. But that would be hurtful, and he would demand an explanation. And it didn't seem like something she could bring herself to do.

"I just want things to be good between us," he said. "I just want to do anything I have to. You know. To make sure we can be happy."

Virginia took her hand back. Suddenly. And in spite of her previous thoughts on the subject.

It was about the fifth time he had said that, or some version of that. And it had made her increasingly edgy each time. Now it struck her for the first time—at least the first time consciously—that it might be exactly what you tell yourself to justify disappearing someone's dog. Especially if you feel the dog has been a point of contention in the relationship.

"What's wrong, honey?" he asked.

She was going to tell him. But just then the champagne came.

She waited for Darlene to retreat again before she spoke. "Dinner, dancing, champagne. You rob a bank or something?"

He averted his eyes. Fixed them on the wood tabletop. "Ah, now don't go and take all the fun out of it."

"I don't mean to. But it's what we'd normally spend in a week."

"Well, if you just have to know, I borrowed a little from one of my sons. I'll be back working soon. You'll see. I don't want you feeling like you're supporting me. It's not going to be like that. Now, come on. A toast." He poured them each a glass, making the champagne flutes too full, so she could barely pick one up without sloshing. "To us."

He raised his glass. She raised hers, but said nothing. They clinked glasses, spilling quite a bit. Lloyd took a long drink.

"You're supposed to say it too, Ginnie. 'To us.'"

"I have to ask you a question," she said.

She could feel Lloyd's energy armor over. And why wouldn't it? Whose wouldn't? It was the way she'd said it. Her tone. Like the tone someone would use to say, "We need to talk."

"Well, that doesn't sound so good," he said, "but fire away."

"I'd like you to look me in the eye and tell me honestly you had nothing whatsoever to do with the disappearance of my dog."

She never looked up from her glass when she said it. She couldn't bring herself to. But in her peripheral vision she saw Lloyd sit back against his chair, hard. She heard the sound it made when he hit it.

"Well, that's a hell of a thing. Where did that come from?"

"I was having a beer with Fern today—"

"Oh. Fern."

"I guess it's no surprise she's not your biggest fan. And I don't want to do anything to make the situation worse between the two of you . . ." She stalled. She wondered briefly if it was wrong, even cowardly, to put it all off on Fern. But then she remembered that it really had never occurred to her that Lloyd might have done something to T-Rex. Not until Fern brought it up. Still, not wanting to be a coward, she pulled the conversation back to herself. "It's just that, four or fives times tonight you've said you'd do anything to make sure we'll be happy. I just wondered if maybe you'd even have . . . done that." She still couldn't bring herself to look up.

"And what exactly do you mean by 'that'? Define 'that' for me, Ginnie. Tell me exactly what you think I did to him."

"I can't really know that," she said. It sounded weak, which disappointed her.

"Give me an example, then."

"Well. I know it sounds awful to say. It's hard to even say it. But you do have a deer rifle."

"You think I took your dog out in the woods and shot him."

Virginia didn't answer. And she still didn't move her eyes from her champagne flute.

"Look up, Ginnie. Look at my eyes."

She did. He didn't look angry, as she'd feared. He didn't look vulnerable or hurt. Just sure. He looked sure.

"I did not take T-Rex out in the woods and shoot him," he said, his gaze never wavering.

Virginia let out a breath that felt as if it had been waiting hours to break free. It was probably loud enough for Lloyd to hear from his side of the table. "Oh, thank God," she said. "Thank the heavens for that. I'm sorry I even asked, then. It's just that she planted the idea in my head. And then it seemed like tonight you were acting kind of . . . like maybe you felt guilty."

"I do," he said. "I do feel guilty. Because you came home last night and you were all worried and I was only thinking about myself. I feel guilty for that. And I'm trying to make it up to you. Now come on. I want the honor of this dance."

They were the only couple on the floor, and so everybody watched. He spun her, and he dipped her, and maybe it was the sweet relief of the thing, but it made Virginia laugh.

Chapter Fifteen: Jody

He woke just before dawn, because it was cold. Actually, technically, it wasn't even the cold that woke him. It was Worthy. The dog pushed and jostled Jody, trying to wiggle under the covers with him. Then, having been wakened by that, it struck Jody that it was drafty and freezing cold.

He could hear the propane heater blowing on high in the living room. But still it felt as though the walls had disappeared in the night, leaving his bed out in the winter temperatures, unprotected.

He got out of bed, shivering and hopping and hugging his arms around himself, slapping his own sides. Anything to ward off the chill.

He skipped the robe and put on his winter coat instead. Sat on the bed and pulled on socks and then warm boots, his teeth chattering. He looked back at Worthy, who was trying to make a nest in the bedding. Jody pulled the covers over the dog, and Worthy settled beneath them.

Then Jody left his bedroom to look around. The front door was standing wide open. A several-inch drift of powdery snow had blown in and stacked up on a small rectangle of rug.

The door to Grampa's room was open. Grampa was not inside.

His heart beginning to race, Jody looked in the bathroom, then dashed out into the snow. He looked for tracks, thinking he could follow them. But the snow was fresh and untouched. If there had been tracks, new snow had covered them.

He felt Worthy's nose bump the back of his thigh.

"Worthy, go find Grampa. You've got a good nose, right? Where is he, boy?"

The dog just looked up into his face, loving and unguarded, and wagged.

"Here, smell this," he said, moving back inside and pointing down at the rug near the door, brushing snow off it as best he could.

The dog put his nose down and sniffed, apparently knowing he was being asked to. Then he looked up at Jody and wagged again. Jody sighed. Worthy was not Lassie. He did not understand what else was being asked of him.

"Do I look for him first?" Jody asked the dog. Well, it was more of a general question. If he'd been alone, he likely would have asked it out loud anyway. "Or do I just call 911 right now?"

He stepped back out into the snow and looked around. It was barely light, but the sky had begun to glow with morning. If Grampa had been standing, or sitting, or collapsed anywhere within a hundred feet or so of the cabin, Jody would see him. But all he saw was snow.

He ran inside and made the call.

———

Jody and Worthy paced the driveway for several minutes, waiting for the sheriff to arrive. Then Jody stopped. He looked at the dog, his mind filling with a terrible thought.

The sheriff's office was in town. So the deputies had probably seen the signs for the missing dog. Maybe a report had even been filed directly with their office. When the deputies got here, they might take Worthy away.

Jody ran back inside, calling for the dog to follow. Then he closed Worthy into his bedroom.

"You wait here," he said.

He ran into the kitchen and picked up the dog's water dish. Poured about three days' worth of food into a mixing bowl. Just in case.

He opened the bedroom to find the dog digging and scratching to build a nest with the bedding again. He didn't say anything, or try to stop him. He put down the two bowls and closed the door.

Then it struck him that Worthy would be too cold in there. The propane heater couldn't heat that room with the door closed.

He ran out to the garage to get the space heater and the stack of blankets. He brought them back inside and plugged the heater into the outlet beside his bed, Worthy tapping his tail against the bedding the whole time.

Jody covered him with all three blankets.

"I'll be back soon," he said. "I hope."

He ran to the front door, opened it, and found a sheriff's deputy on the welcome mat, one hand raised to knock. It was Deputy Rodelle, a man Jody knew fairly well. Because he'd helped locate Grampa twice before.

"Oh, you're here," Jody said, his voice trembling with panic. He hadn't realized how deeply panicked he felt until he heard it in his own voice. He'd worked himself into such a state that he'd simply stepped outside of himself, where he felt cut off from what he was feeling. Even from what he was doing. Or who he was. "Should I help you look?"

"No need to look. We saw him when we drove up. He's out on the side of the road. We're just waiting for an ambulance."

"Can I go to the hospital with him?"

"Come on, then."

They walked down the driveway together in stony silence.

The sun had just come up over the eastern mountains. As they walked, it flashed into Jody's eyes between the green of the pine needles. Now and then he could see the sun in a narrow space between trees, shooting out a perfect mandala of rays that seemed to sparkle with color, like a prism.

Jody blew hot breath into his hands.

Deputy Rodelle spoke, startling him. "I think it might be time to talk about your grandfather being someplace where they can take better care of him."

"You mean like a home?" he asked, his voice still trembly.

"I know that sounds bad. But they know how to deal with things like this. For his own sake, not just ours. He needs to be somewhere he can't wander off and get himself into trouble."

"Did he get himself into trouble this time?"

"I won't lie to you, Jody. It looks bad. He went out there in just pajamas. Bare hands, bare feet. We could be looking at some serious frostbite. Seems like he's been lying out there in the road for quite some time."

Just at that moment they reached the end of the long driveway, and Jody saw Deputy Rodelle's partner, Deputy Lighton, brushing the last of the snow off his grandfather's rigid, unresponsive body. Then he began trying to wrap a blanket underneath the old man, rather than just draping it over him.

Jody walked over to them, not feeling his feet touch the ground. Feeling like he was hollow inside. Light. Floating away.

He stood over the old man and looked into his face. Grampa's eyes were closed, and he had frost on his lids and lashes that looked as though it had frozen his eyes shut. His lips were a startling color of blue.

"Oh, Grampa," Jody said on the breath of a sigh. It sounded and felt like somebody else was talking.

When he looked at the deputies, he saw them both looking back at him. What he saw in their eyes was painfully familiar. In fact, it seemed to be the theme of his life, a sort of cement that fused his whole existence together.

Pity.

———

It was nearly three hours before the doctor came out to talk to him. He was handsome, with jet-black hair, barely in his thirties from the look of it. He looked like a leading man from one of Grampa's TV war dramas.

Jody jumped to his feet as the doctor approached, his whole body tingling with fear the way your foot tingles after it's gone to sleep and is just beginning to feel again.

"You're Edward Schilling's grandson?"

"Yes, sir."

In the doctor's eyes, that look again. That pity.

"I wish I could tell you everything's going to be fine. But we don't know yet. It's a tough situation. His blood pressure is dangerously low. We're trying to get it back up safely. We're trying to warm his extremities as promptly as we can, but without causing additional damage. Be prepared for the fact that, if he survives this, he's going to at least lose fingers and toes. If he's lucky. If he's not . . . Well. Let's just say, 'if not more,' and leave it at that for now."

Jody opened his mouth, but his ability to speak tangled back on itself and got stuck. He couldn't decide which to focus on: the idea that Grampa could lose more than fingers and toes, or the idea that he might not survive.

He felt himself wanting someone. Someone to be here with him, to stick by his side during this. But all he had in the world was his grandfather. And Worthy! He wished he could have brought Worthy to the hospital. Without the dog, he felt helpless. Moored, like a turtle flipped over onto its back. Completely at the mercy of whatever happened next.

He squeezed his eyes closed and worried again that Worthy was not all right. That he desperately needed to go out, or had spilled his water and was thirsty, or had knocked the heater over and set fire to the place, in which case Jody not only had no one, he had nowhere to go.

When he opened his eyes again, the doctor was peering into his face. A little too closely. As if Jody might need emergency medical care himself.

"You okay?"

"What could he lose if it's more than fingers and toes?"

"Worst case scenario, both his hands and feet. And part of his nose."

Jody's head swam alarmingly. He thought he might pass out. He dropped into a sit in the hard waiting-room chair. The doctor reached out and steadied his upper arm, but Jody was seated by then. It was too late to help.

"I don't know how I can take care of him if he loses his hands and feet. I can barely take care of him now."

"I know," the doctor said.

Jody looked up into the doctor's face to try to figure out how he would know. Could he just see these things in Jody somehow?

"I had a talk with the deputies who brought him in," the doctor said. "They suggested he might be better off placed in a care facility rather than returned to the home. They said he's been wandering away more and more often. That he's a danger to himself. More so every day."

Jody shook his head, almost sleepily. Not so much to say no to anything, but more to try to coax it into working order. "That must cost a lot of money."

"There are different options. He has Medicare and a Medicare supplement insurance, so it shouldn't be a burden to the family."

"I'm the family," Jody said, spreading his arms wide. "Just me."

Jody purposely did not look at the doctor's face, having seen more than his share of pity for one day.

"You want to come see him?"

"Yes, sir. I do."

———

Grampa was laid out on his back on a gurney in the emergency room. He had no pillow under his head, which made him look strangely flat, the way you might expect a hospital to lay out a corpse. He was covered with a white blanket almost to his chin. But there were extra thicknesses of something—something more than just Grampa—under parts of that blanket, as though his hands and feet were wrapped in something bulky.

Jody felt relieved that he couldn't see more. He didn't want to know what extremities look like when you might be about to lose them. He looked at the tip of the old man's nose, but it just looked strangely white.

The room spun slightly, and he steadied himself against the doctor's arm.

"You okay?"

"Yes, sir. Seems hot in here. Is it hot in here?"

"No, actually we keep it pretty cool."

"Why does it feel so hot to me?"

"That's usually what people say before they pass out."

"Oh."

They stood in silence for a few moments more. Jody reached out and held the backs of his fingers to his grandfather's cheek. It felt cool to the touch. It also felt wrong, like he should take his hand off Grampa's face. They had never exchanged any affection that involved touching.

"He looks like he's not even in there," Jody said.

"He is," the doctor said. "He's on a monitor, so we know he is."

"Oh. Well, then, maybe he just looks like he doesn't want to be," Jody said.

———

It was nearly eight o'clock that evening when Jody saw the doctor again. The doctor was walking past an open doorway that connected the waiting room to a long hallway. He stopped short with apparent surprise, looking like he might almost topple forward from his own impetus. Then he took two steps closer to Jody and leaned his shoulder in the doorway.

"You're still here."

"Shouldn't I be?"

"You don't need to be. There's nothing you can do for him right now."

"I'm not sure where else to go."

"Home?"

Jody glanced at the clock on the wall. "The bus doesn't even run this late."

"The buses run until ten."

"Not out to the lake they don't. Not in the winter."

"Oh. The lake. Can I call you a cab?"

"It's a long drive," Jody said. "I can't afford one."

The doctor disappeared from the doorway again.

A few minutes later a middle-aged nurse appeared in that same doorway, her big pink parka on over her uniform, pulling on her mittens.

"I'm your ride," she said.

Jody looked up, confused. "I live all the way out by the lake."

"I know. Come on."

"I don't even have money to give you for gas. I mean, not *with* me. I was all upset when I left the house and I didn't think to take any money."

"Don't worry about it. The doctor gave me a twenty for gas. Come on. You must be exhausted. Let's get you home."

———

"You turn right at that little road up there," he said.

It was the first either had spoken since they got into the car. It did more than break the silence. It shattered it, leaving Jody feeling as though he should gather the silence into his arms and apologize to it.

She pulled into his long driveway, her snow tires spinning slightly on the icy, packed surface. She gave that situation her full concentration until the car was stopped in front of the cabin. Her headlights were the only illumination anywhere.

The cabin had not burned down.

Jody breathed panic out of his gut, gently allowing it to leave. He felt a little weak and shaken as it exited. He felt as though a car had run over him. And now the car had driven away, and it was in the past. But he still felt run over.

"Sorry I didn't talk much," the nurse said, startling Jody. It was a silly thing to say, he thought. Because she hadn't talked at all. "You seemed lost in thought, and like maybe you didn't care to say anything, and then I guess I got frozen up right along with you."

"It was nice enough you gave me a ride home. You didn't need to do more."

She was digging around in her purse as they spoke. Apparently not finding what she wanted, she turned on the dome light. Jody winced and covered his eyes.

"But you might want to talk later," she said, while his eyes were still closed and covered. "I know you don't know me. Dr. Benton said you don't have any other family. Maybe you have friends, I don't know. But just in case . . ."

He didn't know why she had stopped talking, so he opened his eyes. She was holding a scrap of paper in his direction. It had a name and phone number written on it.

He took it, his insides feeling a little melty.

"I know I'm a stranger," she said, "but sometimes a stranger is good. Whatever you say, you can just hang up the phone and know you'll probably never see me again."

He ran his fingers across the number she'd written down. As though it would feel different than the rest of the paper. It didn't, of course. The melty feeling dripped down into his thighs. "I won't call."

"But just in case."

"I'll look at the paper and think how nice it was that you liked me enough to give it to me. But then I won't call. But that's a good thing all by itself. So thanks."

"You *could* call, though. If you needed to."

"I don't really like to talk to people. I'm not very good at it. It makes me feel like I'm not okay."

"You're talking to me now. You seem to express yourself very well."

"I mean on the inside I'm not good at it."

They sat a moment in silence. Jody thought about Worthy. How he should go into the house and let him out to pee. But he figured it didn't matter a lot, because Worthy had probably peed in his room hours ago.

"I don't feel anything," Jody said to the nurse.

"In general? Or right now?"

"When I'm scared. And right now."

"That's normal. When something like this happens, a person goes into a mild shock. It doesn't mean you don't care. It just means you can't take it all in. Time will take care of it."

"Maybe not for me," he said. "Even on a normal day I can't seem to take everything in."

They sat in silence for another long moment.

Then she said, "See? You can talk to people."

"I have to go now," he said. "Thank you for this paper." He held it up as he opened her passenger door and stepped out into the stinging cold.

"It's not the paper that matters. It's the number."

"Right. I knew that. That's what I meant."

But that wasn't entirely true.

————

He expected a flood of nasty smells to assault his nostrils when he opened the bedroom door. He braced for it. Then he swung the door wide.

Worthy rocketed past him and headed for the front door.

The room was toasty warm and carried a mild smell of dog, but nothing more. Nothing bad.

He ran to the front door and opened it for Worthy. The dog shot out and stopped at the nearest snow-crusted bush. Lifted his leg. Jody could hear a sound from the dog as he relieved himself, something like a cross between a grunt and a sigh.

Jody looked up to see the nurse still backing carefully down his driveway. But he knew she couldn't see him, because her car headlights were pointing elsewhere.

Worthy was still peeing, even though it had been an absurd length of time. In the light of the moon Jody could barely see steam rising from the bush.

"You're a very good dog, Worthy. Do you know that?"

Worthy finished up his business, then came back to Jody to enjoy the praise.

"And now I feel guilty. Because I had no idea you'd be so good. I thought you'd just pee and poop in my room and then give me a look like, 'What did you expect me to do?'"

As if Jody had reminded him, the dog set out sniffing, looking for a place to squat.

———

The knock came just after midnight. Jody startled awake, looked at the clock, and knew.

He just knew.

Worthy barked. Two deep woofs in the pit of his throat.

Jody sat up abruptly. His arms and legs felt rubbery and weak. He braced himself against the bedside table to stand. Then he made his way to the front door, anchoring one hand on a wall or doorway whenever possible.

Just as he reached the big, heavy wooden door someone knocked on it again, startling him. He nearly fell over backward recoiling from it, but he righted himself. Worthy barked three more deep woofs. Jody hadn't realized the dog was right at his heels.

"Who's there?" he called, realizing as he did how terrified he sounded.

"It's Deputy Rodelle and Deputy Lighton."

"Oh. Just a minute."

Jody grabbed Worthy's collar and ran with him back to the bedroom. He was steadier, because he needed to be.

"Wait here," he told the dog in a sharp whisper.

He closed the dog into his room and made his way to the front door again, which he opened.

The deputies were standing on his welcome mat, their caps in their hands, breathing great clouds of steam, eyes shining with a level of pity even Jody was not used to seeing.

"Sorry for the late hour," Rodelle said. "May we come in?"

Jody stepped back from the door. They wiped their feet carefully on the mat and then lumbered into his living room.

Jody sank into Grampa's chair. The deputies stood. Jody had to crane his neck to look up at them. But of course he avoided their eyes.

"You can sit on the couch," he said.

They looked at each other, then did.

"I think you might already know why we're here, Jody."

"Yes, sir," Jody said, his eyes glued to the intricate patterns of Grampa's Persian rug.

"We didn't want you to hear it on the telephone."

"Thank you."

"He was just too old and weak to come back from that serious a case of hypothermia. His poor old heart gave out."

Jody said nothing for a time. It might have been two seconds. It could have been several minutes, except that the deputies would likely have filled the silence if it had lasted that long. Nobody liked long silences. Except maybe that nurse.

"That's good, in a way," Jody said. "Because now they won't have to cut off his hands and feet. I didn't want that. That sounded like the most horrible thing I could possibly think of that could happen to a person. If Grampa had a thing like that ahead of him, I guess I'm glad he didn't live long enough to get there."

"I think that's a very healthy way to look at it," Lighton said. "No more suffering for him."

Jody realized he had never heard Deputy Lighton's voice before. He tended to stay silent and let Rodelle do all the talking.

"You going to be okay here by yourself?" Rodelle asked.

"I'm not by myself."

"Oh, right. You have a dog now. We heard him bark."

"Yes, sir. I adopted a dog."

"Well, that's good. I'm sure he'll be some comfort to you. I still feel bad leaving you alone. We might talk to Liz first thing in the morning. Have her come by and check on you."

"Liz and Mike are down in the valley for the winter."

"No. Mike is down in the valley. Liz is up here by the lake. They separated. She came back up to do some thinking."

"That's too bad," Jody said.

"We'll have her come check on you."

"You don't have to do that."

The deputies exchanged a look. "How're you fixed for food?"

"Oh. Not so good. I should have gone to the store when I was in town. I didn't think."

"We'll have her come by, see if you need anything."

They stood. Jody stood. He felt a little wobbly, but he did it. He willed himself to do it. So they would trust him to be okay. So they would go.

"You okay till morning?" Rodelle asked.

"Yes, sir."

"Okay, we'll leave you alone to think, then. Here's my direct number." He handed Jody a business card with an official star-shaped badge printed on as a logo. "In case you need help."

"Thanks," he said.

He was thinking he'd put it on the table next to the nurse's piece of paper. And look at them both. And run his fingers over them both. And not call.

————

Liz came by at 7:25 a.m., and hugged him tightly, and wouldn't let go. It made him uneasy, because Grampa hadn't liked shows of affection. And after all those years of living together, he'd pretty much trained Jody not to like them either. But Jody didn't say so, because it might have sounded mean. So he just stood there with his hands at his sides. Wishing she would let go.

When she finally did, she ran back to her car and brought in some groceries. Two brown paper sacks full of them.

He followed her into the kitchen and helped her put them away.

There was orange juice and milk. Lettuce and broccoli. A loaf of bread. Some ground beef. A frozen pizza. Canned fruit. Canned soup. Dried pinto beans and split peas. A very small canned ham.

"I should pay you back for this," he said.

"Don't be silly," she said.

She was in her forties, with hair that looked like it might have started out some other color. Now it was reddish brown with silvery tips. It swept back very nicely and stayed in place. She never said why paying her back was silly.

She looked down at Worthy and patted him on the head, and he wagged extravagantly. Jody hadn't even thought about the dog. It hadn't even occurred to him that he should have put Worthy away in his bedroom.

"How do you feel?" she asked, putting one cold hand on Jody's.

"I'm not sure. I feel like I'm dreaming all this."

"That's normal," she said.

She sat down at his kitchen table. And something broke through. Just in that moment, Jody realized how he felt.

"It was really nice of you to bring all this food," he said. "But I really feel like right now it would be good just to be alone."

She stood. "I understand," she said. But her eyes said she didn't understand.

He walked her to the door.

"I'm sorry about you and Mike," he said.

"Oh. Thank you." She averted her eyes. Looked down. Worthy was down there. "You know, someone in town is looking for this dog."

"No," Jody said. His stomach buzzed with a cold feeling. "Not this dog."

"I saw the signs."

"I saw them, too. And I called. And it wasn't the same dog."

"Sure looks like the dog in the picture."

"It does. But it's not."

"Where'd you get him?"

"At the pound. It was like a month ago. Turns out the dog in the picture has only been gone a few days. So it couldn't be the same one."

"Ah," Liz said. "Right. I see."

But her eyes said she didn't see.

Chapter Sixteen: Virginia

It was about two thirty in the afternoon. Virginia was in the diner's kitchen, doing dishes, because the part-time dishwasher had called in sick again.

She heard the bells of the door jingle.

She heard Fern say, "We're closed. We stop serving lunch at two."

She heard an unfamiliar woman's voice. It said, "I'm not here for lunch. I'm here to see Virginia."

Virginia dried her hands and stepped out into the seating area. "I'm Virginia," she said.

The woman was younger than Virginia by maybe ten years, and spent much more time on her hair, which was nicely highlighted with a silvery shade at the tips.

God help me, she thought, *if she's come here to tell me she's having an affair with Lloyd, I'll burn my way right through the floor of this place like a nuclear meltdown.*

"I called your house," the woman said. "The man who answered—your husband, I guess?—said I could find you here."

Virginia relaxed a little. Since the woman obviously didn't know Lloyd.

"You want to sit down?"

She led the woman over to the corner of the empty diner, where they sat at table five, under the wall of ticking clocks.

"I guess this is kind of a sensitive matter," the woman said. Virginia's gut tightened again. "I'm not sure if I'm right or I'm wrong to come talk to you about it. I just figure I won't be able to sleep if I don't. But . . ."

Virginia waited, but her patience was wearing thin, and she had to work to contain it. She didn't like a lot of prefacing of information, because it scared her to have to wait for what might be bad news.

"Could you just . . . whatever this is . . ."

"I think I might know where your dog is."

Virginia's mouth gaped open, and it took her a moment to get hold of it again. "T-Rex? Oh, my God. I was sure he was gone. I didn't figure there was a chance in hell he could have survived in weather like this. Fern! You've got to come hear this! This woman knows where T-Rex is!"

And to think I asked that poor man if he took him out in the woods and shot him, she thought. She could feel her gut, her whole torso, change with the intense sensation of relief.

"I said I *think* I know where he is. And if I'm wrong, imagine how bad I'm going to feel, because I got your hopes all up and everything."

"Where is he? Let's go see!" She looked up at Fern, who was standing over the table, face eager. "Fern, will you finish those dishes? I have to go see if it's T-Rex!"

"Wait!" the woman practically shouted. "There's a whole bunch more I have to tell you before we go *anywhere*."

"I'll get you both a cup of coffee," Fern said, and disappeared again.

"Sorry," the woman said. "I didn't mean to be harsh. And I can understand how you're excited. But you were getting a little ahead of things for a minute there."

Virginia sat back and folded her arms under her ample bust. "Go ahead and tell me what you've got to tell me," she said.

"Well. The guy who has him . . . at least, who has this dog I *think* is him, is my neighbor. Up at the lake."

"I didn't think anybody lived up there in the winter."

"Hardly anybody does. But my neighbor Jody and his grandfather live up there all year-round. Have for a couple of years now. And my husband and I usually go down to our house in the valley for the winter. We did this winter, but then I caught him messing around with one of his sales associates, so now I'm up there by myself trying to figure out if I should give him the second chance he's been begging me for."

Don't, Virginia thought. *Move on.* But it was none of her business. She didn't even know why the woman had steered the conversation in such a personal direction. Besides, Virginia was a fine one to talk.

All she said was, "I'm sorry to hear that. So go on about the dog."

"Oh. So, Jody. My neighbor. He's this really sweet little guy. Lives up there all alone with his grandfather. Neither one drives, or has a car. Well, the grandfather used to drive, but then he got this age-related dementia."

"Is this all need-to-know type of stuff?" Virginia interjected.

"I'm afraid so. But I'll try to hurry it along. Anyway, Jody's not quite like everybody else. Sweet as hell, but different. I want to say almost handicapped. Not physically. And not really mentally, either. He's plenty smart. But it's like he just can't cope with normal things the way you or I would."

"I really don't mean to be impolite, but I sure would like to know what all this has to do with my dog."

"He's the one who has your dog. Or what I think is your dog."

"Yeah. You said that already. But I still don't see what—"

"He was orphaned real young. He's had a tough life. I know you don't want to hear this, but I'm sorry. It all has to get said."

Virginia poured cream into her coffee and took a sip. It tasted a little old. "Sorry," she said.

"Anyway. His grandfather died this morning."

"Oh. That's too bad."

"It was kind of tragic, how it happened. The old guy wandered out in the snow in nothing but pajamas. You know. Because of his dementia. And Jody didn't know he'd gone out. I mean, not until morning. So he was out all night. He didn't freeze to death. Not exactly. He was alive when they took him into the hospital. But he didn't make it for long. So this morning I went over there to bring Jody some groceries. Everybody who knows him is real worried about him, because we can't really imagine him being on his own."

"How old is this kid?"

"He's not a kid. He's in his twenties. Early twenties, I guess. Well, in a way he's a kid. His mind is all grown up, but in some ways he doesn't act his age. He's just had a hard life. I guess it's some kind of PTSD, or something like that, but I don't know the exact diagnosis. I mean, if there even is one. Or maybe it's just how he is. Anyway, when I was over there, I saw the dog. Just the spitting image of the dog in the picture on your signs. Except his collar was blue instead of green."

"It's not hard to put a new collar on a dog."

"That's what I was thinking. I told him somebody was looking for the dog. But he said no, it wasn't the same one. He said he called the number on the sign, and your dog had been missing just a couple or three days, and he'd had this dog for a month. So it couldn't be the same dog, he said. But I live right nearby and I haven't been seeing him with a dog for any month."

"Nobody called me about the dog."

"See, I had a feeling maybe what he told me wasn't true. Jody doesn't lie—"

"Seems like you might be wrong about that."

"I mean, normally he doesn't. And you know how when someone is a real honest person, if they do tell a lie for some reason, they're . . . just . . . bad at it? That's what it was like. He hemmed and hawed and wouldn't look me in the eye. So I figured I'd best come talk to you."

"Why don't you tell me where he lives, and I'll go check all this out for myself?"

"Because his grandfather just died. He's very fragile. If you go up there and just rip the dog away . . . I think he's really attached to the dog already. I just don't know what he'd do."

"Let me get this straight. You think you know the guy who swiped my dog, but you're telling me I can't go get him back."

"I don't know that he stole him."

"How else did he get all the way up by the lake?"

"I have no idea. But he doesn't even drive, this guy. How could he come down into town and steal your dog?"

"I don't know. He could've gotten a ride. He could've hitch-hiked." She heard her own voice coming up. Felt her ability to control her temper waning. "Fern! You've got to come hear this. This is the strangest thing I ever heard in my damn life, and I need some help figuring out what to make of it."

Fern walked up to their table. Sat down. Sighed. "I heard," she said. "You're not being nearly as quiet as you think you are."

"So what do we do?" Virginia asked, to neither of them in particular. "What am I supposed to do? That's my dog. I want him back. I'm sorry if this kid's got problems, but that's no excuse to take somebody's dog and not give him back."

The woman slid a scrap of paper across the table. Virginia picked it up. Put on her reading glasses, which had been tucked

in her apron pocket. It was an address. On March Road, off
Highway 22.

"I'm not saying you can't go get him back," the woman said.
"I'm not telling you what to do. I'm just trying to let you know
what you're stepping into here. Now that's the address, and none
of this is my business anymore. I just wanted you to understand
his situation. You do what you think is best. But go easy on him.
Please. Even if he did something wrong here, he never did before
that I know of. Just give him a break if you can."

Then she got up and marched straight out the front door, jingling the bells and wrapping her scarf around her neck just before
the wind hit her.

Virginia looked at Fern. "Is that the damnedest thing?"

"Damnedest thing *I've* ever heard. But at least it means T-Rex
is alive. Which is some pretty amazing good news."

"Maybe. Maybe he's alive. If she's right, and this is him."

"I think you better start there," Fern said.

"Yeah. I have to go up there and see if this is him."

Chapter Seventeen: Jody

Jody was sitting in the living room, in Grampa's chair. Where he never sat. Until very recently, at least. Not doing anything. Not thinking anything. Looking at Worthy, who was asleep on the rug near the heater. Watching the light change, on a slant through the curtains. It must have been late afternoon by then.

Worthy's head came up, and his tail thumped the carpet. Only then did Jody hear a car coming up the driveway. Usually he heard cars anywhere on March Road. It was a short road. Jody knew he must have been very far away in his head.

He jumped up, grabbed Worthy by the collar, and ran with the dog to his bedroom.

"Wait here," he said, closing the door. "Don't make a sound."

He ran to the front window and pulled back the curtain. A woman was climbing out of a car, navigating on foot through snow nearly as high as her knees. Jody had never seen the woman, and he had never seen the car. She was middle-aged, a little heavyset, with long hair pulled back into a soft twist. She had a kind face. And yet she also looked a little scared, or mad, or both.

Jody winced, waiting for the knock. Then he decided he could avoid the knock. He could just open the door.

He threw the door wide. A blast of cold and a light drift of snow blew in and hit him. And he was face-to-face with this stranger. It was all quite alarming.

"Hello," she said. It seemed to come from the part of her that was kind, not the part of her that was mad and scared. Her expression had changed, too. She had a curious look on her face now. Like she was trying to figure out something important.

"Hi," he said. "Who are you?"

"My name is Virginia. You don't know me. Well . . . I guess you already know you don't know me."

"Yes, ma'am."

"May I come in?"

He didn't want her to. But he had been raised to be polite. To his elders. To women. To everybody, really. That was the rule. Always be polite.

He stepped back from the doorway and let her by. Then he closed the door, and it felt good to block out all that icy wind.

She sat down on his couch without being invited. Jody perched on the very edge of Grampa's chair, facing her. He wrapped his hands around his knees and tried not to fidget.

"I was sorry to hear about your grandfather," she said.

Jody very nearly burst into tears. It was alarming, really. It was like something was trying to breach a containment wall, explode out into the world with a violence, a force, that would startle him if he allowed it. He didn't allow it. It would be horrible to lose control in front of a stranger. He wrenched it back down with a tightness in his muscles, and by barely breathing. By breathing just enough to stay alive, and not pass out. No more.

"Did you know him?" he asked when he felt he could.

"No," she said simply.

"Why are you here?"

She sat back. Sighed.

Just in that moment Jody realized he could hear Worthy. The sounds had been there to hear for some time, he realized, but he had been too busy wrestling feelings into submission. The dog was not being silent, as instructed. He was whimpering, and scratching at the bedroom door.

"I'm not going to lie to you," she said. It sent a deep shock through his gut. "I was going to make up a story. But that doesn't feel right. I'm not going to play games. My dog disappeared a couple of days ago. And I think you might have him."

"I don't," Jody said sharply. "That dog you hear is *my* dog. I've had him for, like, a month. So if you had your dog until a couple of days ago, then it can't be the same dog."

He could feel his own face turning hot and red as he spoke. He had to fix his gaze on the carpet to keep the words flowing.

"Jody," she said, and he wondered how she knew his name, and that his grandfather had died. "Listen to him. He can hear the sound of my voice. He can smell me."

Jody held perfectly still. He said nothing.

"T-Rex!" she called out, making Jody jump.

The dog let out a sharp yip of excitement and joy.

"I want my dog back," she said. "I know this is a terrible time for you. And I'm very sorry about your loss. But that's my dog. I want my dog back."

Jody felt as though he were shriveling. Shrinking. Like that scene in *The Wizard of Oz* when Dorothy puts water on the witch, and it melts her. Painfully and slowly melts her.

"I know you must be hearing what I'm saying," the woman said.

Jody took a deep breath—for the first time in a long time—and cobbled together all the strength he could find. All the courage he could manufacture, borrow, or fake. He added all of it together, and spoke to her in a firm tone.

"I'm not giving him back," he said.

Her mouth fell open. The dog continued to yip and bark excitedly.

"You just may have to," she said.

"No. I won't. I won't give him back."

An icy chill ran through the energy in his living room, making Jody shiver slightly inside.

"Would you care to tell me how that's in any way honest? Or fair?"

"Because if I give him back, he might end up getting dumped again. And this time maybe I won't be around to save him. I'm sorry if you changed your mind, but you can't change your mind about something like a dog. He's real, and he's alive, and he needs you to feel the same way about keeping him every single day, as long as he lives. Because he would never change his mind about you. You can't just dump a dog and then say you want him back. When you abandon him, he's not yours anymore. As of that moment. He'd be dead if I hadn't taken him in. And if he were dead, you sure wouldn't get him back. At least this way you know he's happy somewhere."

He paused. Breathed again. Felt all the borrowed courage slip away. Or maybe he'd just reached the end of that supply. It was exhausting to be brave. He felt like he needed to sleep until morning just to halfway recover.

"And because I love him," he added.

He braved a look at the woman's face. Her mouth was hanging open again. He'd just met her, and already he'd noticed that her mouth did that a lot.

"I did not dump my dog," she said.

"Well, no, not you personally. But that guy did. And that's bad enough."

"Wait, wait. Wait. What guy? Back up. Slow down. I want to hear what happened. And I mean in *detail*."

Jody breathed for a few beats to steady himself. Then he set off with far less energy and force.

"There was a guy in a red pickup who drove out here after that big snow. He wasn't three minutes behind the plow. He had that dog in the bed of his truck. Which is really, really bad when it's this cold. And he wasn't tied down either, which is illegal. And mean. He pulled over by the lake, and dragged him out of the truck bed. And he yanked off his collar, right over his ears. It hurt his ears. I could hear him yip, and I was all the way up in my driveway. And then he threw the collar away in the snow where I guess he thought no one would find it for a long time and drove off and left that poor dog in the middle of the road to freeze. I went down and got him and brought him inside. You know he would have died pretty soon after the sun went down."

Silence. Long silence. He braved another quick glance at her face. Her eyes were squeezed shut.

"Can you tell me what this guy looked like?"

"Big, bushy beard. Lots of hair on his face. None on his head."

"That son of a bitch," she said on a long rush of exhaled breath.

"That's exactly what I said."

In his peripheral vision, he saw her eyes open again. "Why didn't you just take him to the pound, so his owner could find him again?"

"But his owner just dumped him. So why would he go find him?"

"Oh," she said, sounding tired all of a sudden. "That's true."

"Actually . . . it's not entirely true. I thought the guy might go to the pound and try to get him back. I thought maybe the dog peed in the house or chewed something up, and the guy had a hot temper. And maybe after he cooled down, he'd want to get the dog back. But I didn't think he should have him back. Because if he ever did it again—dumped him again—I might not be there. And that dog doesn't deserve to die."

Another long silence.

Then the woman spoke, but in a voice so soft he found the change alarming. "She was right. You *are* really sweet."

"Who?"

"It doesn't matter. Listen. If I get the sheriff out here, will you tell him the story you just told me?"

"*You're going to call the sheriff on me?*" His voice came out squeaky and too loud.

"No, not on you. If I press charges against Lloyd for cruelty to animals . . . you're the only one who saw what he did. Will you tell the sheriff what you saw?"

"Yeah. Sure I will. He deserves to get in trouble. Is he your husband?"

His gaze still trained on the rug, he heard another great sigh come from her, this time slightly cracked and shaky, as if she might be on the edge of tears. Which made it panicky hard to control his own. If she so much as let out one sob, Jody knew he would lose it.

"No," she said. "I thought he was going to be. But obviously not."

"But he lives with you."

"Yes."

"You can't take him. The dog. You can't. He can't go back and live with that man."

"Lloyd will be out soon enough. Don't worry."

Jody felt the flurry of panic rise, pushing the barriers up right along with it. "Please," he said, looking right into her face. Her eyes were full of shame, or sadness, or pity. Or maybe all three, all at once. "Please. I don't know what I'd do without him." Then he looked away.

"Can I just see him?" Her voice sounded calm. "I'd just really love to see him. See how he's doing. It breaks my heart to think of leaving without seeing him, when he knows I'm here. You're right,

I can't take him home with Lloyd still there. That's all I know for right now. I guess we'll have to work out the rest later on."

Jody pulled to his feet. Walked carefully to his bedroom. Opened the door. Worthy came bounding out, nearly landing in the woman's lap on the couch. His front end did, anyway. She laughed, and hugged him. His whole body wagged.

Jody sat down across from them again, his mood falling fast. Which surprised him. Because he'd thought it had no more room to sink.

She held the blue tag in her fingers and looked closely at it. "Worthy," she said.

"It's his new name."

The woman began to cry quietly.

He looked away again. "Please. If you cry I'll lose it. I mean it. I'll just lose it."

"I'm going to go now anyway. You stay here with Jody for now, boy," she told the dog. Then, to Jody, "He's going to try to follow me out the door. You'll have to hold on to his collar. This is going to be hard. For me, at least. And for him, I think. Well. For all of us, I guess."

She coaxed the dog off her lap and led him over to Jody by the collar.

"Thank you for saving his life," she said.

Then she moved toward the door.

Worthy did not try to follow. He just sat down against Jody's leg, half on his foot, and watched her, and wagged. As if he could wag hard enough to convince her to stay.

She turned and looked when she'd reached the door, when she had one hand on the knob. She looked back and saw that her dog was not trying to leave with her.

Her tears flowed faster. Jody tried not to look.

"He's choosing you," she said. "He's been my dog for six years, and he's staying with you. Thought you said dogs never change their mind about us."

"He didn't," Jody said. "He's not choosing who he likes best. He's staying with the person who needs him most."

She smiled sadly. "Yeah," she said. "That sounds like . . . him." Her eyes bored into Jody, and she asked, "What's your last name? If you don't mind."

"Schilling," he said, hoping it wasn't dangerous to tell her, even though he couldn't imagine why it would be. She knew where he lived and all. That was the danger.

Her face fell. She was disappointed that his last name was Schilling. But he had no idea why it would matter to her.

"Why do you ask?"

"No reason."

"Nobody ever asks things for no reason."

"No reason that matters now," she said.

Then she closed the door behind her, and she was gone.

Jody breathed deeply and let go of Worthy's collar. The dog ran to the window and put his paws up on the sill. But he couldn't figure out how to get his face underneath the curtain. He whined in a frantic way that made Jody's stomach upset.

"She'll be back," he said. "You don't have to worry." Then, more to himself, "I'm the one who has to worry."

He purposely didn't say it loud enough for the dog to hear.

Chapter Eighteen: Virginia

When Virginia stepped inside, the only deputy who seemed to be on duty in the sheriff's office was Roger Rodelle. And he wasn't busy, either. That put her more at ease. Roger had been coming into the diner for lunch at least three times a week for as long as she could remember. He always said their BLT was the best anywhere. She could talk to Roger.

"What can I do for you, Ginnie?" He started to get up from his chair out of respect to her, but she waved him back down.

He nodded at the chair on the other side of his desk. She took it, and sat. But forward, tightly. Rigid, with her back not touching the backrest. And clutching her purse to her belly. It had been a very trying day.

"I would like you to go to my house and arrest Lloyd for cruelty to animals."

"Oh, hell." He rubbed his forehead hard with one palm. "What did he do to T-Rex? I hate to even ask. Kenny was the one who first brought it up—that the dog's disappearance might not've been accidental. I guess I still try to be too much of an optimist. I like to think everybody's a better person than *that*."

"He drove him out to the lake right after the big snow. And he abandoned him out there. There was no way for him to get home. No shelter. And on a night when it was forecast to go down to seven degrees. Fern thought he might've taken him out in the woods and shot him with his deer rifle. And you know what, Roger? Glad as I am that he didn't, I swear it would have been kinder. More humane, you know? At least the poor guy wouldn't have known what hit him. But to leave him out there to freeze to death . . ."

"You know for a fact it happened that way? I need evidence."

"The young man who has him now saw the whole thing."

She watched the deputy's face light up. "T-Rex is alive? Well, that's a cause for celebration!"

It made her like him even more.

"This young man told me he'd be happy to tell the same story to the sheriff."

"Good. Then let's cause Lloyd some hurt for this, the son of a bitch. Who do I go talk to?"

"Jody Schilling," she said. "You know him? He lives out by the lake."

She watched Roger's face fall. Actually "collapse" might have been a better way to describe it.

"Jody Schilling? Has your dog? That dog he told us he adopted? Is T-Rex? Are you sure?"

"I was there, Roger. I saw him with my own eyes."

Roger braced his elbows on the desk. Dropped his head into his hands.

Virginia waited. The waiting seemed to drag on. She wondered how long she was supposed to just sit there.

Finally his head came up again, and he rubbed his face briskly. "Well, that's a bit of a conundrum, then. How well do you know Jody?"

"I just now met him."

"He's . . . sensitive."

"That's what I keep hearing."

"His grandfather just died."

"I know."

"That was the only family he had in the world."

"I still want my dog back."

"That would be the conundrum," he said.

"Are you saying I can't get my dog back?"

"I'm saying no such thing. If that were the case, it wouldn't be a conundrum. At least, not in the way I mean it when I say that word. It would just be a very hard thing for you. But what we've got here is a situation that wants to be a mess no matter *how* we sort it out."

Virginia sat back for the first time. Crossed her legs at the knee. Took a deeper breath than the ones before it. It was a conscious effort to calm down.

"What does the law say about it?" she asked calmly.

"Well, now," he said, making a steeple with his fingers. "Let's see. The owner of a dog loves and wants the dog, but her fiancé dumps the dog without her knowledge. Innocent bystander picks up the dog, rescues him. Knows better than to try to find the owner, because the owner dumped him. Now he loves the dog, too. Original owner did nothing wrong and feels the dog belongs to her. Current owner did nothing wrong and feels the dog belongs to him. So what we've got here is a case of a dog with two rightful owners. Probably legally sways toward you, but Jody's sensitive mental condition mentally sways it back. Actually, I'm not sure what the law says about it, because I don't know that it ever happened before. Might've happened somewhere, sometime, but I sure as hell don't know about it if it did. Only one part of this is clear to me: it's time to pay a visit to old Lloyd, without whom we wouldn't be in this conundrum, and haul his ass off to jail."

"How do we figure out the ownership thing?"

"No idea. Mind if I sleep on it?"

"I guess. You going over there right now?"

"Right now. I'm up. I'm on my feet." Roger stood. Buckled on his gun belt and put on his cap. Shook a heavy coat on over his uniform. "I'll talk to Jody, get his statement. Oh, crap. I just told my wife I'd be right home. Well, that's the job for you. Then I'll go pick up Lloyd."

"I'm not going back to that house until I know he's gone."

"I feel obliged to warn you I might not be able to hold him long. I might have to cite him out. At the very least I have to send him in front of a judge who'll set bail. Cruelty to animals—I wish I could get more going against him. Maybe intentional infliction of emotional distress. Which probably won't stick, because you were never supposed to know what happened."

"But I was going to feel pain losing T-Rex either way."

"True." He walked to the door with her. "Well, it'll stick or it won't. Let's throw it at him. Charge him, anyway. It'll likely bring up the bail amount, and I can justify not citing him out with both those charges hanging on him."

He opened the door for her, and they stepped out into the blustery cold. It had begun to snow again—big, wet flakes that stuck on her eyelashes and made her blink.

"If you need me tonight," she told Roger as he locked up the station, "I'll be at Fern's."

"I'll keep you posted."

He walked one way toward his car. She walked the other way toward hers.

"Ginnie," she heard him say.

She stopped. Turned around. The snow fell harder now, settling onto her hair and the collar of her coat.

"I'm sorry for your loss," he said.

"My loss? You mean T-Rex? I'm still not accepting that I don't get him back."

"Actually, I meant your fiancé."

Virginia spit out a burst of sarcastic laughter. "Turns out losing Lloyd wasn't losing much."

"I know that," he said. "But you didn't know that until just now, today. You thought he was something worth having. You thought you had this new life ahead of you. It's a loss all the same."

Immediately her mind filled with an image of Aaron. What the deputy had just said—that's what she couldn't make Fern see. Couldn't make anyone see. It was that loss of what she'd thought her life was going to be with him.

Once she'd driven under a highway overpass and seen the words "I Love You" written on the side of the bridge in spray paint. First thing that came to mind was Aaron. And he'd been gone fifteen years at the time.

Tears sprang to her eyes, and she didn't know if they were for Lloyd or for Aaron. Or for herself. Or maybe tears don't have anybody's name on them. Maybe they're just tears.

"That's a very thoughtful thing to say to me, Roger. Thank you."

He tipped his cap, and they walked in opposite directions again.

———

"Don't try to sell me that crap about helpless people, Fern, because I'm not buying it." She reached her wineglass out to Fern, who refilled it. "When I was growing up, I had two sisters who pulled this garbage all the time. 'Oh, my feelings are hurt.' 'Oh, I just fall apart so easily.' And my parents totally bought it, so they'd say things to me like, 'Why don't you make the sacrifice for your sister? She's more sensitive. You're stronger.' Hell yeah I was stronger than them, but I didn't want to be punished for it. I buck up and deal with things. That's no reason why I should be the one who always has to lose."

Fern raised both hands as if Virginia were robbing her at gunpoint. "Fine. Go rip the dog out of his arms. Sorry I ever brought it up."

She pushed the box of chocolates in Virginia's direction. It irked Virginia that Fern had a box of chocolates sitting around the house and was skinny as a damn rail. In her fifties, yet. Hell, it irked Virginia that Fern had chocolate sitting around the house, period. If Virginia had chocolate, she ate it. More or less nonstop until it was gone.

She took a deep breath. Everything was irksome to her now. Her best bet, she figured, was to try not to act on anything she was feeling. At least before giving it all time to settle.

"Well, I didn't rip the dog away. You notice I didn't."

"You said you didn't because you couldn't bring T-Rex into the house until you were sure Lloyd was gone for good."

"You're like a damn tape recorder. You know that?"

"Drink some more wine. It'll calm you down."

Virginia took a few sips, hoping Fern was right.

"You never told me that," Fern said. "About your sisters."

"I don't like to talk about it."

"How long have I known you, though?"

"It doesn't matter how long. It's in the past. We were kids. It was a bad deal. Now it's over."

"Doesn't seem very over. Seems like it chews at you a lot."

"Only when I think about it."

Fern let out a snorting laugh. But otherwise she didn't answer. She got up and wandered over to her TV set. There was a DVD player on top of it covered with a hand-tatted doily. On top of that was one of the five cats, and a DVD in commercial packaging from the rental place.

"You want to watch this? Take your mind off things?"

"I doubt I could concentrate. What is it, anyway?"

"Some kind of romantic comedy."

"Good lord, no! What was so funny about that? I told you the thing with my sisters doesn't bother me unless I think about it. And you snorted."

"It colors everything you do, Ginnie. When you said that just now I thought, I'll be damned if that doesn't explain a lot."

Fern sat back down on the couch again. It was lumpy, that couch, with a distinct Fern-shaped dip in the middle. And lots of loose cat fur. And it would be Virginia's bed for the night. Her hips felt sore just contemplating it.

"Three days ago he was my dog, Fern. Lloyd stole him from me while I was at the diner. This guy found him, but shouldn't he be returned to the person he was stolen from?"

Fern lit a cigarette. Virginia wondered what had taken her so long. "That's one way to look at it."

"I can't think of any other."

"You thought T-Rex was dead. You'd just about accepted he was dead. Now you find out he's alive and happy and healthy, but somewhere else. If this guy hadn't taken him in, he *would* be dead. And everything would be worse than it is now. What have you really lost over what you thought you had when you woke up today?"

"I want things back the way they were before," Virginia said.

"Good luck with that."

"When I went over there today . . ." She paused. Pulled the box of chocolates over closer. Picked out a chocolate buttercream, popped it into her mouth whole, and continued talking with her mouth still full of it. "This guy opened the door. He's about in his early twenties. And I looked into his face. And just for a minute . . ."

But she ran out of steam and didn't finish.

"What?"

"No. Never mind. You'll make fun of me."

"I won't make fun of you."

"Promise?"

"Yes, I promise."

"You'll say I have too active an imagination, or—"

"Oh, for God's sake, Ginnie, just say it."

"I thought for a second he was Buddy. All grown up. He looked kind of like I figure Buddy would look. You know. Nineteen years later. Which is hard to know, anyway, because people change a lot between when they're four and when they're in their twenties. But it kind of struck me like that."

"What was Aaron's last name again?"

"Albanese."

"Did you ask this kid his last name?"

"Yeah. It's Schilling."

"Well, that's that, then."

"But that lady said he lost both his parents young."

"But he doesn't have the same name. So he's not the same kid."

"So I was just being delusional like you always say."

"You were having a hard day. And right now I think you need a good night's sleep. I'm going to go get you some sheets and blankets."

Fern stood up. Brushed ashes off the front of her polyester slacks. Then she leaned forward and stamped her cigarette out in the ashtray on the coffee table.

Just before she disappeared into the hall, Virginia said, "Fern?"

"Yeah?" But Fern kept walking to the linen closet.

"I guess this more or less goes without saying. But I'm going to say it anyway. You were right. You were right and I was wrong."

"About Lloyd, you mean?" she called back from the hall.

"About everything. But yeah."

Virginia heard her friend's deep sigh, even from the distance. Then Fern appeared again with a stack of bedding.

"It gives me no pleasure, Ginnie. You have no idea how much I wish I'd been wrong."

———

Just before she climbed between the covers on the lumpy, saggy, hairy sofa, Virginia looked down at her left hand. She was still wearing the ring. It sent a little shock wave through her to see it there, like the feeling you get when you see an old flame unexpectedly, and aren't prepared to defend yourself from those feelings.

She should have given it to Roger to give back to Lloyd, but she'd forgotten she was wearing it. She took it off and dropped it into the ashtray on Fern's coffee table. Then she tucked in for sleep. But she never slept. And not because the sofa was lumpy, either.

Chapter Nineteen: Jody

"How're you holding up?" the deputy asked him. It was Rodelle. He'd come out alone this time, without his partner. He was standing in the open doorway. Jody had not yet invited him in.

Jody hadn't bothered to put Worthy in his bedroom before opening the door. He'd figured it was too late. That all was already lost on that score.

Jody never answered the deputy's question.

Rodelle looked down at the dog, who was wagging around his legs. "Yeah, that's T-Rex all right. I didn't catch your answer to that question."

"What question?" Jody asked, though he was fairly sure he knew. "And also, he has a new name now. It's not T-Rex anymore. I thought that was a silly name. His name is Worthy."

"We'll talk about that by and by," Rodelle said. "Meanwhile the question is, how're you holding up?"

"Good," Jody said.

"Really?"

"I think so."

"But you're not sure."

"I think not all of me knows about it yet. I guess that sounds crazy."

"No," Rodelle said. "It sounds about right. Mind if I come in?"

Jody stepped back out of his way. Rodelle stamped snow off his boots before coming inside.

"What have you been doing all day?" he asked.

"Nothing," Jody said, closing the door.

"Literally nothing?"

"Pretty much, yeah. I was lying on the rug next to Worthy. He likes to lie by the big propane heater. I found out if I curl up with him, and hold him real tight, things seem to go okay."

Deputy Rodelle's brow wrinkled. He opened his mouth to speak, then seemed to think better of it.

"I didn't get up until you knocked," Jody said.

"When did you eat last?"

Jody thought briefly. Nothing came to mind. Literally. Nothing. He could have been searching for anything in that head of his. Nothing would have come up.

"I don't know."

"Was it before or after your grandfather passed away?"

He briefly ran the events of the day through his head. It seemed easier to replay everything than to ask a question of himself and expect information to come back. Which it wasn't doing. "Before," he said.

"Before or after he went missing?"

"Before."

"Well, that's no good."

Jody felt something, sharply and clearly, for the first time in a long time. He had disappointed the deputy. It sent a pang of remorse through his gut, which felt surprisingly empty, tender, and disordered.

"Walk into the kitchen and sit down," Rodelle said. "First we're gonna put some food in you. Then we're gonna get your statement."

———

Jody sat at the table with one hand on Worthy's soft back and watched Rodelle. The deputy was plowing through the cupboards.

"Ah. Here we go," the deputy said. "Soup. You want split pea or chicken vegetable?"

"Chicken vegetable," Jody said.

Rodelle got a pot down. Rummaged around in the kitchen drawers. "Tell me you have a can opener."

"We do. I mean, I do. But it's not in that drawer. It's in the one next to the fridge. Are you going to take Worthy away?"

"Oh. Here. Can opener. No. That's not why I came here today. I'm just going to take a statement from you. Fill out a report."

"Okay, so not today. But later. If she comes to you and says he's her dog, and you have to come take him back . . . are you going to do that?"

"No." He poured the soup into the pan, then peered closely at the label. Probably he was trying to see if you're supposed to put any water in this brand of soup or not. At least, that's what Jody would have wanted to know.

"So you're on my side."

"I'm not on anybody's side. I'm not taking sides. That's the whole point."

"Then what are we supposed to do?"

"I don't know, Jody. I just don't know. But I'm no damn King Solomon. It's my job to enforce the law. So I'll go pick up Lloyd and throw his ass in jail. But this other situation is beyond me." He stirred the soup with a wooden spoon he'd found sticking up out of a crock on the counter. "I have no idea how you two will work it out. I'm just trusting you will, and with no violence. No additional lawbreaking. One of you is going to have to yield. That's all there is to it. Somebody has to back down. And everybody needs to stop looking to me to dictate who it should be and start looking into themselves to see who actually lives in there. And I hope this next part goes without saying: that's territory well outside my jurisdiction."

Jody said nothing. He watched the deputy put two slices of bread in the toaster and push the lever down.

"You got butter for toast?" Rodelle asked.

"I don't think so. I think we're out. I mean . . . I think I'm out."

"Can you bear it dry?"

Actually, Jody didn't think he could bear anything in the way of food. He'd known it for some time, ever since the subject of food came up. But he hadn't had the heart to break it to Deputy Rodelle.

"There's peanut butter," Jody said. "Peanut butter is good on toast."

"Fair enough," Rodelle said.

"Is she nice?"

"Who? Virginia McCarthy?"

"Yeah."

"You met her."

"Yeah. But she was upset. I think she wasn't the way she would normally be."

"I'm surprised you haven't met her before."

"How would I have met her?"

"She's one of the two women who own the diner down where the highways intersect."

"We never eat in a diner," Jody said. "It's too expensive. And too far away."

"Oh. Well, the answer to your question is yes. She's very nice."

"Why is she with that awful man, then?"

A bowl of soup appeared on the table in front of Jody. He'd been hoping for just a little cup so he wouldn't have to eat so much.

"That's more of a was. She *was* with him. I doubt she'll have anything to do with him after this."

"Why was she with him?"

The deputy sighed deeply. The toast popped up, startling Jody.

"You've got to stop asking such hard questions, Jody."

"Why?"

"Because nobody knows the answers. Nobody knows why perfectly nice people hook up with somebody who's all wrong for them. Well, maybe a psychiatrist knows. But I'm not a psychiatrist. Now eat your soup."

"I'm really not very hungry."

"It really wasn't so much a request. I'm saying you need to eat something."

Jody stirred it around as if it were too hot. But it wasn't. He was just stalling. He took a small sip, but it didn't taste like anything. Well, probably it did, really. But he couldn't taste anything. And his stomach turned slightly as the hot liquid filtered down.

Rodelle sat at the table and pushed a plate of toast and peanut butter in his direction. "Now I don't want to spoil your appetite, so we won't talk about anything difficult while you're eating. But as soon as you're done, I want you to tell me exactly what you saw Lloyd do."

———

"Who does she have?" Jody asked, stirring the last of his soup in the hopes it might substitute for finishing it.

"I don't understand the question."

"The lady."

"Ginnie."

"You said something else for her name."

"Virginia. Ginnie is short for Virginia."

"Oh. Okay. Who does she have?"

The deputy sighed. Looked into Jody's soup bowl. "I still want you to finish," he said. "I'm not trying to be a hard-ass. But I figure you won't eat much after I go away again."

Jody took another sip of the soup. It was pretty cold by that time.

"Who does she have," the deputy repeated. "Well. She had a fiancé, but now she doesn't anymore."

"And she had a dog," Jody said. "But now she doesn't anymore."

"She has Fern. Her partner in the diner. They're friends."

"But Fern doesn't live in her house."

"No."

"So when she goes home now, who does she have?"

"I guess nobody," Rodelle said. "So if you decide to get generous and give the dog back, that would be a very nice gesture."

"But I've got nobody, too."

"I know," Rodelle said. "It's a conundrum. Now I think it's time we get this report done."

———

He didn't look into Grampa's room as he let the deputy out. He realized as he passed Grampa's doorway that he'd been very careful not to. All this time.

"The hospital wants to ask you some questions," Rodelle said, hovering in the doorway, snow flying all about his shoulders. Drifting down onto the rug. "About . . . well . . . there'll need to be some arrangements. I asked them to hold off. Give you a little time."

"Thank you," Jody said.

He closed the door.

He stood a minute, listening to Deputy Rodelle's engine rev in the driveway. Then he passed Grampa's room again. This time he looked in.

The room was empty, the bed unmade. Grampa never left his bed unmade. He never forgot, even when he'd forgotten who Jody was, or even who he was himself.

Jody shattered. He shattered without consciously realizing that shattering had been waiting patiently for him all this time. And yet, the minute he did, he felt surprised that he hadn't shattered long before.

He sank onto the rug next to Worthy, who was asleep in front of the heater again. And held the dog. And nothing more.

He never got up and went to bed as the hours wore on. He never slept that night, even though he had barely slept the night before. He didn't even get up and go to the bathroom for a very long time. He just held the dog, and was shattered.

———

Sometime in the wee hours, Jody got up off the floor. His bones and muscles were sore and stiff from lying in the same position for so long.

He picked up the cordless phone and carried it over to the kitchen table. He dialed the number on the scrap of paper the nurse had given him. He knew it was too late to bother somebody with a phone call. He did it anyway.

He carried the phone back to where Worthy curled near the heater, and lay back down against him, listening to the ringing.

She picked it up.

"Hello," she said.

Jody didn't say anything back.

He expected her to hang up, since she didn't know who it was. And since he wasn't saying anything.

She didn't.

A minute or two passed in silence.

Then she said, in a voice that was nicely gentle, "I know it's you."

"How?"

"Your grandfather's name came through on the caller ID."

"Oh."

Another minute or two of silence. Jody found it a comfortable silence. He wondered if she felt the same.

Finally she asked, "Do you want me to stay on the line? Even though you're not talking?"

"Yes, please," he said.

Sometime later he was able to sleep briefly, the line still open.

Chapter Twenty: Virginia

It was still pitch dark outside when Fern served morning coffee. No breakfast, because neither woman liked to eat first thing in the morning. And unlike some other people's jobs, theirs included plenty of opportunities to snack as the morning wore on.

"Think he's gone?" Virginia asked.

Fern looked asleep, except for the fact that she was sitting more or less upright with her eyes open. "Lloyd?"

"Who else?"

"There are other males in the world. There are other males we've been talking about recently."

"I meant Lloyd."

"I wouldn't know," Fern said.

"I don't want to go back there unless I know. I want to go home and change. I really don't want to drag into work in yesterday's clothes. But I don't want to go back there if he might not be gone."

"Guess I don't blame you," Fern said, and lit a cigarette.

"Funny how Roger Rodelle never called. He said he'd keep me posted."

"Your cell phone turned on?"

"No. I kept it off last night. I didn't feel like talking to anybody. But I told him I'd be here."

"He probably thought you meant this's where you'd be if he wanted to drop by in person. I'll bet anything he left a message on your cell."

Virginia regretfully left her much-needed coffee behind, though only for a moment, to dig her cell phone out of her purse. She brought it back to the table. Turned it on.

She had a voice mail message.

"He called."

"Not surprised," Fern said.

Virginia called her voice mail, listened to his message, and repeated it out loud, slightly paraphrased, for Fern's benefit.

"He picked up Lloyd and he has him in a holding cell at the county jail . . . He wants me to go back to the house as soon as I can, like right after work today, and gather up all Lloyd's belongings and put them in the bed of his pickup truck . . . and he'll come by and get them and put them in storage . . . That way when Lloyd gets out, he won't have any need to come sniffing around my house."

"Smart," Fern said.

"Oh. And he says to get the locks changed."

"Also smart," Fern said.

Virginia pushed the button to end the call. "Think he'll want his ring back?"

"Or he could just buy another box of Cracker Jack."

"Very funny. Do they even make Cracker Jack anymore?"

"How would I know? I guess they do. I just woke up, Ginnie."

"Right. I'm going to go home and change. When you empty the ashtrays, do me a favor and fish out that ring and rinse the ashes off it. I think I'll sell it."

"And when you do, you can buy us both dinner at the McDonald's with the proceeds."

———

Virginia turned the lock gingerly. Turned the knob slowly, opening the door into her dark house. She flipped on the light switch by the doorway. Blinked until her eyes had adjusted. Then she waited. Looked. Listened.

She told herself it was silly to be so cautious. Roger would have called again if Lloyd was out of custody. But the caution felt built in. No longer optional. Lloyd had reduced her home to a land of possible enemies, a place where she did not dare let her guard down.

She resented him deeply for that.

Just for a split second she imagined T-Rex running to the door to greet her. Then she remembered.

She resented Jody Schilling deeply for *that*.

It was one thing to lose your fiancé. That was bad. It was another bad thing to lose your dog. But both at right around the same time?

She thought about Jody losing his grandfather. It was sad. Very sad. But so was the situation over here, at her house. And somehow he had won. Somehow he was coming home to a happy, loving dog. And she was the one stuck with silent and empty. With utterly alone.

She marched to the phone and picked it up. Dialed the diner by heart. She was going to tell Fern she'd be late. That she was sorry for the extra workload, but that Fern would just have to start serving breakfast without her. Because she was going to drive up to the lake and get her dog.

She heard one ring on the line.

She hung up the phone.

Because she realized if she drove out and got T-Rex, she'd have to bring him back home and leave him alone all day while she worked. He'd always been good about staying alone. But now it didn't seem fair. Because now, if she just left him where he was with

Jody for the time being, he'd have someone with him every minute of the day.

Also, she hadn't changed the locks yet. And Lloyd might manage to get himself bailed out today.

But really, even if Lloyd had been fully removed from the picture—which she hoped he would be soon—it still felt wrong to leave T-Rex alone all day just a minute after bringing him back home.

She changed her clothes quickly and got herself to the diner instead.

———

"What did you try to call me about?" Fern asked the minute Virginia jingled through the door. "Kind of scared me, that you'd ring once like that. I thought maybe something bad happened."

"Oh. I'm sorry," Virginia said, shucking off her coat. "I just changed my mind is all."

"About what?"

"I was thinking I'd drive up to that guy's house and get T-Rex back."

"Glad you changed your mind," Fern said.

Virginia slipped the strap of a starched white apron around her neck. It was almost too starched. She would have to have a talk with the linen service guy about that. "I didn't change my mind forever. I just hated to go get him right before work. You know. Drop him back and then leave right away. And just leave him home all day by himself."

"That's true. He's got somebody now who's with him all the time. That's a nice thing for a dog."

Virginia felt herself bristle slightly. She wished she could change the subject. She wished she could get in gear, and start on the side work necessary to set up for breakfast. But she felt drained from the lack of sleep, and so downhearted that every tiny movement felt like just too much trouble.

She sank into a chair at table two and watched Fern bustle. "He's always been fine home alone during the day."

"He didn't used to have two options," Fern said, not missing a beat.

"So you think I should leave him there."

"I think it's worth considering."

"He's my dog."

"I honestly don't think that bears repeating, Ginnie. You gonna do any work at all? Or am I on my own this morning?"

"No, I'll work. Just give me a minute. I feel lousy because I hardly slept. It's making my eyes feel all grainy and sore. And my stomach is rocky."

"Want a glass of buttermilk?"

"Yeah. That might help. Thanks."

The diner fell blissfully silent.

What might have been a minute later the glass of buttermilk appeared on the table in front of her. A huge iced tea glass full. Maybe three or four times what one might consider a normal serving of buttermilk. On the table next to it Fern set the little plastic bottle of eyedrops she kept in her purse.

"Thank you," Virginia said. Her own voice sounded so dispirited it made her even sadder.

Surprisingly, Fern sat down across the table from her.

"Breakfast'll be late," Virginia said, hoping to avoid what Fern might've come to talk about.

"Cook's not even here yet. Two minutes won't set us back much. Heard about the big storm?"

"No. I haven't listened to anything."

"I had my car radio going on the drive in. Supposed to hit late this afternoon. Might be a twenty-five-year storm, they're saying."

"You didn't sit down to talk about the weather, Fern. Go ahead and say what you came to say."

"Two things. First of all, take that kid out of the picture and you've got a dead dog. So it's entirely to his credit that T-Rex is living on this borrowed time. So maybe it's not so unrealistic that the boy deserves the time with him, since he's the one who caused that time to exist in the first place."

Silence as Virginia tried to allow that thought to sink in. She took a sip of the buttermilk and waited for it to settle the queasy feeling.

"What's the second thing?" she asked Fern after a time.

"Remember when you said you looked at this kid and thought he looked like Buddy?"

"But he's not."

"But what if he had been? What if this was Aaron's son who saved T-Rex? And then the dog was the only thing he had, because his granddad had just died. Would you go yank the dog back?"

"No. But that's because he'd be Buddy. He'd be Aaron's son. He's not Aaron's son."

"He's *somebody's* son," Fern said. Then she got up and brushed off her apron. Even though there was nothing on it to brush off. "Drink your buttermilk. Take all the time you need. I'm going to get back to work."

———

It was around eleven. Long after the breakfast rush. Fern and Virginia were working together on the dishes, because the part-time dishwasher had called in again. And the lunch rush would start soon enough.

"Think he's really sick?" Virginia asked. "He's been calling in a lot lately."

"Yeah, I think he's sick. But I don't think he has the flu. I think it's not that kind of sick."

"You think he's drinking too much?"

"Crossed my mind," Fern said.

"Yeah, I think so, too. Figure we ought to let him go? Long as we're already hiring a new waitress . . . I mean, the idea is to get time off for us, right? So we might as well replace the one who keeps not showing up."

The bells on the front door jingled.

"You ladies here?" a voice called in. It sounded like Roger.

"Go ahead," Fern said. "I'll finish up here."

Virginia dried her hands and stepped out of the kitchen, surprised by the level of fear in her gut. It was Roger, all right.

"Whoo," he said, shaking off his coat. "Warm in here."

"Too warm?"

"No such thing."

"What's up, Roger? I'm nervous to know."

"Good news and bad news," he said.

Virginia sank onto a stool at the counter. The deputy walked over and sat two stools away. So they could sit facing each other and still have room for their knees.

"Tell me the bad news first," she said.

"Lloyd made bail. He called his daughter and she came and posted bail for him."

"So he's out."

"Yeah."

"What's the good news? I could use some."

"He's leaving town. Or so he says. I'll be monitoring his movements for a while. But he says he's going back to stay with his daughter. And that he won't be coming back to town except for the hearing. And I guess to stand trial, if there is one. He might just plead guilty and be done with it. In which case he'll stay around to serve some kind of sentence, but they have bars on those cells, so

I wouldn't worry. Anyway. New plan. If you'll trust me with your front door key, I'll go over to your house with him. You know. So he can gather up his things. I won't let him touch the key, and I won't leave him alone in there for a second. I won't even turn my head. You don't need to give me *your* copy of the key. I have his key to your house in what we took off him when I arrested him. I just need your permission to take it out of that envelope of belongings before I give the rest back to him. And mostly I need your permission to open the door with it."

"Yeah," Virginia said. "Of course. I trust you. So does this mean I don't even need the locks changed?"

"I still would if I were you. We don't know but he could've had a copy made."

"Oh."

"I can even call the locksmith if you like. Though I doubt he'll make a same-day visit to your house. Especially not this day. The storm'll slow him down. But at least we'll get on his schedule. You hear about the big storm?"

Virginia noticed she was shredding the paper napkin on the counter in front of her. She hadn't even been aware she was doing it. She made a mental note to replace it before the lunch customers rolled in.

"Fern said she heard something on the radio."

"I'm getting some pretty alarming storm warnings come through the office. They think it's going to be an ice storm. And you know that's not pretty when it happens. I mean, it's pretty. To look at. The trees and such. But the damage is not pretty. So I want you to promise me you won't be slow getting out of here this afternoon. And that you'll go right home."

She looked at the shredded napkin for an awkward length of time. There seemed to be an extra helping of gravity in that last sentence of his. She looked up from the counter and into his eyes.

"As opposed to what?"

"As opposed to driving up to the lake to get your dog back. I'm not going to tell you not to go get him, because I'm staying out of that. But don't try it after work today. That's a dicey road even without a sheet of ice on it. And there's bound to be trees and power lines down. At least, if it goes like the weather service thinks it will. You go up there today, you might get yourself killed, or you might get stuck for three, four days or longer waiting for trees to be cleared off the road."

"And if I don't go get him today, it'll be days before I can. And Jody'll be getting more attached to the dog every day."

"I don't know how to advise you on that, Ginnie, except to advise you not to get yourself killed over it."

———

"I'm leaving," Fern said. "And I think you should leave, too. Leave the damn dishes in the sink. You don't want to get caught in an ice storm."

"It'll only take me maybe ten minutes to finish them. I don't live as far as you do. It'll be okay."

"Ten minutes tops," Fern said. Sternly. As if she were Virginia's mother and had a right to set curfews. "After that, leave what's left and go."

It dawned on Virginia that maybe they wouldn't make it in to open the diner tomorrow. And maybe it wouldn't matter. Because maybe nobody would make it in to eat there. It was a surprising comfort, to think about an unexpected day off. She hadn't had a day off in over a month.

It would be so different when they got that new waitress in. And fired the drunken dishwasher and hired one who actually showed up for his shift.

"Lock the door. Okay, Fern? You know. Just in case."

"That sounds smart," Fern said. "Ten minutes."

Then she disappeared from the kitchen. Virginia heard the bells jingle as Fern let herself out.

Chapter Twenty-One: Jody

Jody picked his way downhill along Highway 22, Worthy trotting along beside him on an improvised rope leash. Jody didn't like the rope. It looked shabby, and the last thing he wanted was to mark the dog's value that way.

I should have bought him a nice new green nylon leash at the pet mart, he thought. Then again, that would only have been more money he didn't have.

He was struck by a frightening thought: there would be no more of Grampa's Social Security checks on the third of each month. Because there was no more Grampa. What would he do without even those most basic funds?

He stopped suddenly in the highway. There was no way to walk off-road. No shoulder. Because the snow that had been mounded up by the plows had not melted away. If anything, it had only gotten colder.

Worthy looked up at him with his tail swinging, asking what would happen next. Could they continue with their outing? Please?

Maybe nobody will come by to give us a ride, Jody thought.

He looked around and above them. A strong wind was picking up. The air felt crisp, and just above their heads the sky was a steely blue. But at the edge of the world there was weather blowing in. Jody could see it in the clouds. His only hope was that maybe it wouldn't come exactly their way. Wouldn't make a direct hit.

He looked back uphill, knowing he would have to hike up that steep slope again if he couldn't get a ride. But the big trucks always came through in the afternoon. He decided to chance it.

He turned downhill again and they walked. Into a situation where only luck could save the day.

————

About a mile from the cabin Jody heard the first engine sound. He turned and stuck his thumb out. A compact red Ford pulled up and slowed. Maybe to get around him safely. Maybe to help him out. He stuck his thumb out farther, more eagerly. Maybe even pleadingly.

The driver was a woman, a little older than Liz. Maybe a little younger than the lady from the diner. She stopped and powered her passenger window down.

"Jody," she said.

But Jody didn't think he knew this lady. Or, at least, if he knew her, he didn't know it.

"Yes, ma'am," he said.

"Not the best day to be out. Even in a car. Where're you headed?"

"Down to the intersection with the 132."

"Not much down there."

"There's that diner."

"Oh," she said. "Okay. Hop in."

"I don't think my dog and I can both fit in the front."

"You can put him in the backseat."

"Would you be offended if I sat back there with him? I don't want to treat you like you're our limo driver or anything. It's not that. I just want to be with him as much as possible. You know. While I can. Never know when you're about to be out of chances."

The woman's face melted into the pity Jody knew so well. "Oh, I know. I was so sorry to hear about your grandfather, Jody. It just broke my heart."

Who are you? he thought. But he said nothing.

"I know you two were very close," she added.

"No, ma'am. We weren't at all."

"Is that a joke? The two of you in that tiny cabin, together all day?"

"Oh, that kind of close. Yes, ma'am. In that sense I suppose we were."

"Well, don't just stand there freezing. Get in."

Jody opened her back door and climbed inside, and Worthy jumped in after. Jody had to reach over him to slam the door. Then he wrapped his arms around Worthy's bulky neck and buried his forehead in the dog's fur. It would be impossible not to cry. So he would at least cry in relative privacy.

"I didn't know you had a dog," she said.

That pushed at the tears. Made them harder to hold in.

"Yes and no," he said.

"Looks like that lost dog on all those signs in town."

"Yes, ma'am."

"Who does he belong to?"

Jody squeezed his eyes shut hard and willed her to stop talking. Or at least stop asking questions.

"We're still working that out."

"Who put up the signs?"

"The lady at the diner. Virginia."

"Oh. Of course. That's why you're out in this weather. Because of her lost dog."

"Yes, ma'am," he said.

"Well, you're very sweet."

They drove in blissful silence for a time.

"You should get yourself and the dog indoors and safe as soon as you can," she said after a couple of miles. "Weather report's not looking good. They're issuing warnings. Emergency travel only. That's why I decided to get back down to the valley. You know how quick this road is to close."

"Yes, ma'am," he said, pulling his face back from the dog's fur to be heard. Worthy took that opportunity to crane his neck around and lick Jody's nose. It always made Jody laugh when he did that. Except this time. This time it made him cry.

He looked up to see the lady watching him in the rearview mirror. Their eyes caught. Snagged on each other's. Then Jody looked away in shame.

"I don't blame you for being upset," she said. "I'd feel bad too if my grandfather'd just died. Especially if I lived with him and he was all the family I had."

"Yes, ma'am," he said, wishing they could talk about something else.

It wasn't his grandfather he was crying about. Except maybe it partly was. Maybe when you put tears away uncried, everything you cry about from that day on contains a little of those tears. Whether you wanted them released or not.

"But I won't talk about that if you don't want," she said.

They drove in silence for several miles. Jody stared out at the sky, mildly alarmed by the gathering dark of the clouds. Had the lady said something about the weather? He hadn't been listening, and couldn't remember.

"I have a question," he said. "Do you think when we do something good, we get . . . I don't know. Not rewarded. I don't mean it like that. Do you think anything or anybody notices?"

"Well now . . ." she said, and paused. "I believe when we do the right thing, it comes back to us."

"How?"

"Lots of ways. People like us more. We feel better about ourselves."

"I would like it if people liked me more," Jody said. "I always feel like I don't quite fit with anybody."

She didn't answer for a few seconds. Then Jody looked up and saw the diner in the distance. And, unfortunately, the railroad bridge off in the distance behind it. Jody had never liked the look of that bridge. It filled him with a dread he couldn't explain, even to himself. Now, with the way the black storm clouds framed it, it looked like a movie cue that nothing good could happen from here on out. All that was missing was the ominous music.

"Oh. We're here already," he said, holding more tightly to the dog. He tried to disguise the fact that he wished they weren't.

He was seized with an idea. He'd jump out at the highway intersection, wait for the lady to drive away, then turn around and hitchhike back up to the lake. Forget the whole crazy thing he'd started.

Just at that moment the rain let loose, drumming on the roof of the car, splattering the windshield. The lady turned her wipers on to that super-fast position, but they still couldn't keep up.

"Hoo!" she said. "You got a ride out just in time. Nobody's going to want to go out in this."

"How can it rain if it's below freezing?" he asked, knowing he was probably too upset to take in the answer.

"Something about a warmer area above us in the atmosphere. Then it refreezes when it touches down." She pulled into the diner's parking lot, the tires of her small car crunching over gravel. "I think it's closed," she said.

"The lady is still here. I recognize her car."

"Go see, okay? And let me know. Wave or something when you see for sure she's there. I don't want to just drop you in this weather. I don't want you stranded out here if her car battery died and she got a ride home from someone else."

"Yes, ma'am," he said.

Jody and Worthy stepped out into the violent rain. It pounded on his knit cap and turned to ice when it hit the shoulders of his coat. Worthy winced, squinting his eyes half-closed against the freezing drops.

They ran together to the diner's porch. Up the three wooden steps. Something twisted into Jody's stomach at the look and feel of the place—that sensation like waking up after a bad dream you can't remember, but can't shake either.

They stepped up to the wood-and-glass doors, where the big red sign said, "Closed." He could see a light on in the kitchen, and hear dishes being moved.

He ran back to the lady's car. She powered down her window, even though it allowed rain to come in and hit her in the face. She used her hand to shield her eyes.

"It's fine," he said. "She's here."

"You're sure? You saw her with your own eyes?"

"Yes, ma'am," he said, even though he hadn't, because he wanted her to stop worrying about him and drive away.

"Jody? Do you mind if I ask . . . are you okay?"

Jody stood a moment in the freezing rain, trying to figure the fastest way out of this moment. He decided, under the circumstances, to plow forward and get this over fast.

"Honest answer, ma'am? Not really, no. But I keep thinking I could be. If I just . . . I don't even know what. But I'll figure it out, I suppose."

She smiled. Patted the gloved hand he'd set on her car door. Then she shifted into reverse and Jody took his hand back and watched her power up her window and drive away.

He stood a moment in the miserable weather, looking up to the lake. Wondering what had happened to all that clear weather and steely blue sky he'd been enjoying not an hour before.

He would have fled back up there in a heartbeat if that option hadn't been closed and locked to him. Part of him was glad he couldn't. He needed help doing the right thing. And he was getting it.

He and Worthy ran back to the diner's scary door.

Chapter Twenty-Two: Virginia

Virginia ran her hands through the hot, soapy water, feeling like she was on vacation already. That wonderful feeling like a snow day when you don't have to go to school.

Her mind drifted to Lloyd, examining the strangeness of having loved him not even a week ago. Going from planning a future with him to locking the door against him in just a matter of days. She poked at the feeling again and again, as if to dispense with the conscious registering of those emotions. But every time she ran through the timetable, it stung just as much as the time before.

She thought about Jody, and how differently she might have felt about him if it turned out he'd been Buddy all grown up. After all, Buddy had only been a nickname. She knew it hadn't said Buddy on his birth certificate. He had a real name, only all these years later she still didn't know what it was.

Just for a minute her hopes rose again. Somehow her mind backtracked, papering over a basic fact. Then it came back again. She might not have known Buddy's first name, but she knew his last name. And it wasn't Schilling.

But he was *somebody's* son.

A hard rap on the glass of the front doors jarred her back to the moment.

She looked at the clock over the grill. It had been almost twenty minutes since she'd promised Fern she'd leave in no more than ten.

Her stomach icy with fear, she pulled the biggest carving knife out of the woodblock of chef's knives. Maybe it was only Fern coming back to tell her she'd broken curfew. Maybe. Or Roger Rodelle to tell her all was well and the coast was clear.

Or maybe it was Lloyd.

Roger said he'd keep an eye on him, though. But once he gets in his truck, or in his daughter's car, how do you really do that? How do you know he didn't just turn right around and drive back into town?

Virginia could hear the sound of freezing rain hitting the roof. Then a much greater torrent let go, as if the skies had burst open, showering the roof with hail that sounded like it must be the size of peas. It made her jump. She thought about her car, parked out in the open. She'd just barely finished paying off the body shop for the last time it was parked outside during a big hailstorm.

She crept to the two swinging doors of the kitchen, the knife held cautiously at her side, partially behind her back and out of sight. She placed her fingers on one half of the door and pushed it open just enough to see through. No more than an inch or two.

Under the roof of the front porch, the only sheltered spot outside the door, stood Jody Schilling. Well, maybe "stood" was the wrong word. He was bent over, brushing ice off T-Rex's back. He had the dog on a leash that was nothing more than a length of braided rope, frayed and unraveling at both ends. His knit cap and the ends of his own tousled hair were coated with ice, and the shoulders of his coat were thick with it. But he seemed more concerned about the dog.

She opened the kitchen door wider to watch.

Then he straightened up, and their eyes met through the glass.

Virginia hurried over and stood holding the diner door open for them, icy wind blasting into her face and onto her bare arms.

"What are you doing here?" she asked. Then she realized it might not have sounded as welcoming as she had intended.

Her dog came racing in and jumped up, but not on her. He'd been trained not to jump on people. He was too big to get away with that. Instead he just reared up on his hind legs, his face almost level with hers, wagging so hard that the motion of his rear end nearly knocked him off balance.

Virginia laughed and kissed him on the nose, and his front paws touched the linoleum again.

She looked up at Jody, who was still waiting outside on the porch in the cold. When she looked into his face, he looked so sad that she shifted her eyes away.

"I shouldn't let him in," she said to the young man. "I'm sure the health department would have a thing or two to say about that. But it's so cold out there. Come in, honey. Come in before you freeze."

He stepped inside, but then backed up nearly to the front windows. As if to stand as far away from her as he could.

"I don't like this place," he said.

Virginia rose up to be offended, but then decided not to bother.

"What's wrong with it?" she asked, closing the three of them in from the cold. Well, from most of the cold. A fair portion of it was now inside with them. It would take time for the heater to overcome it.

"Nothing's wrong with it. It's a perfectly good diner."

"Then why don't you like it?"

"I don't know. I just don't. It makes me nervous. Even when I go by on the bus, and it's a long way away, and I'm only seeing it from the outside, it still makes me nervous."

"Well, that's a strange reaction to a diner," she said.

She watched his face fall into even more sadness, if such a thing were possible.

"I'm sorry," she said. "I didn't mean *you* were strange."

"You sort of did," he said. "But it's okay."

He sank into a sit in one of the chairs at table four. Virginia could feel the thwack of the dog's tail beating like a metronome against her leg. She reached down and scratched him behind the ear.

"What are you doing here, honey?" she asked again. "I don't mean to make it sound like you're not welcome. Of course you're welcome. And of course it's wonderful to see . . . my dog. But you just about couldn't have picked a worse day to come down here. Everybody's trying to buckle in for the big ice storm."

"Ice storm?" he asked, as if just waking up from a dream. As if he'd never considered such a thing.

"You must have noticed all the hail and freezing rain."

"It was nice when I left," he said. "Cold. But clear."

Virginia sighed and walked the few steps to his table. Sat down across from him and leaned forward onto her elbows.

His gaze remained trained down to the tabletop. He wouldn't look up into her face.

Virginia noticed some crayon marks on the table, from one of the kids who had been in that day. She wondered why Fern hadn't cleaned it off, or at least mentioned it. Probably in a hurry to get home safely before the storm set in. At the back of her mind Virginia knew she should feel the same sense of hurry, but it didn't translate into action. The new developments had displaced everything that came before. Even caution.

The dog settled at her feet with a sigh. Jody pulled off his knit cap and set it on the table.

"How did you even get down here?" she asked him. She kept her voice gentle, because he looked like he was about to cry.

She understood more clearly why Roger had refused to drive out there and tear the dog away from this young man. Legally she still figured she had the lion's share of rights to the dog. But she saw more about the situation now. Or felt more. She felt his fragility, like Jody was a raw egg in the palm of her hand, emotionally at her mercy.

"Walked some. Hitchhiked some."

"And nobody who picked you up warned you about the ice storm?"

"Um. Yeah, the lady who gave me a ride said I should get myself and the dog inside as soon as I could. I thought she meant just because it's cold. I don't think she said anything about an ice storm, though. Or maybe she did and I wasn't paying attention. Sometimes when I'm upset, I'm not a very good listener."

"Don't you watch TV or listen to the radio?"

"No, ma'am. My grampa used to. All the time. He'd tell me if he heard anything interesting, like something that happened close to home or a weather report. Until lately, anyway. Before he got so bad he couldn't even remember what he heard. But it didn't matter, because he had the TV up so loud I could hear everything anyway, even if I was in the next room. Since he's been gone, I've had it turned off. The quiet is nice. In a way. And then in another way, it's not." He looked up and around at the diner ceiling. The hanging hats. "I still don't like this place. I thought it would stop making me nervous in a minute, but it's not stopping. I think I should go."

He rose to his feet suddenly, then just stood, looking a bit disoriented. As if he'd forgotten what he was going to do.

"Go? Go where, honey? You can't get back up to the lake now. The storm's already on us. Listen to it. Listen to it on the roof. Nobody'll be going up to the lake to give you a ride. It'll be like a ghost town out there now. I'd drive you home on any other day, I swear I would, but I specifically promised Roger Rodelle I would *not* try to drive up there today. He says there'll be trees down and power lines falling. I'll have to take you to my house."

A long silence. Then he sank back down into a sit again, all at once and almost automatically, like a kid's blow-up water toy when you pull the plug and it deflates itself instantly.

"I'm going to ask again," she said, "because I've asked twice, but I still don't know. Why did you come all the way down here today?"

To her alarm, he began to cry. As if his tears were operated with a simple on-off switch. No dimmer. Just all the way off or all the way on.

"To bring you your dog back," he said miserably.

Then Virginia began to cry, too. It was only partly the gesture he'd made. Usually when anyone cried in front of her, she caught it like a cold.

She pushed up from the table, moved around to Jody's side, and threw her arms around him. He remained small and tight and did not return the gesture in any way. If anything his shoulders felt stonier as the seconds ticked by—literally—punctuated by the wall of clocks. Virginia couldn't shake the feeling that her touch was not welcome. She let him go and straightened up again.

"You don't like to be hugged, do you?"

"No, ma'am."

"Sorry."

"It's not your fault."

She sat back down again. "Didn't you *ever* like to be hugged? Even when you were little?"

"I think so," he said. "I think I liked it when my dad hugged me. But that was a long time ago."

His tears continued to stream, and his nose was running. Virginia handed him a paper napkin from the table, but he only used it to wipe his eyes. She'd always wondered why when you hand crying people a tissue or hankie, they only wipe their eyes. It seemed to her they'd feel better if they would just blow their noses. And in this case, so would she.

"What made you change your mind?" she asked him.

"I don't know. I think because my grampa never did touchy stuff like that. I got out of the habit. Plus I knew he thought it was a bad thing. So I guess after a while I decided I thought so, too."

"I meant about bringing the dog back."

"Oh," he said. And then he went silent.

"You were so set on keeping him," she said, after a time. When it was clear he didn't plan to go on without her urging.

"I love him," he said through the tears. "I love him so much that I kept thinking about how much you must love him. And how much I'd love him if I'd had him six years. And I thought about how much it hurt to even think about losing him. And I didn't want to be the one who made you feel that way."

Virginia almost jumped to her feet to embrace him again, but she stopped herself in time.

"That's just about the sweetest thing I ever heard in my life," she said.

"There's one condition, though."

He braved a brief glance up toward her face. She felt her insides tighten. "Okay . . ."

"That's not the right word, though. It's not really a condition. Because I'm giving him back even if you say no. But it's a nice thing I'm doing for you and it's hard, so I'm going to ask you to do something for me in return."

"Okay, shoot."

"Shoot?" he asked, sounding confused and slightly alarmed.

"It's just an expression. It means go ahead and say it."

"Oh. Okay." He stopped. Wiped and blew his nose on the paper napkin. Much to Virginia's relief. "I don't want you to go back to the name T-Rex. I want you to let him keep his new name. He deserves it. I don't think T-Rex is a very good name. Why did you name him that, anyway?"

Virginia sighed and sat back, the tightness in her gut easing.

"I didn't, really. I mean . . . I didn't mean to, anyway. I named him Rex after my great uncle. But the shelter where I got him, they told me he was a cocker spaniel mix. Well, obviously not. More like golden retriever or golden Lab. But I guess it was hard to tell when he was barely six weeks old. So I figured he'd get to be twenty-five, thirty pounds. But he just kept growing. Around the time he hit sixty, my friend Fern started calling him T-Rex as a joke. Because she said he was as big as a dinosaur. I guess it just kind of stuck. But you're right. It's silly. It's just a joke, and a dog shouldn't have a name that's a joke, because then it sounds like you think the dog is a joke. Worthy is better. He deserves that."

A long silence except for the freezing rain on the roof. The sharp tapping of it.

Get safely back home, and take them with you, her brain said. *Stop messing around.*

But still she sat and let the moment melt her.

He looked up into her face. "So . . . you'll do it?"

"Call him Worthy?"

"Right. That."

"Yes. Sure. I will."

His tears began to flow again.

"I got him a great big bag of dog food," he said. "Cost me a fortune. I hate to see it go to waste. You should come pick it up. I had no way to get it down here with us. But you should come get it."

"I think you should hang on to it."

"Why would I do that?"

"I've been doing some thinking, too," she said. It was a lie, but a harmless one. There had been no premeditation to what she was about to say. The ideas were forming on the spot, appearing just in time to be spoken. "He's alone during the day while I work. We're just about to hire a new waitress and a new dishwasher. So I'll be going to a five-day week. I have to. Fern and I both have to. We're just getting too damned old for this nonstop schedule thing.

Shame for him to be alone at my house and you alone up at the lake. I was thinking maybe he should be with you for five days while I work, and then I could come get him when I'm ready to take my two days off."

His face came up. Not all the way up to meet her eyes, but his gaze rose from the crayon-marked tabletop. "You mean share him?"

"I'd sure be willing to give it a try. But, you know what, honey? We need to work out the details some other time. We've been here way too long as it is. Those roads are going to get real bad real fast. We need to get back to my house while we still can."

She pulled to her feet, trying to think what was left to do. Most of it would just remain undone, but some of it was essential. She would have to unplug the toasters and the coffeemakers. And turn off the heater. She couldn't think of anything else that wouldn't wait.

She grabbed her coat and met Jody at the door, Worthy wagging at her to hurry up and join them.

Virginia opened the diner door. Stepped out into the gathering dark of a winter late afternoon.

The porch steps were already coated with ice. The road looked slick with it, shimmering in the illumination from the light pole in the diner's parking lot. In its light, Virginia could see a long, even strand of icicles hanging off the power line as it began its descent to the diner roof.

As she stood looking, the freezing rain turned to hail again, hail the size of marbles. The sky let loose with millions of whitish marbles, clattering everywhere with a nearly deafening racket. A small limb came loose from a tree and fell onto the highway in front of the place, shattering into several pieces and sending chunks and shards of ice flying in every direction.

The hail gathered quickly as she watched, piling up on every surface. Porch steps. Parking lot. Driving surfaces. The land turned into a flat sheet of ice scattered with ball bearings made of still more ice.

She stepped back inside. Worthy wagged at her in greeting, as though he'd been wondering why it took her so long to come to her senses and come back into safe cover. Jody was crouched near the door, under the window, bent over his own knees, the heels of his hands pressed hard to his ears.

A moment later the hail turned to freezing rain again. Virginia listened to the change in the sound of it hitting the roof. She watched out the window as it covered the collected hail in a bumpy sheet of ice.

Jody took his hands away from his ears cautiously. He looked up into her face.

"I think we might have missed our moment," she told him. "I think we'll need to hunker down right where we are."

Chapter Twenty-Three: Jody

She offered him food. And he was hungry.

It was nearly dinnertime, and he hadn't eaten since breakfast. But being in this place was making him sick to his stomach, and he was afraid whatever she gave him to eat wouldn't stay down.

And besides, he didn't want to stay long enough to eat.

"I have to go," he said. "I have to get out of this place. I don't like it. I want to go home."

Instead of answering straight away, she turned around and headed for the kitchen. He edged toward the door the minute she turned her back.

"I don't think you understood what I said a minute ago, honey," she called over her shoulder. "It's too late. We're well and surely stuck here until those roads improve. Now what do you want? I could make you a sandwich. Smoked turkey? Ham and cheese? Tuna? Roast beef? Or maybe you're too cold for cold food. We have soup left. The soup of the day was chicken rice. You like chicken rice?" She disappeared through the swinging kitchen doors as she spoke.

"Yes, ma'am," he said, still moving quietly in the direction of the front door. "How long?"

"Oh, I could whip you up a sandwich and some soup in less than five minutes."

"I mean until the roads are clear and I can go home."

Her face appeared again, holding one kitchen door open.

"Well, that's anybody's guess, isn't it? It might be days before you can get back up to the lake. If a bunch of trees come down onto Highway 22, it's going to be quite a project to clear them. But don't worry. I have a guest room."

Her face disappeared into the kitchen again.

"How long till we can get out of here and get to your house?" he called to her. "Because this place makes me nervous."

"So you said," she called back. "Definitely not tonight. Maybe tomorrow if we're lucky. Depends on how much ice we get, I suppose."

His hand was on the diner door by that time. He pushed lightly and quietly to see if she had locked it.

She hadn't.

It pushed out an inch or two, letting a blast of cold air in.

Jody looked at the dog, who was watching him with an amiable look on his face. He didn't want to say anything to Worthy out loud, so he tried to say, telepathically and by the look on his face, "Stay here, you'll be fine."

Then he darted out into the night. As he did, the bells jingled. But Jody couldn't think how to fix that. So he just kept moving.

The minute he came out from under the porch roof, he realized he had forgotten his hat. The freezing rain fell on his hair and soaked down onto his scalp in an instant. It didn't freeze, probably because his scalp was warm. But it sure did chill him through and through.

He thought about going back.

He turned and looked behind him to see if she was still in the kitchen or had noticed he was gone. The diner glowed with light from the inside, and looked warm. To someone else it would have looked welcoming, he thought. But to Jody it was like the wrong end of a magnet. The farther he got from that place, the better he would feel.

He picked his way along fast, trying to be careful of his footing. Hoping the lug soles of his winter boots would prove traction enough. But he slipped and slid on every second or third step, always managing to right himself.

When he'd crossed the parking lot, he stepped out onto the road. He looked up Highway 22 in the direction of the lake, and he knew he would never get up there. He'd never get a ride, because no one was out driving. It was too far to walk even in ideal conditions. And the road would turn steeply uphill, which would not be helpful when your footing was precarious anyway.

But he had to get somewhere that wasn't the diner.

He turned the other way, toward town. Town was only a few miles, and the road was relatively flat.

He took one careful step. Then two. On the third, his feet came out from under him and he pitched forward, landing hard on his hands and knees.

"Ow!" he shouted out loud. But he was still not clear enough and settled enough to assess the damage that had caused the jolt of pain.

He crouched there for a few beats, feeling the rain gather and turn to ice on the back of his coat.

He pulled up to his knees, which were banged up and sore, but apparently uninjured. He looked at the heels of his hands, because they hurt. But they weren't bleeding, or otherwise visibly damaged. Then he tried to move his wrists. The right one moved normally. The left one made him cry out loud again.

Then Worthy was there, licking his face.

I must have left the diner door open, Jody thought.

"No, you can't come, boy," he told the dog. "We'll have to get you back inside. It's not safe for you out here."

"If it's not safe for him, it's not safe for you."

Virginia's voice made him jump so much that he unbalanced, slipped off his knees, and fell on his right side on the ice. Again he held still and experienced the sensation of the freezing rain falling on his face and hair.

He looked up at the lady. He could barely see her in the dark. The only light was from the streetlamp in the diner parking lot, but it was behind her, and it only backlit her silhouette like a halo, making it even harder to see her face. Jody could just barely see that she was hugging her coat tightly around herself. He couldn't make out much more.

Again Worthy loomed over him and licked his wet face. Then the dog slipped on the ice and landed flat on his belly, legs sprawled out in four different directions.

"Where did you think you were going?" Virginia asked him.

"I don't know. Town. Anyplace. I don't like it in there."

"How could it be that bad? Why would the place make you *that* nervous?"

"I don't know," he said. "It just does."

Silence for a moment. She stood over him in silence, and he lay on the road in silence. Worthy tried to struggle to his feet but only ended up sprawled on the ice again.

Then she said, "Do you get it now? That it isn't going to work?"

"Yes, ma'am."

"Do you understand that no matter how you feel about my diner, it's the only safe place within reach?"

"Yes, ma'am."

"Ready to go back inside?"

"I suppose so," he said.

She reached a hand down to him, but he didn't take it. Not because he didn't want to touch her hand, but because he didn't want to pull her down if he slipped again.

"I can do it," he said.

He cautiously pulled to his hands and knees again—well, *hand* and knees—careful not to put weight on his left wrist. When it seemed he might slip again, he put his left elbow down to steady himself.

As he straightened slowly and carefully to his feet, she steadied his arm.

Then she helped the dog by holding his collar to keep him from going back down until he got his legs under him.

She linked her arm through Jody's and they inched their way back to the diner, slipping and sliding, their heads wet and cold, the shoulders of their winter coats weighing down with ice in the freezing rain.

———

"You hurt yourself, didn't you?" she asked him.

He had just sat down at a table again. The one closest to a heating vent. She handed him two or three thin white dish towels as she asked it.

"No, ma'am," he said, shrugging out of his icy coat.

"I heard you yell out when you fell."

"Oh," he said.

He took the towels out of her hand and began to dry off his head as best he could with only his right hand to work with.

He thought of saying more, but then he decided he shouldn't.

"Is it that left wrist?"

"Why do you say that, ma'am?"

"Because most people towel off their hair with both hands. Especially on the left side there, where you have to reach over."

She pulled the towels out of his hand and moved around behind him, where she began toweling his hair briskly. She used enough pressure that his head moved back and forth with her motions. Which he wasn't too happy about. It made him feel like someone else was in control of him. But the friction began to build up some relative warmth. So he sat still and put up with it.

"Lift your left arm," she said.

Jody did as he was told.

"Now show me whether you can wiggle your fingers."

He did. It hurt his wrist to use those muscles. But the fingers moved.

"Good," she said. "It's probably not broken. Let's hope you just sprained it. There's a first aid kit in the bathroom. I think it might have one of those elastic compression bandages in there. Unless someone used it and didn't replace it. Honestly, I haven't looked inside that first aid kit in years. But Fern thought it was a good idea to have one."

"It's okay," he said. "I'm fine. I just won't try to use it much."

"Compression," she said, still toweling.

"What?" he asked dreamily.

He figured his hair must be as dry as it was going to get by toweling, but he was warming up nicely, so he didn't say so. His feelings were changing on the subject of being out of control. He was beginning to like it now. Instead of feeling like he was being overpowered, it now felt more like he was a kid letting a parent take care of everything.

"You're supposed to use compression on a sprain. And ice."

"Great," he said. "Just what I need. Ice."

"It'll help, though."

"I'm trying to get warm, in case you hadn't noticed." He looked up and around, into her face. Her eye makeup was running. And her own hair was still soaking wet. She was toweling his first. Before her own. "Sorry. Did that sound rude? I didn't mean to be rude."

She threw the towels on the table in front of him.

"Whatever," she said. "I guess we're both having a bad night. Get nice and warm in front of the heater for a while and then I'll get you a plastic bag of ice for that sprain. And I'll get some aspirin. I think I have some in my purse. What do you want to eat?"

His stomach twisted into a painful pang at the mention of food.

"Um. Whatever you're making for yourself is fine."

"How about tuna sandwiches and soup? Or don't you like tuna?"

"I like it fine, ma'am. Thank you."

She disappeared into the kitchen.

Jody looked down at Worthy, curled at his feet. The dog looked back into his face, tail thumping.

It hit Jody again that he was stuck here, which brought a wave of nausea. First he looked around the place, but that only made it worse, as if he might really be sick. Then he closed his eyes, and that was better.

Maybe a minute later, maybe two, the light on the other side of his closed eyelids went dark. The hum of the heater's fan wound down to silence.

He heard the lady spit out one hard word from the kitchen.

"Shit!"

He opened his eyes.

Nothing. The diner lights were gone. The light on the lamp-post in the parking lot was out. It was too cloudy for a moon. Jody could see nothing. He felt his stomach ease.

He heard the movement of the lady as she crossed the room to join him.

"Well, I guess I should chalk that up as no big surprise," she said.

"Can you still make food?" he asked, hungrier than ever now that the tension in his gut was melting.

"Oh, yeah. I can still get sandwich makings out of the fridge if the batteries are good in the big flashlight. If not, I can still take out food, but it might be hard to see what I'm getting. And the burners are gas, so that's no problem. Yeah, I'll still make food. But it looks like we'll be stuck here all night in the dark. Sorry, but what can you do?"

"I don't mind the dark," he said.

"You don't? I thought you would."

"No," he said. "Not at all. I like this place a whole lot better when I can't see it."

Chapter Twenty-Four: Virginia

Virginia set the flashlight on the table, pointing it up toward the carbon monoxide detector on the diner's ceiling. But then she couldn't see well enough to dare to stand on a chair, so she pointed its beam toward the chair.

It was already cold in the dining area, even with her coat on.

She stepped up onto the chair, then felt around for the detector. Just before she pushed its button, she called into the kitchen.

"Brace yourself, Jody! There's about to be a big noise."

"Okay," he called back, sounding like his mouth was full of food.

She pressed the button, and the device shrieked out three long, ear-piercing beeps. It frightened her, even though she was the one who had caused it. She hadn't expected it to be so loud and startling.

I should have told myself to brace myself, she thought.

She climbed down off the chair, picked up the flashlight, and made her way back into the kitchen. It was warmer in there, because both ovens were going, their doors open wide. But still not warm enough to invite Virginia to take off her coat.

Jody sat in a chair pulled up to the central kitchen island, which was a mix of cutting boards and stainless steel food-preparation surfaces. He winced at the light and turned his face away. He had finished his sandwich and was spooning up soup with his right hand. His left forearm was flat on the cutting board, his wrist draped with a plastic bag of ice. Worthy sat close to his side, his chin on Jody's thigh, begging semi-politely.

She turned the flashlight away so as not to blind them.

"T-Rex, you come away from there," she said sharply. "I'll make you some hamburger." The dog, knowing the word "hamburger," left Jody's side and came wagging around her legs. "I'm sorry," she said to Jody. "I didn't mean T-Rex. I meant Worthy. I just need a little time to get used to it."

"So does he," the young man mumbled, his mouth full of soup. "He really doesn't answer to it yet or anything."

"We'll both get used to it."

"What was that noise?" he asked.

"The carbon monoxide detector."

"Oh," he said. "We have one of those. Grampa and I do, I mean. But it never made a sound like that."

"It makes that sound when you push the test button. Or when it's warning you there's too much carbon monoxide."

"Is there too much?"

"No, I don't think so. I was just testing it."

She placed the flashlight on the table, its beam angled off toward the wall. She leaned her elbows on the wood cutting board, across the island from him, and tried to absorb the warmth coming from the ovens. It was barely enough.

"Why were you testing it?" he asked, his mouth full of soup again.

"To make sure it's working."

"But why would there be too much carbon monoxide?"

"Because you're really not supposed to use ovens for heating. It can be dangerous."

"Are you still worried? Or are you not worried now that you tested it?"

"I'm a little worried. Because *it's* out there. And *we're* in here."

"Maybe we should turn the ovens off, then."

"But if we do, it'll get very cold. And the cold is also dangerous."

"Oh," he said. "That's true."

He ate in silence for a few minutes.

Virginia walked around to the oven side of the island and sank down to her knees in front of one, reaching out her cold hands for warmth.

Worthy appeared beside her and licked her cheek and nose, and she laughed.

She sank into a sit on the hard linoleum floor.

"Why were you with him?" she heard Jody ask.

She just kept looking into the dark oven. Thank goodness they were old-fashioned gas ovens and didn't have those new computerized controls that required electricity. Just good old "gas on, gas off" units with pilots. Fern had wanted to replace them, but Virginia had held out for putting the money into hiring another waitress instead, a decision which might prove lifesaving.

"With who?" she asked. But she had a feeling she already knew.

Worthy plunked into a sit beside her and she wrapped her arms around his neck, burying her face in his fur.

"That terrible man."

"Lloyd."

"The guy who drove Worthy out to the lake and left him."

"Yeah. That's Lloyd all right."

"Why were you with him?"

"Well, that's a question for the ages, isn't it?"

She looked over her shoulder at Jody, but there wasn't much to see. Just the beam of flashlight pointing at nothing, and a vague dark shape of him hunched over his soup.

"I don't know what that means," he said.

"It means it's a hard question to answer. It means nobody really knows."

"That's a pretty complicated way to say nobody really knows."

Then all went silent for a time. Virginia leaned on Worthy and listened to the sounds of the young man finishing up his soup and placing the bowl in the sink with the other unwashed dishes.

"You want me to wash these?" he asked.

"No, you don't have to do that. Especially not in the dark. I'll wash them in the morning."

"We can work on them together in the morning," he said.

Then, much to her surprise, he came and sat near her. Right on the other side of the dog. *He just wants the heat*, she thought. But then she realized there was a second oven going, and he had voluntarily come to share hers.

"I don't mind the kitchen of this place," he said. "It's only that other room out there where the customers eat that makes me sick."

"Don't take this the wrong way, but that doesn't make a lick of sense."

"Well, sure it does. I've never been in the kitchen before, so how can I think bad things about it?"

She looked over at him, but it was much too dark to see his face.

"You've been to my diner before?"

"I don't think so."

"Well, then why did you just say that?"

"I don't know," he said. "It seemed like a normal thing to say at the time. Maybe it's because you didn't think you deserved better."

"Now what on earth does what I think I deserve have to do with you not liking my diner?" But then she realized her mistake. "Oh. We're talking about that other thing again, aren't we?"

"Lloyd."

"Oh. Well. It's not that I don't think I deserve a nice person. Exactly. But I'm not a young woman. I'm fifty-six years old."

"How old was he?"

"Fifty-nine."

"So if you're fifty-six . . . well, what does it matter? If you find a man who's the same age, how can he mind? He's the same age."

"It's different for women."

"It shouldn't be."

"You're right. It shouldn't."

"It's just stupid."

"Yes. It is."

"Well, why don't you just ignore it, then, and act like it's stupid?"

Virginia didn't answer. She was busy asking herself similar questions. She was thinking of Lloyd's bald head and potbelly and wondering why she'd still always felt *she* was the one who didn't quite measure up.

While she was thinking, he startled her by speaking again.

"I still think it's about what you think you deserve."

"Well, what about you?" she asked, slightly irritated now. "Are you just all brimming with self-confidence?"

"Not really," he said, seeming to take none of the offense she had intended. "But I still think I'd rather be alone than with a guy who would hurt my dog. I'm not saying I would be with a guy if I was with someone. You know. I just mean if I were you. You know what I mean."

"I didn't know he would hurt my dog. As soon as I knew that, I put him right out of my life."

"But you must have known something. He couldn't have been this perfect, wonderful guy and then turned around and done a thing like that."

"I wouldn't say he was perfect and wonderful, no. I guess there was something there to see. Fern saw it. She never liked him. She tried to tell me he wasn't very good husband material. But it's not like I had a bunch of offers to choose from. It was Lloyd or nothing. So I guess I overlooked a few things. Probably more than I should have. I don't like to be alone. Fern doesn't mind it. I think she actually enjoys it. She's happy just living with her cats. I think she literally likes it better that way. I think a great guy could stand right in front of her and ask her to share the rest of their lives together, and she'd probably tell him she prefers to leave well enough alone. That it's simpler her way. But me, I've never liked an empty house. It's lonely. And scary. And kind of sad."

He didn't answer. She waited for a good minute, in case he wanted to speak.

Then she said, "What about you? Do you like to be alone?"

"I'm not sure," he said. "I never really have been. Just in the last couple of days. Before that, Grampa was always around. I guess I like it and I don't like it, both. The house feels empty, and that I don't really like. But it's quiet. And sort of . . . predictable. When there's a person around, you never really know what's about to happen. When you're alone, things happen just the way you make them happen. So . . . I don't know. I guess I have mixed feelings."

They sat quietly in the dark for a minute more. The heat from the oven was edging out her chill at long last.

"Do you ever plan to have a wife and a family?" she asked him.

"Oh, I can't picture that."

"Why not?"

"I don't even drive. I can't even work. How would I support a family? And I'm not very good at being close to people."

"How do you get by if you don't work?"

"We had Grampa's Social Security check. It wasn't much, but we managed. But I guess Grampa's check is gone now. I'm not sure what I do from this point on. I haven't had time to figure that out yet."

"What are you going to do with your life?" she asked him.

"What do you mean? What does anybody do with their life? You live every day. What else can you do?"

"But no job. No family. No one in the house but you."

"And Worthy five days a week," he said.

"Right. But still. Seems kind of . . ."

"Can we talk about something else?"

It made her slightly grumpy and resentful. Because he had dragged her into equally uncomfortable conversational territory. But, as was so often her decision, she simply let it go by.

She rose to her feet—noting that it was not as easy to get up from the floor as it once had been—and began to fix Worthy something to eat.

A moment later they heard the first branch hit the roof.

They had a few seconds to brace for it, because they heard it break. It seemed to fall for a long time. Long enough that Virginia thought it had given the diner a miss. And she wondered why they were close enough to hear it break but not close enough to hear it land.

Then it hit hard on a spot that must have been just above their heads from the sound of it. Jody let out a strangled sound of alarm. The ice shattered on impact, and Virginia could hear chunks of it rolling and bouncing down the roof.

"At least the roof held," she said, her heart hammering. *That time*, she almost added, but she figured Jody was spooky enough without her helping his fear along.

"What if it doesn't?" he asked.

"But it did."

"But what if another one falls, and this time it doesn't?"

"I don't really know how to answer that," she said.

He was silent for a few seconds. As if thinking the idea through in his head.

"I guess that's a question for the ages," he said.

It wasn't, exactly. But Virginia didn't correct him.

Chapter Twenty-Five: Jody

"Hey," he whispered. "Are you asleep?"

He sat with his back up against the kitchen wall. It was a little farther from the ovens than he might have liked, but he needed to get his back up against something when he sat. He hugged his coat more tightly around himself to try to stay warm.

He could barely make out the shape of Virginia and the dog sprawled on the kitchen floor. They'd turned off the flashlight long ago, because its beam was growing weak. And the lady didn't think there were any extra batteries in the place. The only light was just a faded glow from the gas flame underneath the cast-iron bottom panels of the ovens. There were a couple of small cutaways that allowed light to glow through.

It felt like the middle of the night, but Jody had no way to know.

A few seconds passed, and he figured the answer to his question must have been yes, she was.

Then he saw and heard her stir.

She sat up and slid across the floor until her back was up against the same wall as Jody's.

"No," she said. "I haven't slept a wink."

"Me neither."

"I think it's partly because I'm cold," she said. "But mostly I'm just waiting for another branch to fall. Or maybe a whole tree. What about you?"

"Well, that. Sure. Hard to let go of the idea that a huge tree might be just about to fall on the roof right over your head. But also I can't stop thinking about what you said."

"What did I say?"

"About the whole rest of my life and what I'm going to do with it. No Grampa. No family. No friends. No job. Just me in that little cabin all by myself."

"I'm sorry if that was a bad thing to say."

"Not bad, exactly. It just started me thinking."

They sat quietly for a long time. There was no more rain or hail on the roof, but Jody could hear the occasional tinkle and crash of ice hitting the ground and shattering.

Then she said, "Want to talk about it?"

"I'm not sure," Jody said. Actually, he felt fairly sure. That he didn't.

"Well, you think about it," she said.

Then, much to his surprise, Jody found himself talking. "It's just that you said you had a friend. Fern. And you had that guy you were going to marry even though he would have been a terrible person to marry. But I was sitting here thinking you add people to your life. New people. Everybody does, I think. Except me. I haven't added anybody new to my life . . . well . . . ever, I guess. I'm not even sure how you do that friend thing."

"You didn't have friends in school?"

"Did I? I don't know. There were lots of other kids there. I'm not saying I hated them or they hated me. I talked to some of them. Stayed closer to some than others. You know, during the day. When I had to be at school. But I don't think they were my friends.

When Grampa and I moved back here after Gramma died, there wasn't anybody I wrote to or called. If you have a friend and you move away, you keep in contact. At least, I think you do. I didn't have anybody like that."

Then he stopped talking, and realized it was weird to have said all that. Very weird. Because it was exactly the kind of talking he'd always said he didn't do.

Or couldn't do. He wasn't even sure how to tell the two apart anymore.

It was because he hadn't slept, he decided. The lack of sleep was grinding him down. But then that made him wonder why losing his faculties to exhaustion would make him better at something instead of worse. He would have to think about that when his brain was in better shape.

"You lived here before?" she asked, knocking him out of his thoughts. "I didn't know that. I thought you and your grandfather had only lived here for a couple of years."

"He lived here before. He had that cabin up by the lake forever. He always wanted to live in it, but Gramma couldn't stand the cold. He liked the cold. The minute she . . . passed away, he moved us back here."

"But did *you* live here before?"

"They tell me I did. But I must have been awful little, because I don't remember that."

"Where did you live in between?"

Before Jody could open his mouth to answer, they both heard the horrible sound of a tree fracturing. Not a branch. They had heard enough branches give in the night. This was the breaking of a big tree. It started with a series of frightening squeaks and screeches, followed by a cracking report, like a massive gun being fired. Maybe even a cannon, though Jody had never heard a cannon fired except in the movies.

Jody dropped his head between his knees and instinctively covered the back of his head with his hands. As he did, he pictured the tree hitting the roof above them, and knew his posture was ridiculous. If a many-ton tree is going to squash you flat, it really doesn't matter what position you're in when it crushes you. It's just one of those things you instinctively do when it all happens too fast.

The sound of the tree hitting the earth was a terrible thing. It didn't seem to happen all at once. First there was the boom of the trunk striking the earth so hard that Jody felt the jolt like a small earthquake. It did not strike the roof of the diner. That much was clear. But the sounds continued for a bizarre length of time as the impact caused branches and twigs to snap and fall, and shed their ice coats. And each of those events had its own impact with the ground, every one sounding smaller than the one before it.

Then there was silence.

Jody lifted his head and tried to breathe. He hadn't been breathing for those few seconds, but he hadn't even noticed. He put one hand on his heart, feeling it pound.

"Wow," Virginia said. "Thank God that one missed us."

"Okay, now I'm really scared."

She put one hand on the back of his neck, as if to try to massage out the kinks.

"No, don't," he said, pulling away. "Don't try to make me relax, because I can't. I'm sort of freaking out here, and when I'm freaking out and people try to make me relax, I only get more freaked out."

She didn't speak for a few moments.

Then she said, "I could go outside and see how it looks."

"I don't see what good that would do."

"I could tell you if it looks pretty clear over us. It's stopped raining. So maybe this is all the ice we're going to get. Maybe there's nothing more over the diner that's really dangerous. Maybe I could put your mind at ease."

"Okay," he said, strangely surprised that he could speak. He felt immobile and generally not in working order.

She rose, turned on the weak and dying flashlight, and disappeared from the kitchen.

It hit Jody that he was now alone. Then he looked down and saw the dark shape of Worthy lying on a bed of laundry—mostly dish towels and aprons—in front of the stove. He moved closer to the ovens and curled up behind the dog the way he had in front of the propane heater in the cabin.

He tried not to think about what he would do if something happened to the lady and she didn't come back.

Jody had no idea how much time passed. It might only have been a minute or two. But, if so, it was a long minute or two.

Then he heard her come back in.

"You have to see this, Jody. You have to."

"Is it bad?"

"No. It's beautiful. It's the most beautiful thing I've ever seen. I could never describe it to you. You just have to come look."

He rose to his feet and she hooked her arm through his. They moved through the dark dining area and out the front door, Worthy padding behind.

Jody stepped out into the bitingly cold night.

"Come here where you can see the trees better. But watch your step. It's really slick."

He allowed himself to be led down the porch stairs.

As they picked their way along, Jody realized it wasn't as dark as he expected. He looked up to the sky and saw it was perfectly clear. A big moon, two or three days before or after full, bathed the scene with light. And the stars were out in numbers, looking sharp and distinct in their contrast against the black sky.

They stopped, and she turned them around to face the diner.

Jody sucked in an audible breath.

The trees had their heads down. The hugely tall but whip-thin evergreens were so thick with ice that their tops bent over and rested on the ground, like an actor taking a dramatic bow.

There was nothing directly over the diner roof anymore. Every tree, every bough, was crouched down to one side of it or the other.

And the trees were not green now. They were a clear and brilliant white. The moonlight glinted off thousands of points of their ice coatings, making it look like the whole world shone. The diner roof shone and glinted. The phone and power lines shone and glinted. Even the mailbox glittered, icicles dangling from its bottom. The wind had died completely, leaving an unearthly still. Except for the walls of the diner, the entire world was made up of this same glittery clear-white ice.

"How can they bend over like that and not break?" he asked her, his breath billowing out in visible clouds as he spoke.

"That one broke," she said, pointing to a sheared trunk rising up into nothing. "But at least if any more break, you can see it won't be onto the roof."

"They have their heads on the ground," he said. Not so much because she needed to know, not because she couldn't see it with her own eyes, but because he wanted to say it. It was an amazing thing that felt like it needed to be said. "Have you ever seen anything like that in your life?"

"Never," she said. "And I've lived in these mountains for thirty-six years. I've even seen some other ice storms. But nothing like this."

Just as she finished that last sentence, another tree let go. Again it began with a terrible screeching squeak, then a huge bang like a gunshot. But this time Jody knew there was nothing over his head except stars. So they just stood and watched it hit the ground. Watched its boughs bounce on impact, and break. And fall. And shed their ice coats, which also fell.

Then all was silent again, and still, and still beautiful. And Jody felt surprisingly unshaken, because the falling trees didn't feel like a direct danger to his life and well-being anymore.

"You're right," he said. "It's the most beautiful thing I ever saw in my life."

"How's your wrist?"

"Oh. It's not too bad."

He held it up in the moonlight. It looked only slightly swollen.

"Looks so-so," she said. "Not as bad as I thought it might be. I forgot I was going to wrap it in an elastic bandage. If I'm even right that I have one. Might be hard to find in the dark, but I'm going to try. And you probably need some more aspirin by now."

"Yes, please," he said.

She started back to the diner. He didn't.

"You coming?" she asked over her shoulder.

"Yeah. In a minute. I just have to stand here and look at this some more."

"The dog's sniffing around looking for good spots to pee," she said. "So I'll leave him out here with you. Make sure he comes in when you do, okay?"

"Sure. Okay."

Then she left him. Alone out in a world that was suddenly different than the world ever had been before.

Maybe I'll just make friends with the world, he thought.

He looked all around himself again, and this time he saw the hulking shape of the railroad bridge's truss in the distance, coated with ice and shining in the moonlight.

Then the world didn't feel like a place he wanted to be friends with anymore. So he called Worthy to him and they carefully made their way across the ice and back inside.

Chapter Twenty-Six: Virginia

Because she knew the moon was out, Virginia raised the blinds on the only window in the kitchen, the one set into the back door. By that soft glow, she carefully wrapped the young man's sore wrist.

"I hate that railroad bridge so much," he said.

It hit hard and vibrated in a place in her gut. So much so that at first she couldn't say anything in reply.

"Was that a weird thing to say?" he asked. "Is that why you're not answering?"

"No. I wasn't thinking that. I was thinking how much I hate it, too. Why do *you* hate it?"

"I don't know," he said. "I just do."

She finished wrapping in silence, and used the little metal fastener with teeth—the one that was supplied in the box—to hold the bandage in place. Then, without any forethought, she bent her head down to the injured limb and kissed it. Kissed him on the bandage on what would have been the inside of his wrist if it weren't completely covered.

"What was that for?" he asked. He didn't seem to object to the gesture. Neither did he seem to particularly like it. He just sounded emotionally blank.

"Oh, you know. Like a mom does. When you hurt yourself, a mom kisses it and makes it better."

"Oh. I didn't know that. Does it really make it better?"

"Well, not the actual injury, I don't suppose. I think it just makes the patient feel better. A little. Or it's supposed to, anyway."

"Oh," he said.

Then he wandered away and sank down in the same spot as before, his back sliding down the kitchen wall.

She walked over and sat a suitable distance away.

"It feels better," he said. "A little. But I don't mean because you kissed it. It just feels better to have . . . what's the word you used?"

"Compression."

"Right. I thought it would hurt to compress it, but it feels better. Like there's something supporting it. I don't know how to explain it. Were you ever a mom?"

"Where did that come from?"

"Seems like a logical question. You were telling me what moms do. I didn't know, because I didn't really know my mom. I just wondered how you knew."

"No," she said. "I was never a mom. But I *had* a mom."

"You're lucky," he said. "Did she used to kiss the things you hurt to make them better?"

"Yes. She did."

Silence.

Virginia felt stunningly tired from lack of sleep. And yet she was not the least bit sleepy. The adrenaline from falling ice and trees had left her wide awake and almost shaking from exhaustion and cold. She had no idea what time it was and whether she would get even a minute's sleep before the sun rose.

Just for a split second she almost questioned whether it *would* rise. Because the world was so new, so changed. But she pushed that thought away again. It would. Of course it would. And it was a comfort that it would. Some things never changed.

"Did you ever want kids?" he asked, startling her.

"Um. Yeah. I guess at one point I did."

"Why didn't you have them?"

"I never got married."

"This guy, this Lloyd . . . was he the first guy you wanted to marry?"

"No. He wasn't. There was a man when I was younger. We were together for years, and I thought we'd get married. But it didn't work out. And then there was this really wonderful guy. He had a child, and I guess I thought I'd get to be the mother of that child, or . . . I guess I would have been the stepmom, but it would have been a lot like being his mother, especially since he was so young. And I had this dream that maybe this guy and I would get married and have another of our own. But he died before any of that could happen. And then a bunch of years went by and I met some guys, but they never seemed to measure up to the one I lost. Fern said that was because I didn't get to know him very well. That I was still idealizing him, and that's why no other guys measured up. And then I realized a lot of time was going by, and I was at that age where most women had paired up a long time ago. Hell, women my age were having their grandchildren by then. And Lloyd asked me, and I guess I felt like it was time to settle. You know. In more ways than one."

"I'm glad you didn't settle for him."

"Yeah," she said. "Me, too."

Then she just breathed in the silence for a few moments, noticing how much more peaceful everything felt without the mental image of ice-laden trees hovering directly over their heads. It felt good to be relatively relaxed. Virginia wondered how long it had been.

"I would be your friend, you know," she said. It surprised her. She hadn't known she was about to say it. "You say you never add people to your life. But you added Worthy. Well, granted, he's not exactly people. But he's an addition. And he's a friend. And now I'll be coming over to get him right before my two days off and dropping him back when I go back to work. So I'll be a new person in your life."

A long silence. She even entertained the idea that he might have fallen asleep sitting up.

Then he said, "Is a new person different from a friend?"

"I suppose. But I'm telling you I'd be your friend."

"How is that different?"

"Well, it's just . . . it's different. But it's hard to explain. I guess you just have to try it and see for yourself. We could do things together."

"Like what?"

"Like when I come to drop him off or pick him up, I could bring food from the diner and we could have dinner together. That's the kind of things friends do. Or you could come to my house and we could watch a movie or something."

A pause, which Virginia wondered if she should fill.

"Yes, please," he said.

———

"You still awake?" she asked.

It was maybe an hour later.

"Oh, yeah," he said.

"When I first met you, I thought you were him." Then she realized it had been a while since she'd talked about Aaron and Buddy. And that he couldn't possibly be expected to know who "him" was.

So she raced on. "That little kid I told you about. I said there was a man I loved and he had a kid and I thought we'd be together and he'd be my kid, too. Even though that was all a little premature. And I guess it might not have worked out like that. But it might have. You never know. Well. Now we know. But we don't know what might have happened if he hadn't died."

First he said nothing. After a time of listening to his silence, it occurred to her that he might not care in the slightest about her life.

Then he said, "A lot of people have died in my life, too. So I really do know how you feel."

"Thank you," she said. "That's nice."

"What was his name?"

"The man or the kid?"

"The kid."

"Buddy. Everybody called him Buddy. But I didn't know his real first name. So it could have been anything, I guess. That's why when I first met you, I asked you your last name. But then when you said it was Schilling, I knew you couldn't be Buddy. I mean . . . nobody ever called you Buddy, right?"

"I don't think so."

"Right. I figured. But then my friend Fern . . . I said something about how you weren't this man's son. And she said maybe not, but you're somebody's son. And I've been thinking about that since. You lost both your parents, just like him. So I'm not sure why it should have made so much difference whether you were the same boy or not. You were a boy. And you lost just as much."

"Did you ever see him or talk to him again? After his dad died?"

"No. His grandparents came and got him and took him away."

"Wow. We did have a lot in common."

"You did. So you can see why I wondered. Anyway, I didn't know their names or their address. At first I thought I'd still find him. I'm sure if I'd hired a private investigator or something, it wouldn't have been that hard. But Fern thought it was more important to me than to him. That he didn't have any attachment to me, which was probably true. So I just let it go. But I think about him sometimes. Actually, I'll be honest. I thought about him every day for years. And then after a while I thought about him less. But when I met you, I thought you looked like maybe he might've looked grown up. And then I started thinking about him again."

At first he just waited, as if he expected her to go on.

Then he said, "I'm sorry I'm not Buddy."

"That makes two of us," she said. "But that's okay. You're you. That's good enough."

Chapter Twenty-Seven: Jody

A thick crust of sleep released him. Quite suddenly. And it left him frightened, because he didn't know where he was. He was not at home. Not in his bed. Not in any bed.

He lifted his head and blinked into the light. And remembered.

Somehow it had become morning. It must not have been very late in the morning, though, because the light through the one small window in the kitchen door seemed murky and muted.

He thought he smelled coffee, but it must have been his imagination. Wishful thinking. Because surely the coffeemakers were electric.

It was cold. The ovens were still going strong, and Jody imagined it would have been even colder without them. In fact, they might both be dead without them. But no matter how powerfully those ovens blasted, they just couldn't seem to make much of a dent in the cold.

Jody sat up and rubbed his eyes. His hip hurt. It was pinched and achy from sleeping on the hard linoleum floor.

He looked around. No Virginia. No Worthy. He was alone.

"Ma'am?" he called, hearing the alarm in his own voice.

No response.

He pulled stiffly to his feet.

"Virginia!" he called again as he stepped out into the dining area.

This time something bothered him about not just the diner itself, but about the woman he was calling. About the name Virginia. Or maybe it was the combination of the room and the name, but it all felt so foreign and distant to him, like looking for something small in a vast, dark room. So he tried to shake the whole set of feelings away again. Tried to soothe his expanding alarm.

Through the window, he saw them. And felt better.

She was standing out on the porch, hugging her coat around herself, her breath puffing out in great clouds. Worthy was sniffing around looking for a good spot to lift his leg, occasionally slipping and skating on the ice in the process.

Jody stood and watched them for a moment, surprised at how good it felt to see them. Like they were his people, his only tribe, and because he was no longer separated from them, he was saved.

He stepped out onto the porch. Into the bitter chill.

She glanced at him over her shoulder. "Oh, you're up," she said.

"How long did I sleep?"

"At least four or five hours. That I know of."

"What time is it?"

"Nearly ten a.m."

"You're kidding. Why is it so dark?"

She pointed up at the sky. Well, out and up. The porch had a roof. And Jody couldn't simply go to the porch railing and look up, because the icicles that hung from the roof were so thick and so long that there wasn't room for him to put his head between them. They reminded Jody of bars on a jail cell.

He walked to the porch stairs, ducked under those icicles, and looked up. It was no longer clear. The sky was black with more storm.

"Oh, hell," he said to Virginia, ducking back under the icicles and onto the porch. "It's not done, is it?"

Worthy saw him and came wiggling in his direction, tail wagging. Jody could tell the dog wanted to run to him, but it wasn't a good surface for running, and Worthy knew it. So he walked quickly but carefully, with an odd gait that might have made Jody laugh if he'd seen it in a happier and less stressful moment.

"The storm? No. Doesn't look that way. Sure wish I had a radio. Well. I have a radio, but I wish I'd put fresh batteries in it. You're always supposed to have a radio for emergencies like this. And you're supposed to check the batteries a couple of times a year. But I sure dropped the ball on that one."

Worthy wiggled his way up the porch steps, and Jody crouched down and hugged him. When he pulled away again, he could swear the dog was wearing a grin.

"Think it'll be more ice?" he asked Virginia. "Or just regular snow?"

"I think I have no idea. But it's not looking good for us getting out today, is it?"

Jody let the news sink down. Into his gut, his heart. He felt things collapse inside him at the thought of at least another full day in the diner, in the cold. Surrounded by names and places that made him edgy for reasons he couldn't reach.

"Maybe it's time to call for help," he said. "I know it's a big decision to do that, because when they send somebody out in weather like this, it puts their life at risk . . ."

"The phone is out," she said. Her voice sounded flat and emotionless. "Those lines must be down, too. And my cell phone's not getting any reception, which it usually won't in bad weather. Especially out here at the diner."

"Oh." They stood, breathing icy fog, for a moment more. Then Jody realized he was tired of being cold. "I'm going back in," he said.

"Yeah. Me, too. I just wanted to give T—I mean Worthy a chance to go. There's coffee. You want coffee?"

"Oh, yeah," he said, moving to the door. He held it open for her, and for the dog, and they all moved into the diner, where it was only a few degrees less freezing. If that. "How did you make coffee?"

"It wasn't hard. I just boiled water on the gas stove and poured it through the grounds."

"Oh. Right."

They made their way back into the kitchen again. Jody sat cross-legged as close to one of the ovens as he could get without its open door pressing into his belly. He rubbed his gloved hands together, imagining a mug of coffee between them, the hot steam rising into his face.

A moment later, that dream came true.

"Take anything in it?" she asked as he took it from her.

His numb, stiff hands felt clumsy as he gripped the mug. Especially with his heavy gloves still on.

"No, ma'am."

"You can call me Virginia, you know."

"Yes, ma'am," he said, careful to avoid her eyes.

"Don't tell me, let me guess. You hate the name Virginia just like you hate my diner and that railroad bridge off in the distance. But if I ask why, you'll say you don't know, you just do."

He could feel her towering over him, but he continued to avoid her eyes. He brought the mug up to his face. It was still too hot to drink, but the steam felt comforting. Just the way he'd imagined it would.

Then he said, "I wish you wouldn't make fun of me or give me a hard time about the things that scare me. Because I would change them if I could."

A long silence, followed by what sounded like a sigh. Then she sat down on the floor next to him, her shoulder nearly touching his.

"Sorry," she said. "You're right. Won't happen again. Just give me a few minutes to warm up a little and I'll get us some breakfast. Bacon and eggs sound okay?"

"Yes, ma'am. Sounds great. But don't hurry. I usually can't eat until I'm good and awake."

"Me, too," she said.

And they fell into another awkward silence.

"What if the gas goes off?" he asked. "Or runs out? We'd die. Wouldn't we?"

"I don't know if we'd die or not. We're inside. We're dry, and out of the wind. And we have our coats and hats and scarves and such. I guess it's possible, but I'd say our chances are good. Besides, it's not like we have a propane tank. We can't exactly run out of gas. There are gas lines that run out here. And they're buried, so it's not like they'll break under the weight of the ice."

"Can anything happen to them if it gets cold enough?"

"I don't know. I don't know, Jody. I just know the gas never went out before."

She sounded irritated with him, or at least with the line of questioning, so he stopped talking.

He blew on his coffee and took a deep gulp. It burned the roof of his mouth and his throat, but he didn't mind.

It was heat.

He could feel something bristly pouring off her. Like he had scared her, or made her mad. Or both.

He pulled to his feet, setting his mug of coffee down while he did. Then he picked it up and headed for the kitchen door.

"Where you going?" she asked after him.

"Just out."

"Any special reason?"

"I don't know. No. Maybe. I started feeling weird, so I wanted to see the trees with their heads on the ground again. I thought that might help me feel better. It did before."

"Oh. Well, don't stay out too long. You'll freeze."

"Yes, ma'am," he said.

But he figured he'd stay out as long as he damn pleased. Or as long as he could stand it. Or until she'd forgotten that he'd made her mad by asking all the wrong questions. Whichever came first.

He slipped and slid out into the middle of the parking lot and fixed his eyes on the white trees, still bowing.

They didn't help much.

But he stood and looked and sipped at his hot coffee, blowing into the mug between sips to send steam up into his face. Because part of him still believed those trees would help in a minute.

But then Jody was on his chest and belly on the ice, his ears ringing with a terrible sound. Like the world had exploded. At the corner of his eye he saw a burst of fire, many feet up off the ground, maybe a hundred yards away. It leaped and shot in all directions, haphazardly in the icy wind.

It felt like dying. It was the end of everything when something that terrible happened.

He couldn't breathe. No matter how badly he needed the oxygen. No matter how hard he tried.

Then, seemingly with no elapsed time in between, he felt himself spilling and skidding down a road. He didn't know what road. He had never seen it before. And he could no longer locate the diner in any direction. There was no coffee mug in his hands. He stopped and spun around. Nearly unbalanced, he fell but caught himself. He had no memory of leaving the parking lot. Yet the parking lot was nowhere to be seen.

He turned and began to run at the edge of the road, where ice had formed on a wide curb of snow left by the plow. Because he could keep his footing better that way. His feet broke through the ice on every step, so he didn't fall. He had to pull his knees up high, and try not to trip as he brought his feet up out of the holes again. He did trip, many times. But he did not go down.

It was awkward and exhausting, but he didn't stop. His chest ached, and he could hear the desperate rasp of his own breathing. But he didn't stop.

Soon he was no longer aware of the labor of his exertions at all. His brain, which had briefly turned on, turned off again.

Jody just kept running.

———

When his brain chose to function again, he was huddled under a bus bench, inside a shelter. The bus stops in town all had little booths built around them to keep the bus riders out of the weather. Rain, snow. Ice. Wind. Whatever.

Jody realized he had been huddled in the corner of this shelter, under the bench, for whatever warmth the small space could provide. He could hear the steady, aggressive tap of more freezing rain over his head.

He guessed he must have been hiding in that place for some time, because his hands and feet were entirely numb. Without feeling.

He thought of Grampa, faced with losing his hands and feet, and it sent a jolt of fear like lightning through his gut.

But Grampa had only been wearing pajamas. His hands and feet had been bare. Jody was wearing good thermal gloves and heavy wool socks under winter boots. Still, it wasn't out of the question, and he knew it. Sooner or later frostbite will find you.

The layers of clothing only slow it down. Nothing holds it back forever except getting indoors and warming up.

He carefully slid out from under the bench and pulled to his feet. Everything hurt. Both hips and one knee hurt, and the heels of both hands. He could feel the evidence of hard falls on the ice. He must have fallen several times. But he couldn't remember that. He couldn't remember much of anything after that terrifying burst of noise and fire.

He stuck his head outside the little shelter and looked around. Freezing rain whipped into his face, stinging his not-quite-numb skin.

He was on a road he'd never seen before. Which wasn't too surprising, since he always took the same bus to the same area of town. And he'd only been back from Florida for two years. He didn't know the area all that well.

The sun would not help him find his direction, because the sky was a dark and solid gray. And what if he *had* seen the sun? Without knowing which direction he'd blindly run after leaving the diner, what use would it be?

He pulled his head in just enough to keep the rain off his face, and took stock of his situation. The way Grampa would have told him to do.

There were no buildings, no homes, no businesses on this lonely stretch of road. No cars. And there would be no cars any-time soon. Because the road was in no shape for them.

He pulled all the way back inside and carefully slid underneath the bench again, in the corner, the closest he could get to any space that would hold in his body heat.

He expected to feel panic rise. He waited for it. Monitored the spot where he knew it always rose. But he felt nothing. Just a sense of being jangled, sandpapered, exhausted. Yet there seemed no way out of his situation, except to hope the storm broke and emergency crews came out and found him before he froze to death.

He wondered how long that could be.

For a minute he wondered why he was not more afraid, but then he knew. There was nothing he could do to change his fate. He had to accept his predicament.

And apparently he had.

In that blissful lack of trying, he might even have slept.

Chapter Twenty-Eight: Virginia

Virginia waited a good forty-five minutes before she went out to check on Jody.

He was nowhere to be found.

The dog came out with her and slipped and slid around, sniffing at everything and seeming to ignore that there was nothing to smell except ice. But Virginia had read once that tracking dogs followed the smells of the skin cells we shed everywhere we go. Maybe Worthy was wondering where Jody had gone off to as well. Maybe he even had the skills to figure it out.

Then again, he'd never exactly been a keen canine detective.

Virginia made her way carefully around the outside of the diner in a big arc, one hand on the wall of the place where possible, calling Jody's name.

Nothing.

She looked down at Worthy, who looked up into her face.

"That's strange," she said.

Then Worthy took off toward the road.

"T-Rex! You come back here!" She called him that on purpose, in case he wasn't used to his new name yet.

He did not respond, which was unlike him.

Grumbling, she inched her way along after him. Maybe the dog thought he could find Jody. And they would have to find him—Worthy was right about that. Preferably before he froze to death. Though why he had put her in such a position she could not imagine.

She'd only managed to inch a few dozen yards down the highway before she lost the dog from view. He'd gotten so far ahead she couldn't see him anymore.

She stopped. Called for him again. Called for Jody again.

Nothing. She was out on the ice alone.

Just for a minute she thought about going back inside. She still didn't know why the young man and the dog would be foolish enough to strand themselves outdoors in this weather. But what seemed even crazier was the fact that she was allowing herself to be drawn into doing the same.

She stopped a moment, watching her breath puff out in great clouds. The rain hadn't started again. Not yet. But from the look of the sky it didn't plan to wait much longer.

She seriously considered going back without them. Whatever Jody was doing, it had been his own idea. A terrible idea, but his. It might well kill him. But did it need to kill her as well? Were two victims of the storm better than one?

But she shuffled on again. Away from the diner. Because she couldn't imagine going back there alone. No Jody. No Worthy. Just a lot of doubts and regrets over whether she could have—and should have—done more.

———

The rain let go, bouncing off her mittens and her knit hat, and freezing her face. She wanted to call to them again, but she could barely move her lips. It seemed like too much effort for something no one could hear anyway.

Halfway over the part of the road that formed a bridge—where the river ran beneath the highway—the fresh rain on the ice surface made the going even more treacherous. It froze fast, but not instantly. And the rain just kept coming.

She realized something in that moment. The rain was freezing more slowly than it had when she'd left the diner. The weather was getting warmer. In one way, that felt like a comfort. But it wouldn't make the walking any easier.

Virginia tried to move over to the concrete railing of the bridge for purchase.

Before she could reach it, she slipped. Her feet went out from under her and she landed hard on her left hip. She shouted out loud, instinctively, half from pain and half from the surprise and fear of it.

She sat for a minute, miserable in the cold rain, dreading that moment when she would have to stand up and assess the damage. Maybe she had just bruised her hip. Maybe she had injured it. She wouldn't know until she tried to put weight on it. Until she tried to walk again.

And if she couldn't walk? Well, then here she would sit. And either she would be saved by some miracle—such as the first emergency vehicle to move down the highway—or these would be the last few hours of her life.

Virginia felt a deep swell of resentment against both Jody and the dog. Why hadn't they had the simple common sense to stay put? They'd had ovens, hot drinks, a roof over their heads. Who walks away from all that on a day like this? And how had she been drawn into doing the same?

For a second time she considered simply making her way back alone. But she decided to at least go down to the next intersection and look both ways. See what she could see.

If she could.

She slid over to the concrete bridge rail and used its upright columns to lever to her feet. She put her weight on her left foot. It held. The hip hurt. A lot. But it didn't hurt much more when she put her weight on it. It just hurt no matter what she did. It was apparently not structurally injured.

Slowly, like a woman on a tightrope, she inched her way another eighth of a mile or so to the first crossroad.

She looked both ways, off into the distance in the lightening rain. Trees lay across the road in both directions. But it was flat here, and she felt as though she could see a mile. But she saw no signs of life anywhere.

She cupped her hands around her mouth and called the name T-Rex again.

She heard his bark as an answer. But it was distant. He was much farther away than she'd hoped she'd have to walk.

Sighing, she turned in the direction of the sound. She couldn't stop herself from wondering if it was a mistake. Maybe the last mistake she would ever make.

She had to inch around four downed trees. But, though it added distance to the trek, their branches gave her a way to steady herself.

When she'd navigated around the last of them, she could look down the road again. Still no signs of life as far as she could see. She could see much farther than she felt prepared to walk, but there was nothing there.

She shouted one more time for the dog, this time using both of his names.

"T-Rex! Worthy!"

The dog came blasting out from one of those bus bench shelters. It was still a good way down the road. Just a speck in the distance. He hurried to her with a trotting, wiggling gate, stopping now and then to shake freezing rain off his face.

As he got closer to her, and she to him, the dog broke into a run. He built up a good head of steam, then lost his traction and began to slide. His back end went down, and he slid on the ice on his butt until he was only a few hundred feet from where she stood.

Then he barked twice. And got up and made his way—much more slowly and carefully—down to the bus bench shelter again.

Jody must be in there, she thought. But it was still a long way off. A long and dangerous way. Every step she took could be the one that led to an injury. And then, like they said in that documentary Fern made her watch about Mount Everest, that was only half the way. She still had to get back.

She felt herself at the edge of tears of fear and frustration. Because she had to walk all the way down to that shelter before she would know if Jody was there. And if he wasn't . . . if Worthy had only gone in to get out of the rain . . . well, she just felt she wouldn't be able to bear it.

But that's not useful thinking, she told herself. *It doesn't help anybody to say, "I'm overwhelmed" or "I just can't." If you have to, then you just do.*

She tilted her head down to keep her face out of the rain. It didn't. But it helped a little. She put every ounce of attention into her balance, her footing. She didn't fall.

She just did it. Because she had to.

"Jody?" she called, when she thought she was in shouting distance of the covered bench. Her lips felt numb, and the word sounded slurred, as if she'd been drinking.

For a moment, nothing. Her heart refused to beat while she waited. At least, it felt like it missed a beat or two.

Then, very faintly, "Virginia?"

Virginia bent over, resting her hands on her thighs, and let a few tears go. But not tears of fear or frustration. Not that kind of overwhelmed. This was overwhelming relief.

———

"How'd you find me?" he asked.

"I didn't. He did."

Virginia plunked down next to him with a sigh. He glanced over at the side of her face, then looked down at his gloves again.

Just at that moment the rain let up. Virginia had mixed feelings about that. If the storm was passing that would be great, of course. But it seemed ironic that it should rain half the way out here and then stop the minute she got a roof over her head.

"You want to tell me what happened?" she asked him.

He began to pet around Worthy's neck ruff with both hands. "I don't know what happened."

"Well, you're the only one who was there, so that leaves us in a bind."

A long silence as he stroked Worthy's fur. She was hoping he would say something. Volunteer anything. When it was clear he wouldn't, she continued.

"I'm wondering if you have any idea how bad our predicament is right now."

"I do, actually," he said. "I thought I was going to die out here."

"Then why come out here in the first place?"

"I didn't do it on purpose."

"You covered all that distance over ice accidentally?"

His calm demeanor broke. He pulled his knees up onto the bench. Folded over them and held them tightly. He pressed his closed eyes against the knees of his jeans. Before he did, Virginia could see the beginning of tears. Frustrated tears.

"There's something wrong with me!" he shouted, half into his own legs. "I don't work right. And you can't fix me; nobody can fix me. And you shouldn't have come out here to find me. Not you and not Worthy, either. You shouldn't die out here. Not for me."

She tried to put one mittened hand on his upper back, but he shrugged it away again. Hard. Almost violently.

"Don't," he said. "I got scared. Sometimes when I get really scared, my brain turns off. And then I don't know what I'm doing until later. I told you. It's not normal. I'm broken, and you should have just let me go."

Virginia pulled off her wet mittens, blew into her hands, and let those words sink in. She wanted to tell him she would never let him walk off into the storm alone and not even try to find him and bring him back alive. Those would have been good words. But she couldn't say them. Because she very nearly did let him go. Out of fear for her own safety. Twice.

"What scared you?"

"I don't know."

"Well, now you're really not working with me."

"I don't know what it was! I just know what it looked like."

"Describe it to me."

"It was fire. But not fire like in a woodstove. Fire like when electricity goes crazy. It was sudden, like an explosion. And it was in the sky, but not too high."

"Like maybe as high as the power poles?"

"Yeah. Maybe."

He wiped his eyes on the knees of his jeans and turned his face to the side, resting one temple on a knee. His eyes looked red and swollen, and Virginia thought it was possible that she'd never seen a look of misery to top the one she saw now.

"Probably just an electrical transformer exploding," she said. "That happens a lot during ice storms. There's usually moisture around, because the explosion melts some of the ice, so it arcs in every direction. It's very chaotic. Does that sound like what you saw?"

Jody gave a barely perceptible nod.

"I'm not sure why it would send you into a panic like that."

"I told you. My brain's not normal that way. Besides, I just wasn't expecting it. And it scared me."

"I have to say I'm a bit surprised myself. I figured most of those power lines going to the transformers weren't even live right about now. But I guess you never know. Anyway, I suppose I can see how that would have scared you to see a thing like that just out of nowhere. But it can't really hurt us. You get that now, right? I mean, even if a power line arcs, or if the transformers start exploding, there's nothing under them but ice. Even the tree branches are coated with ice. There's nothing to set on fire. Now we better get back. It's getting warmer fast. That's the good news. Bad news is we're burning daylight. Last thing we want is to get stuck out here after dark."

"You know how to get back?"

"Well, sure I do. I know this whole area like the back of my own hand. Come on. We have to make some tracks."

They stood, and stepped out into the weather. Except there really was no weather now. Nothing exceptional. Just a dark, overcast, blowing sky. Even the wind had calmed some.

It felt to her like the first break they'd gotten in quite a long while.

She hooked her arm through his and they began to move, Virginia using the careful skating motion she'd tried so hard to perfect on the way out.

"Maybe there's something wrong with you that can be fixed," she said.

He only shook his head glumly.

"Maybe a doctor could diagnose something."

"No. My grampa had me tested for everything. He thought I had some kind of mental disability or autism or something. I think he wanted to find a *thing*. An actual thing that was real. He didn't like situations he couldn't understand. But there was nothing nice and clean like that."

"What did the doctors say? That they just didn't know?"

"They said probably trauma."

"Trauma? Like head trauma from an injury? Or emotional trauma from a bad experience?"

"I have no idea," he said. "I was six."

They walked—stumbled and skated—a few more steps in silence.

"Are you always so scared of stuff like that?" she asked. "Fire and explosions and stuff? Well, never mind. That was a stupid question. How can anybody not be afraid of explosions? But me, once I see it's a transformer blowing under the weight of the ice, then I'm okay again. What about fireworks? I'm guessing you're none too fond of the Fourth of July."

She looked over at his face again. He had his eyes squeezed shut.

"I don't want to talk about the Fourth of July," he said.

"Well, that's tough," she said. "Because when you live in a country that celebrates with—"

Before she could finish the sentence, Virginia slipped. She tried to hold on to Jody, but he couldn't keep his balance with her weight pulling him down on one side. So they ended up in a pile on the icy tarmac. But at least holding on to him had broken her fall.

Virginia didn't get up right away. She didn't even try.

Jody got carefully to his feet and held a hand down to her. But she only put her face into her mittened hands and sighed.

"This is a mess," she said.

"What is?"

"Trying to walk on this. I'm scared of trying to walk on this. If I take a bad fall, I'm about five times more likely to break a bone than you. Because I'm older and heavier. If I fall and break my hip—or anything else I can't walk on—I'm as good as dead. I'll be out all night and that'll be that."

He squatted down onto his haunches and leaned in closer than usual.

"So what do we do, then? I mean, we still have to try. Right? Why just sit here with nothing broken and freeze anyway? That makes no sense. We have to try. Now come on. I'll help you up."

But Virginia still didn't move.

"There's a shortcut," she said.

"Well, why didn't you say so?"

"Because you won't like it."

"If it gets us back faster, and you're not scared, and you don't break any bones, I'll like it."

"I don't think you will. You see up ahead? Those railroad gates across the road? Well, they're not across the road now. But those red and white gates that come down onto the road when a train comes through?"

"Yeah. I see those."

"If we make a right and walk on the tracks, we can cut over the railroad bridge. If we did that, it would only be a quarter of a mile back."

She waited. But he only remained silent.

"Otherwise we'll have to go a long way on this ice if we need to get to a road that bridges over the river."

She waited again through his silence, watching his face whiten.

"I know it's one of those things that you have an irrational fear about, but I really think it's our best bet."

"It has ice on it," he said, barely over a whisper.

"True. But it doesn't have trains on it. No way they're running the trains in these conditions. Icy tracks shut down the whole system. So that's half the danger out of the way."

"It has ice on it," he said again.

"So we'll go over on our hands and knees. On our bellies if we have to. We can hook our arms over the railroad ties so we don't slip too much. Probably safer than this road that's just a solid sheet of ice."

Another long silence. Then he shook his head slowly.

"I can't do it," he said.

"Well, I think I just have to. So I'll explain to you as carefully as I can how to get back the long way—"

"No!" he said, his first word at full volume since the railroad bridge idea was raised. "No, I don't want to split up. If I get lost, that's it for me."

"Well, those are the choices, honey. I'm lucky enough I haven't broken anything already. I'm not willing to push my luck much further."

They sat a long moment in silence. Virginia was half-aware of dark clouds, black and gray, moving away above the horizon. The bad stuff seemed to be clearing out. Moving south.

"Maybe we'd be okay overnight," he said. "It's getting warmer fast. You said so yourself."

"But when night comes, it'll get colder again. And once it gets dark, it's hard to change our minds. I'm not willing to take that chance. I'm going over the bridge and getting back inside and in front of those ovens and staying alive."

Jody pulled carefully to his feet and held a hand out to her. It still wasn't easy to get up. But she reached down and used the ground for balance as long as she was able.

Then they were slipping and sliding down the road again.

Virginia still didn't know what he had decided. But they would reach the tracks in a minute or two. So she would know soon enough.

———

"I don't think I can do this," he said.

Virginia stood with her feet between two railroad ties. It was a huge relief. The tracks were built with deep layers of gravel on both sides, and between rails. The gravel was coated with ice, but bumpy ice was far easier to navigate than flat ice.

"I wouldn't wait too long to decide," she said. "If you take the bridge with me, we have plenty of daylight. But if you decide to go the long way, you're pushing it. You don't want to get stuck out after dark. Then you *will* get lost."

"I don't want to split up," he said again. Weakly.

They stood in silence for a few moments.

"Look," Virginia said, hearing the strength rise in her own voice. "These are our lives at stake here. I realize your fear is very real, but at this point so is mine. So it's time for some tough love. I'm walking away now, down these tracks and over that bridge. And I'm taking the dog with me because if you get lost, I don't want to lose you both. Follow me or don't. But make a decision. Don't make any decisions that put me in more danger. And don't put either of us in danger by not making a decision at all. Got it?"

He nodded while apparently trying to swallow. It didn't seem to Virginia that the swallowing worked out.

She turned away from him and walked down the tracks, planting her feet carefully on the icy gravel between ties. She called to Worthy over her shoulder, and he bounced along, got ahead of her, then stopped and looked back at Jody.

"Come on," she said to the dog. "We're going."

Worthy obeyed, but reluctantly. And he didn't stop looking back.

She must have walked twenty steps before she realized she hadn't given Jody directions to get to the diner on his own. But maybe that had been purposeful. Because maybe she wanted to force him to make the better choice.

But it sure was one of those decisions you could regret later if things went wrong. It felt like turning a puppy loose on a busy highway and then walking away.

"Wait!" Jody called. "Virginia! Worthy! Hold up! I want to come with you!"

———

Halfway to the bridge, Jody stopped, and didn't seem inclined to start again.

Virginia figured he was just scared. But he was staring at a fixed spot in the trees, a foot or two over his head. Was that the kind of thing fear did to his brain?

"What are you looking at, honey?" she asked him. "We need to move on."

"That red necktie," he said, his voice sounding dreamy and thin.

"What red necktie?"

"Right there." He pointed.

Virginia saw *something* hanging from the tree, right where Jody pointed. But it did not look red. And it did not look like a tie. It did resemble an ancient strip of fabric, but shredded beyond recognition. And it was faded to no color at all, then coated with dirt.

Jody walked carefully over to the tree and reached up for it. He loosened the knot, which Virginia had to admit did look a bit like a Windsor knot. And as he did so, she thought she saw a patch of red underneath. But then the fabric disintegrated in his gloved hands, and fell to the ice at his feet.

Jody picked it up and tucked it into his coat pocket.

Then he joined her on the tracks again.

"Why did you even want that?" she asked as they inched along toward the bridge again.

"Not sure."

"How did you even know that used to be a red tie? It didn't look like much of anything anymore."

"Not sure," he said again. "I just knew I needed to keep it."

———

"Why doesn't the water freeze?" he asked her.

He was on his belly, looking over the first wooden tie with a view down to the river. It flowed beneath them almost violently, at an abnormally high volume and brown with mud, which meant it must have been much warmer to the north. The ice must have been melting upriver. But there was plenty of ice in the water. Smaller pieces that made the whole river look like a giant slushy snow cone. Bigger chunks, some the size of refrigerators.

"It moves too fast to freeze solid," she said. "If we go on our bellies, we can bend our elbows and knees between the railroad ties. That way we won't slip so much, and even if we slip, we won't go over. It'll be almost like holding on to something. Worthy can walk beside the tracks where it's solid."

"What if *he* slips?"

"I'll just have to hold his collar."

"But I can look down and see the river."

"So close your eyes."

She expected an argument from him. She got none. Instead he just squeezed his eyes shut and began to inch along.

Virginia found her system for traction effective. It was, however, painful on her elbow and knees. And it was hard to keep one hand up as high as Worthy's collar. She couldn't help wondering how her body would feel in the morning, after yet another cold night on the diner's kitchen linoleum.

But it didn't help to think such thoughts now.

They moved slowly and silently for several minutes. Now and then she looked over at Jody and was amazed by how well he was doing.

"You're doing great," she said.

He stopped. Then Virginia wished she'd never spoken.

"Only on the outside," he said weakly.

He sat up, twisting around to rest one hip on a railroad tie.

"Don't stop!" she told him.

"I can't do this," he said.

Virginia looked around. Forward and backward along the bridge.

"You're going to have to finish what you started. Look. We're halfway across. No harder to go over than to go back."

"I can't. Either way. I can't move."

"I won't accept that, Jody. Move."

"I can't."

He buried his head in his thickly gloved hands.

Virginia sat a minute. Taking in her options. She could get him to move. Or she could move without him. Those seemed to be the only two plans at her disposal. She thought about moving on and leaving him where he sat. It seemed impossible. Unbearable. It was one thing to leave him out on the road to find the street that crossed over the river. Knowing he might or might not. But leave him out in the middle of the bridge and go inside herself, knowing he would freeze?

No. She had to get him moving.

"How can I get you moving again?" she asked him.

"You can't," he said.

Chapter Twenty-Nine: Jody

"First of all," Jody said, his eyes still pressed hard against his gloves, "you have to stop yelling at me."

"I didn't think I was yelling."

"Well, you are. You're getting scared, and when you get scared, you get screechy. And that's only making it worse."

"Okay," she said calmly. He could hear her force the calm into place.

She was still on her belly on the icy railroad ties. As if about to inch forward any minute and leave him. He wished she would sit up. So he wouldn't have that one additional terror weighing on him.

"Okay," she said again. "Yelling makes it worse. What would make it better?"

"I don't know. Maybe talk to me. Take my mind off of things."

"What do you want me to talk about?"

"Anything."

Virginia sighed. She changed position, rolling away from him and carefully settling with her rear on the solid steel at the edge of the bridge. She felt behind her to make sure one of the upright girders was there to support her. Then she leaned back and sighed again.

"You have to help me out here. I'm a little scared myself. My mind is not exactly full of lovely conversational ideas. So pick a topic. Please."

"Okay. Tell me why you hate this bridge so much. You never told me. You asked me why I did, and I didn't know. But you didn't tell me why you did."

She paused before answering. Looked up at the sky, which Jody realized had grown decidedly lighter. It made her squint to look up.

"The man I was telling you about. He—Oh. You know what? I just realized. This is *so* not the time for that story."

"Too late now, though. Now what I'm imagining will be worse."

"He died here," she said.

"Fell into the river?"

"Yes."

"Well, I guess I was wrong. I couldn't have imagined anything worse."

A silence, during which Jody grasped how stranded he really was here. He'd made it halfway through hell. Now he felt stuck in hell indefinitely.

He talked more, to try to pull his brain away from the clear understanding of his situation.

"So this was the guy with the kid."

"Yeah."

"Why did he fall in? And please don't say there was ice on the bridge."

"No. It was summer. Some kids were setting off fireworks on the bridge in the dark. It startled him."

It startled Jody, too. Just to hear about it. It led him toward a mental image he didn't quite understand, but which frightened him. So he pushed it away again. He looked over to see Worthy lying with his paws over the edge of the bridge, looking down into the river.

Something clicked into something in that moment. That mental image of Sheila came back. Sheila jumping. Pushing out and off. But now he could see *from what*. He could have seen before, if he'd needed to. The steel girders had always been there in the image. It just hadn't mattered until now. It hadn't matched with anything else until that exact moment.

"And he had Buddy and his dog with him," he heard her saying. She sounded distant and muted, as if he were only dreaming about hearing her speak. "And Buddy nearly got hit by a train. And the dog—"

"Jumped into the river," Jody said. Actually, they both said it. At exactly the same time.

"How did you know—" she began. But she went no further. At least, not in that direction.

He looked up, and into her eyes. He usually didn't look anybody right in the eye, but this time he did. Because he needed to know if this meant what he thought it meant. It did. He found his answer there in her face.

"And your dog's name was Sheila," she said quietly.

"Our dog's name *was* Sheila."

"And your father's name was Aaron Albanese."

"My father's name *was* Aaron Albanese."

"Why didn't you tell me your father's name?"

"I don't know. You're the one who wants to know all this stuff. Why didn't you ask me?"

A long pause, during which he did not dare look at her again. Maybe she was angry with him for not doing this right.

Then she burst into laughter. It struck Jody as a sound he hadn't heard for a long time. He couldn't even remember when he'd last heard a hearty, genuine laugh.

"Now *that* is a very good question," she said. "Because I'm an idiot?"

"You're not an idiot."

"Look," she said. "Buddy. I know nobody calls you that anymore, but . . . we still have to get over this bridge and back to the diner."

"You're right," he said.

And he carefully rolled onto his belly onto the ties again.

A moment later she was on her belly next to him. Which felt good. He needed somebody next to him.

"I'm a little surprised," she said. "I didn't think what just happened would help. I thought it would make it worse."

"It didn't. It made it better. It made everything make more sense. You know. Like I am the way I am for a reason."

"We're all the way we are for a reason," she said.

They began to inch along again. Over three or four more railroad ties. Then a rush of light hit Jody's closed eyelids. It took him a frightened second to realize it was only the sun. The bulk of the clouds had blown away. Virginia squinted and raised her only free hand—the one not holding Worthy's collar—to shield her eyes.

"Wow," she said. "That feels good for a change. Huh?"

"It does. But we'd better keep going."

Jody closed his eyes again so he wouldn't see the river of muddy ice raging beneath.

What seemed like a few seconds later, Virginia said, "You should open your eyes now."

"Why should I do that?"

"Because we made it. We're over the bridge."

———

They tromped along for a while in silence. It was easier and more comfortable crossing the massive field between the railroad bridge and the diner. Because instead of a flat sheet of ice, the field was made up of low scrub and fine branches with ice coatings that cracked and yielded as they stepped on them. It was slow going, but not the ice rink he'd grown so tired of navigating.

"I guess I let the name thing throw me," Virginia said. "Plus Fern is always telling me I rewrite reality into what I want it to be. So I kept thinking that's what I was doing. Why do you not have your father's last name?"

"Because my grandparents raised me."

"But most kids would still keep their father's name."

"Oh. I didn't know that."

"But . . . I still don't get it. Why did your grandparents have a different name than Aaron?"

He glanced over at her again, surprised. Her mouth was open, that way it tended to be when she was trying to process information.

"Because they weren't his parents. They were my mother's parents."

Another long silence. Then she shook her head and they walked again. "I am so stupid," she said.

"You're not stupid."

"It never occurred to me. How could that not occur to me? I was so focused on Aaron. So wrapped up in Aaron. When I heard the word 'grandparents,' I just assumed they were on his side of the family. Holy cow. Fern's right about me. My brain is a weird place. I can't believe I could have been so stupid."

"You're not stupid. I wish you'd stop saying that."

She said nothing more. So Jody decided to fill up the silence.

"Maybe my gramma was right," he said. "She hated the cold. Hated it. The minute Grampa retired, she got them out of here. She insisted. I never used to mind the cold much. Then again, I could always put the heater on. The cabin is so small. You run the propane heater on high, it heats up fast. It's like sitting in a nice, warm little oven. In the two years we've been back, I never really got stuck where it was cold and where I couldn't get back to warm. I mean, maybe for twenty or thirty minutes if I was waiting for a bus, or out walking or something, but then I'd go inside and get warmed up and it all seemed okay again. I was never stuck in the cold for a day or anything, not knowing when I'd ever get warm again. This is a lot of talking for me, isn't it?"

She didn't answer right away, so he glanced sideways. She was smiling with only one corner of her mouth.

"It is," she said. "But it's kind of nice."

He braved another quick look over at her. They both stopped. She looked back at him, her eyes shining with something he hadn't seen since his grandmother died. Something that felt precious and frightening in equal measure.

Then she looked away.

They walked on again.

The diner, which had seemed so much like an enemy to him just a few hours earlier, loomed on the horizon like heaven. He could see it clearly now, and every icy inch of it looked like safety and warmth. Relative warmth, anyway.

It made him feel more relaxed.

"Tell me about my father," he said.

Then he waited. Walked, but waited. But she didn't say anything for a long time.

"The night I remember best was the night he kissed me," she said. "And I'm not sure you want to hear about that. That was also the last thing I remember. It was the last time I saw him. Before that, we had dozens and dozens of conversations. And you swear they're burned into your brain and you're going to remember them, always. Every single word of them, because every single word is so important. But nineteen years is a long time. It's not even so much like you forget. It's not like the information gets less valuable, and you let it go. I think it's actually something that happens to our brains. It's like a 'disk full' message on your computer. The only way your brain can save anything new is by dumping something old. It's not really voluntary. It just happens."

"I don't have a computer," he said. And he always wondered why everybody assumed he did. But he never said so, because he was worried it might hurt somebody's feelings to treat them like they shouldn't say certain things to him.

"Really?" she asked, which only made it worse.

"Really," he said. He clomped along for a few more crunchy steps, listening to the sound of the ice as they broke it. Then, anxious to change the subject, he said, "So you really didn't know my father very well at all." It was not a question.

"Hmm . . ." she said. And then stopped. She squinted in the direction of the diner. Shielded her eyes from the sun with one hand. "I guess you would say we were just beginning to get to know each other well. We were in the process of it, all right. But we got rudely cut off before we could get too far. But I remember some things. Like how funny he was. He could always make me laugh. But he didn't tell jokes or anything like that. It wasn't even that he said things that you could tell were outwardly meant to be funny. It was just the *way* he said them. But I can't produce one single example for you, and I'm sorry."

She waited. Maybe in case he wanted to say anything. But they just stood there together. Jody was watching the sun begin to melt the ice on the brush under their feet. Watching the new warmth send drips of water down low branches.

He waited for her to say something, or to walk on.

In time they set off again for the diner.

"And another thing I remember about him," she said, when she seemed sure he didn't want to speak. "He never held a grudge. He wouldn't stay mad at people. He'd come in for lunch sometimes from the motorcycle shop. And he'd complain about something a customer did. Or said. He was very close to his emotions. He'd have this flare of anger about it. But then it was gone. Just gone.

If I asked about it later, there was absolutely nothing left. No bad feelings, I mean. He'd say, 'Oh, we worked that out.' Or, 'I think he was just having a bad day.' I envied that about him. I always stew over old things. I can't seem to let anything go. Any little slight. But he just got it off his chest and moved on."

Speaking of moving on, they were only maybe a hundred yards from the diner's parking lot. Jody felt he could throw a rock and hit it. If he'd had a rock.

"I'm sorry I don't have more to tell you about him," she said.

"It's okay," he said. "You remember more than I do." They walked a few more crackling steps before he added, "At least you'll talk to me about him. Which is more than my grampa would do."

She glanced over at him, but only briefly.

"Was he a nice man, your grandfather?"

"Um. No. Not really."

"Sounded like he might not have been. But you loved him, though. Right?"

"Yeah. I loved him. He was my grampa. Who else was I supposed to love if I didn't love him? Besides. You can love somebody and still look back and see that he wasn't a very nice man."

She barked a short laugh that sounded hoarse and bitter. And maybe louder than appropriate. At first he didn't understand why.

"Tell me all about it," she said.

"Oh," Jody said. "Right."

They walked a few more steps before Jody spoke again.

"That was my father's red necktie," he said.

Virginia stopped short. "Are you sure?"

"Yeah."

"How do you know?"

"Because I was there when he hung it on that tree. I told him nobody wears a tie to the diner. So he put it there and said we'd get it on the way back. But we never did."

He watched her face as he spoke. But it turned emotional. Too emotional for him to want to see. To process. So he looked away again.

He pulled the ancient scrap of shredded cloth out of his pocket and held it in her direction. "Here, you can have it. Because you loved him, too."

But that made her cry. So after she took it from him, Jody turned and walked back toward the diner again, trusting her to follow.

"I can't believe you remembered that," she said when she'd caught up with him again.

"Me neither," he said.

"I wonder if this means you'll start remembering other stuff now."

"I hope not," he said.

———

They let themselves in the front door. Virginia had to open the door for him because his hands were numb and frozen. It made the bells jingle.

They stepped inside and looked around. Both of them. As though they hadn't seen it, or at least not recently. But in Jody's case he was just comparing the feeling—the relief of being back—to the way he'd imagined it.

"Why did I convince myself it would be warmer in here?" she asked.

"I was just about to say the exact same thing," Jody said.

"I'll make us some coffee."

"I'll look at Worthy's paw pads and make sure he's not frozen."

She smiled distractedly and moved off toward the kitchen.

"Virginia?" He called to her before she could get away.

She stopped in the kitchen doorway to listen.

"Thank you for finding me," he said. "And getting me back here in one piece. I said you shouldn't have, but I'm glad you did. I guess I felt like I didn't deserve it. But I'm glad I'm not dead."

"That makes two of us," she said, and went off to make the coffee.

Chapter Thirty: Virginia

Virginia woke on her side—fully dressed and bundled for the cold—on the floor of the diner's kitchen. It took her a moment to remember why. She looked around for Jody and Worthy, but they didn't seem to be in the room with her.

It was day, with early light streaming through the one small window.

She had only been able to sleep on one side, to favor the hip she'd bruised in the fall. So now both hips screamed at her.

She sat up and stretched. Climbed to her feet with a grunt, which, when she heard it feed back to her, made her feel old. It hurt to move her knees. They were bruised up and swollen from the railroad ties. They throbbed. She limped a few steps to the swinging kitchen door and pushed one side open, peeking out into the dining area.

Jody was sitting at table three, staring out the window at the bright morning. As if the coating of ice were a thing one could watch forever without ever getting bored. Worthy sat with his chin on one of the young man's thighs, and Jody stroked the dog's head absentmindedly. He still had his coat on and had put on his knit hat, gloves, and scarf—which had been carefully dried on the ovens—to go with it.

It seemed strange to Virginia to see clouds of frozen breath come out of someone seated indoors in her normally warm diner.

She hobbled over to his table and eased into a chair.

His gaze flicked away from the window, but only briefly. Then he stared out at the icy world again.

It made Virginia think that if anyone could spend the rest of his life in that tiny cabin by the lake, with no one, doing nothing, it was this little guy.

"I'll tell you one thing," she said. "I'm too old to be sleeping on a hard linoleum floor."

"You okay?"

"I will be, I suppose. It's not like there's a cure for it, though. I'm just getting older, is all. And my knees are still sore from those railroad ties."

"You fell, too. Didn't you?"

"How did you know?"

"I could tell by the way you were walking. Even before the bridge. I figured you didn't want to tell me because you knew it would make me feel guilty. You should take some of those aspirin," he said without ever averting his gaze from the view.

"Yeah, I might. I don't like to take them on an empty stomach, though. But in a minute I'll get up and make us some breakfast. And then maybe I will. I'm surprised to see you out here. You know. Voluntarily and all. I guess I expected you to sleep in the kitchen."

"Oh," he said, after a pause. As though it took time for her words to travel to him. "Well. I bundled up."

"I wasn't talking about the cold. I thought you hated it out here."

"Oh. That. Well. Yeah. I still sort of do. But now I know *why* I hate it. And now I know I shouldn't. So now I feel like it's time to start getting over it. It's not the diner's fault, what happened. Just because we had dinner here right before it happened doesn't make the diner a bad thing. I think we all do that. But we shouldn't. At least, not in my opinion. Like if you're passing a corner on the way to school, and some bullies jump out and start hitting you. Then every time you pass that corner for, like, a year, your heart will pound and your forehead will get sweaty. But it's silly. Because the corner has nothing to do with it. It's as likely to happen anywhere else and no more likely to happen there. So why do we do that?"

"I suppose it's a reptilian part of our brain," she said, knowing she'd learned something in school about that and wishing she could remember what. "I guess it's trying to protect us."

"I think we should just decide if we're animals or people," he said. "It's weird to be a little of both."

"It may be weird, but I don't think it's something we can stop doing. We *are* a little of both. Have you seen anybody go by out the window? Even emergency crews?"

"No. There's nobody out there at all."

"Guess we might as well settle in, then. Shall I make us something to eat?"

"What if trees fell down on my cabin? There are trees all around it. What would I do? I'd have nowhere to go."

"Well. There's my guest room. Like I said."

"I meant more like permanently."

"So did I."

He looked over at her again, but she couldn't read what she saw in his eyes. "I can't just live with you."

"Why can't you?"

"We're no relation to each other."

"We could have been. We almost were. I was going to be your stepmom."

"But we weren't. And you're not."

Virginia drew back. Literally. Rocked back in her seat as if he'd slapped her. She didn't feel much about it, though. Just a tightness in her gut. But it made her want to go do something. Not just sit there.

"I've been thinking about it," he said. "A lot. Ever since you told me. And I know you think it's an important thing that we were almost a family. But I just don't think this is one of those situations where almost counts. I'm sorry. I don't want to sound mean. And it's not that I don't appreciate everything you've done for me. But I've been thinking about it for hours. And that's what I decided."

"I'll go fix us something."

"Or *I* could," he said. "For a change."

"No. Let me. I need something to do."

She got up, a tiny bit more limber, and limped quickly into the kitchen. But the minute she got through the swinging doors and out of his view, something changed. It was as though she'd been emptied out inside. Next thing she knew her back was up against the wall. She slid down into a sit, and crouched over her swollen knees. She didn't cry, but she questioned why she didn't. It felt like something that could happen easily enough, but then it never did.

A minute or two later she heard the kitchen door swing open.

She looked up to see him looking down at her.

"You okay?" he asked.

"Why wouldn't I be?"

"I don't know. But you look really sad."

"I'm fine. Why would you even say that?" She knew why. But she wanted to fend off his empathy.

"Can't you tell when someone is sad? I always can."

"You don't know if you always can or not," she said. "Because if someone was sad and hid it from you, you wouldn't know." To her embarrassment, her lip quivered slightly on the word "sad."

He came and sat beside her, Worthy wagging behind. In fact, he sat so close that his shoulder pressed up against hers. Which seemed like a touching thing to do. Especially for him.

"What's wrong?" he asked.

"I don't really know."

"Yes, you do."

"If I say I don't, how can you say I do?"

"Because you're you," he said. "If you don't know, who does? You're in there with whatever you're feeling. It's part of you. Sometimes I say I don't know how I feel about something. But even while I'm saying it, I know it's not completely true. It's more like I know, but I wish I didn't. Want me to get you some aspirin?"

"I have to eat first."

"Oh. That's right."

They sat in silence for a few moments. Worthy plunked down at her feet with a deep sigh.

"I guess it's about that thing Fern told me," she said. "About how I didn't mean anything to you. You meant something to me, but not the other way around. You were just a kid, and you hardly knew me. And you hadn't accepted me yet at all. I knew it was true. But it didn't feel this sad until now. Now that you're right in front of me, it seems sad. I guess I got all excited when I found out it was you. Like I'd found some wonderful thing I thought I'd lost forever. But now I guess I feel like it doesn't matter much. So I found you. What good does it do? We still don't really know each other. This big bond I thought we had was mostly just in my head."

They sat in silence for a time. Then he shifted away from her, which seemed almost tragic. But it turned out he was just getting his arm free. Once it was free, he draped it loosely over her shoulders.

She held bizarrely still, the way one would near a wild animal. A deer, or something else that could be easily frightened away.

A moment later he began to lightly stroke the back of her hair. It was impossible not to notice that it was nearly identical to the motion he used to absentmindedly pet Worthy.

Under the circumstances, she chose to take it as a compliment.

"But I don't remember you," he said.

"I know. I understand that."

"How can I feel like we know each other when I don't even remember that we met before?"

"You can't, I guess."

"Well, help me, then. Tell me something."

"What do you mean? What kind of something?"

"I don't know. Something. Just something from when we knew each other before. I'm not saying I'll remember if you remind me, because I can't remember anything from when I was four. Except that tie thing. But I had to see the tie to remember. So tell me anyway, and maybe that'll help. And even if it doesn't, I'll believe you. And then maybe it'll feel more like we know each other."

Virginia pulled in a couple of deep breaths. They were audible, and unusually deliberate. As though breathing all on her own, unconsciously, was an old talent that had recently abandoned her.

"Well," she said, "let me think."

But she knew there wouldn't be much. Her history had been with Aaron, not his son. When they had come into the diner, she'd small-talked with the boy, but not much more. And who remembers their small talk nineteen years later?

"I used to always put water in one of those Styrofoam to-go containers," she said, "and I'd leave it out on the porch for Sheila while you and your dad were eating. She was one of the best, nicest dogs I ever met. She's the reason I got a dog. Especially after the way she . . . well, you know. She was a hero. So that really sold me on dogs."

"So that's why you got Worthy?"

"I got another dog in between. That was nineteen years ago."

"Oh," he said. And that seemed to deflate the conversation, which skidded to a halt.

"Wait!" she said suddenly. "Wait! I know! You told me to buy this place."

"I . . . what?"

"This place was for sale. And you said I should buy it."

"I did? Why did I say that?"

"You and your dad came in, and the owner had just put it up for sale. And I was feeling bad, because I wouldn't be able to work here anymore. Actually, I was mostly upset because your dad used to come in and visit me here and I was scared I'd have to work somewhere else, someplace where he couldn't come in. Or I thought maybe I'd even have to leave town. So I guess I was making a big deal of how awful it was that the owner was selling the place. You told me I should buy it, because if I owned it, then I could work here as long as I said I could."

She heard a sound come out of him that sounded like a wispy little laugh. She tried to remember if she'd ever heard him laugh before. Then again, they hadn't met under the best of circumstances. When would he have laughed, and why?

"I don't remember," he said. "But it sounds like something a four-year-old would say."

They sat in silence for a moment or two. His hand stopped moving on the back of her hair. Stopped petting her like a dog. But he didn't move the hand away. It just sat there, resting on her head.

"Maybe if you hadn't mentioned it," she said, "I'd never have thought of even trying. To buy it, I mean. So you're kind of the reason I own this diner."

"Business advice from a four-year-old," he said. "I guess I'm just glad it worked out."

"That's almost exactly what Fern said. The first part of it, anyway."

"So you loved my dad?"

Virginia lost a battle with tears she'd forgotten she was even waging.

"I did. More than you know. More than I could ever really tell anybody, because we hadn't known each other too long, and people just didn't seem to understand."

"I guess that gives us something that ties us together," he said. "Because I loved my dad, too. I don't remember him. But I remember that I did."

Then, as if he'd forgotten who she was, as if he'd lost track of what they'd been saying, he got up and wandered back into the dining area. Worthy stayed at her feet, which she appreciated.

Virginia wiped her eyes and blew her nose with a tissue from her coat pocket. Then she struggled to her feet and looked out through the swinging doors. He was sitting at table three again, staring out at the icy world, his breath puffing out in great clouds. Virginia sighed and let the door swing shut.

Chapter Thirty-One : Jody

He stood at the sink, his hip just a few inches from hers, his bare hands deep into a sink of warm, soapy water. He'd left the compression bandage off. He didn't need it. He knew now that it was not a bad sprain.

Even Virginia hadn't known if the sink would run hot water or not. The water heaters were gas, of course, but some appliances required electricity to ignite a flame, and others didn't. At least, according to Virginia. It didn't run hot, exactly. There was just too much cold to overcome. But it ran warm. And it felt good, except on the tips of his frost-nipped fingers. There it ached something fierce.

His hands were only partially mobile. They were beginning to thaw and warm slightly, enough that he figured they were not deeply frostbitten. Which was one reason they were doing dishes, to warm their hands and assess any damage.

He had to be extra careful of his grip on the plates. His fingers still didn't move right. So he worked slowly.

He handed her a clean plate. She looked at it closely, which hurt his feelings a little. As if she didn't trust him to wash a dish properly.

He didn't say so out loud.

Then he reached for another dish and saw, to his surprise, that it was the last one in the stack. The only one left to be washed. Which meant he must have been a long way away in his head, because he hadn't noticed sooner.

He was sorry to get to the end of the job, because it was a comfort to do something. Anything. Just hunkering down on the linoleum wishing he were warmer was starting to get old.

Then she spoke, startling him. "I've got a job for you. If you want it."

"I've never worked at a job before."

"Doesn't mean you never could."

"What's the job?"

"You're doing it."

"Oh. Dishwasher."

"I told you we're about to hire a new dishwasher and a new waitress. And I know you wouldn't want to wait tables. I know you're not that comfortable around people. But it's pretty quiet back here in the kitchen. Just me and Fern coming in and out, and the cook, but he'd pretty much have his nose buried in what he's doing. Your job is the only one in the place that doesn't require any rushing around. And you're doing a good job on these. I've been watching you, and I've been looking at your work. You're very meticulous. You're careful about what you're doing."

"I'd be a lot faster, but my hands don't quite work yet."

"I know that. I was taking that into account."

"Oh."

"It's not the greatest job in the world, and it doesn't pay a fortune. But it's work. And you wouldn't have to interview for it and fill out a form and say where you worked before, because I know you never did. And I don't care. You wouldn't have to convince anyone to hire you. If you want the job, you've got it. Just like that. I just figured you'd do better in a familiar place. And this place ought to be pretty familiar by now. I figure you're already pretty used to it."

But Jody didn't feel used to it. And he didn't feel like someone who could hold down a job.

"How would I get all the way out here from the lake, though?"

"Oh. Yeah. I forgot about that. That *is* a pretty long commute. But if you had a job, you could buy a car."

"I don't even know how to drive."

"I could teach you to drive."

He handed her the last dish. Then he dried his hands on a towel and walked away from the sink, his coat sleeves falling back into place as he moved. He sank into a squat on his haunches in front of one of the ovens, his hands pressed firmly over his ears. It hurt his wrist a little to press. He did it anyway.

He heard her say something, but it was blessedly muffled. He couldn't make out the words.

A moment later she took hold of his right wrist and pulled that hand away from his ear.

"Why are you doing that?" she asked.

"Because it's too much. Too much is changing. You want me to get a job, and learn to drive, and take that test you need to pass to get your license, and buy a car. And fill it up with gas, and pay for the registration. And I'd have to get insurance on it, and that's expensive. And everything is changing, and it's too much. All I ever did was live with my grampa and maybe haul wood and shovel the driveway. That's all I know how to do. I want to go back up to the cabin where there are things I'm used to. Things I know. I can't keep being in this place where everything is new and scary. It's too much for me."

They didn't talk for several minutes. Jody listened to the wind with his eyes squeezed shut.

"Besides," he said, "if I was driving back and forth from the lake to here . . . not only would all the money I make go to gas, but then you wouldn't leave Worthy with me during the week. Because he'd only be alone more than ever."

More silence, except for the wind and the light rain of falling twigs and the ice that had coated them.

"There's still my guest room," she said.

He breathed a minute before answering. "Pretty sure that's the second time you've asked me to come live with you. But I don't know you and I don't know your house. I know the cabin. I want to go back to the cabin."

"I know, honey. I understand. But you were living on your grandfather's Social Security. You're going to have to do something. You have to eat."

"I want to talk about something else," he said, fighting a rising panic. For Jody to notice panic meant that his anxiety level had far exceeded the norm, a norm which he didn't tend to notice anymore at all. Any more than a fish notices it's swimming in water. "This is really starting to freak me out."

"I'm sorry, honey," she said.

She was rubbing her hands together as she spoke, then holding them out toward the heat of the oven. Then rubbing them together again.

For the hundredth time since they'd been pinned down here, Jody imagined how good a deep, hot bath would feel.

"I guess I just figured if you have to get used to it soon anyway, then the best favor I could do for you would be to talk about it. Sometimes that's how we get used to things. You know? We imagine ourselves doing them. And then after a while it starts to feel like something we could do. It's like mental practice."

"Yeah, well maybe your mind practices. My mind just freaks out."

———

A light tap on the glass startled him, propelling him out of his unscheduled nap and into an upright position. He'd been sleeping in a chair at one of the diner's tables, his top half sprawled across its crayon-marked surface. When he straightened, he realized his back was in spasms from that bad position.

He looked out through the glass of the window to see what had made the tapping sound.

On the icy boards of the diner's front porch stood Deputy Rodelle. He still had one hand poised in a rapping position, the backs of his knuckles facing the window. His cheeks glowed red, and his breath billowed out in great clouds of steam. Behind him a big one-ton four-wheel-drive pickup truck sat on the ice of the parking lot, also billowing steam from its exhaust and wearing chains on all four of its huge, knobby snow tires.

Jody briefly met the deputy's eyes and noted the surprise he saw there.

He was still half-asleep, so he walked most of the way to the door before realizing the simple truth: this meant they were saved.

Jody unlocked and opened the door, and the deputy ducked inside, causing the bells to jingle. The deputy blew on his own hands and rubbed them briskly.

"Damn," Rodelle said. "Not warmer in here, is it?"

"No, sir. Not much."

"Now, don't take this the wrong way. Because I'm awful damn glad to see you. Been worried about you, and it's nice you're in one piece. But I sure as hell didn't expect to find you *here*. I came looking for Ginnie, because I went to check on her house and she wasn't there. I figured *she* might've got stuck here in the diner. But what in God's name are *you* doing here?"

"Oh," Jody said. "Right."

Then, much to his surprise, he had to think. He had to remember. Why was he here again? It might have been some leftover sleepiness gumming up the works. But it didn't feel that way. It felt as though it had been weeks since he'd arrived here, not days. And who he'd been upon arriving seemed an ancient history to him. It felt hard to recall.

"Oh," he said again. "I remember now. I came to bring the lady her dog back."

He watched the deputy's face, because it was changing. Watched his eyes soften as the words settled in.

At first neither spoke.

Then Rodelle said, "Well, then in that case I'm proud to know you, Jody. That was a damn fine thing to do."

Jody looked down at the diner's worn but clean linoleum. He didn't speak, because he was embarrassed.

"Tell you what I'll do. I'll take you down to the county shelter in the valley," Rodelle said, "and we'll get you a dog of your own. I bet I can even get some local folks to chip in if you can't cover the adoption fee. Won't be the same dog, but you'll get to love him given time."

"Well, thank you, sir. That's very nice. But it won't be necessary. We're going to share the one dog we've already got." He waited in case the deputy wanted to interject. Then he plunged on. "Because she feels bad leaving him alone all day for the five days she works. So she's going to bring him up to the lake for those five days a week. And then she'll come get him back when it's time for her two days off."

Again, silence. Jody's eyes remained trained to the floor.

"Well, that's a nice thought, son, but . . ."

"But what?"

268 *Catherine Ryan Hyde*

"Ginnie works seven days."

"They're hiring a new waitress. So they can both take days off."

"Huh," Rodelle said. "See that? Now I just had no idea how much progress was taking place in these last bunch of hours. But I knew the two of you were decent adults who could be counted on to hammer out an equitable solution. Where's Ginnie?"

"She's in the kitchen. It's warmer in there, because she's got the ovens going. I think she's asleep. Last time I looked in there, she was asleep."

"So if it's warm in there, what're you doing out here in the cold?"

Jody braved a glance at the deputy's face, then quickly deflected his gaze again. He sighed. Sank into a sit at one of the tables.

"I think I broke her heart," he said.

This time it was Deputy Rodelle's turn to sigh. He plopped into a chair across from Jody and tried to meet his eyes. Jody made sure he didn't succeed.

"Well, damn it all to hell," Rodelle said. "Just when I was feeling so good about two of my favorite locals. Why'd you have to go and hurt her feelings, Jody? She's a nice lady. What'd she ever do so wrong to you?"

"Nothing," he said, tracing the blue crayon lines with the tip of one numb index finger. "She just keeps trying to act like she's my mom. Or maybe my stepmom, I guess. But anyway. She just keeps trying to mother me."

"Still waiting for the bad news," Rodelle said.

"That was everything."

He heard the deputy sit back hard in his chair. "Isn't a little bit of family just what you're fresh out of right about now?"

"Maybe," he said. "But what difference does that make? No matter how bad you need family, that doesn't turn a stranger into one. Need has nothing to do with it. She's not my mom. She's no relation to me. She knew me when I was little. Turns out she knew my dad. And I guess she thought she was going to be my stepmom. But I don't remember that. She remembers but I don't. So she feels like we know each other. Like we mean something to each other. But I don't feel like we do. And no matter how many times she tells me—or you tell me—that I should feel a certain thing, I just don't feel it. And I'm sorry. But that's just the way it is."

Silence. Jody lifted his numb fingertip from the blue lines and began tracing the purple.

"Jody," Rodelle said. "Look at me."

Jody's heart fell. He could feel it. Sinking. "Do I have to?"

"Please do as I ask."

Jody looked up into the deputy's face. He couldn't read any one emotion in the man's eyes, which came as a relief. Rodelle didn't look angry. Also a relief.

"What?" Jody asked when the silence and the eye contact wore him down.

"Just listen, Jody. Open your ears and take this in good. You got nobody in the world just now. Nobody. And, no offense, but you're not the guy voted most likely to make it all on his own. Ginnie is a good woman and she's offering you something important here. If you can't let her be a mother to you, then at least let her be a friend. I'm not telling you to feel something you don't feel. I know you can't just automatically be comfortable with someone. Fine. Then don't do it automatically. Do it manually."

Jody waited. Looked down at the table again.

"I'm not sure I know what you're telling me to do," he said. But he was actually pretty sure he did.

"I'm saying you ought to give her a chance. You feel like she's a stranger to you. You don't know her. Fine. *Get* to know her. Do the work on this. Don't reject it because it doesn't feel right at the beginning. Hang in there until it does. You think people get to be friends overnight?"

"I have no idea how people get to be friends," he said.

"Well, here's your chance to find out. Now come on. Let's go wake her up and get the two of you back to her place. I just went by there, and it's looking good. Lots of trees down all around, but nothing hit her house."

"Oh, thank God," Virginia said.

They both looked up to see her standing in the open kitchen doorway, holding one of the swinging doors, Worthy wagging at her heels. The dog wiggled over to Deputy Rodelle and offered him a lick on the hand.

"Good to see you all in one piece, Ginnie," Rodelle said, patting Worthy's broad forehead.

"Maybe we just keep the part about the dog in the kitchen between you and me," she said in reply.

"Now it just so happens I always thought that rule was silly anyway. Do you know that in France they take their dogs right into the restaurants with them? And last I heard, the French were *not* dropping like flies. Now come on. Let's get you guys home. Well. To *your* home, Ginnie. Too soon to get anybody up to the lake. That road is one hundred percent impassable. You mind if Jody goes home with you for the time being?"

"He knows he's invited," she said. She tried to meet Jody's eyes, but he wouldn't allow it. "In fact, he knows he's invited for more than just the time being. I've asked him to live in my guest room and take a job here as a dishwasher. But so far he's not seeming too inclined to take me up on it."

"Funny you should mention that," Rodelle said, rising to his feet. "Because he was just now telling me he's going to reconsider that decision. Weren't you, Jody?"

He waited. Jody did not reply.

"Weren't you, son?"

This time there was a different note in the deputy's voice. This time he was serious.

"Yes, sir," Jody said. "I guess I'm reconsidering those matters."

———

It was cold in the bed of the pickup. But Jody could understand how all four of them were never going to fit up front in the cab. He wrapped his arms tightly around Worthy, as if the dog might be about to fly away.

He really needn't have bothered. Rodelle never drove much over five miles per hour anyway.

Now and then the truck slowed to carefully steer around a downed tree, or some big branches fallen from one.

Jody watched the power poles ease by. Some still had lines in between, strung with icicles like Christmas decorations gone too far. Others had just a blank space in between where the lines had come down.

Closer to town the highway had been cleared of major obstacles, but both sides of the highway were littered—more than a foot deep in places—with tangles of ice-covered twigs and branches. Jody could only guess that a plow had pushed them into those even borders.

He leaned his head against the back window of the pickup's cab.

He could hear them talking.

"I reached out to him just about as many times as a person can reach," he heard Virginia tell the deputy. "I'm sorry, Roger, but I just think there's no getting through to him."

Then Jody wished he'd heard what came before. Or maybe that he hadn't heard any of it. He wasn't sure which.

"I don't think there's hardly anybody on earth there's no getting through to," Rodelle said. "Some just take longer than others. Longer than you might like. Now what's this I hear about your having known his father?"

"Did he tell you that? He's *Buddy!*"

"Buddy who?"

"Oh, that's right. You weren't even in town yet, were you? But you must have at least heard about Aaron Albanese. He was the guy who drowned going off the railroad bridge."

"I've heard tell of it," Rodelle said. "Couldn't have told you the guy's name. I use the story sometimes when I go talk to the kids. Try to convince them not to shortcut over the bridge. But it's a funny thing about what we tell people. We're all going around trying to tell other people not to make the mistake we made. Or the mistake somebody else made. But seems until we make the mistake ourselves, and really have to pay the bill, nobody gives a damn bit of attention to the stories. Some weird quirk of human nature, but damned if I can figure it out. So you were close with this guy?"

At first it seemed to Jody that she never planned to answer. Then, when she finally did, it was so quiet he couldn't hear. But he saw her nod her head slightly.

"Well, then maybe the kid's worth another try or two," Rodelle said.

If she said anything, he couldn't tell.

"I can hear you, you know," he called in to them through the glass.

"We'll take that under consideration," Rodelle shot back. "But don't expect it to change much."

They rode in silence for a few minutes more.

The roads had been salted in town. Jody could feel the difference immediately. He could hear and feel the crunch of it under the chained tires, and he could feel the difference in the traction. The deputy sped way up. To about ten miles per hour.

He heard Virginia say, "What made you think to even go by my house looking for me?"

"Well, I told you I'd keep an eye on the place," the deputy said. "You know. In case Lloyd came back."

Something icy and tight grabbed Jody's stomach. He'd just assumed Lloyd was in prison. He'd had no idea that coming back was an option for that terrible man.

The truck stopped. Jody sat up straighter to try to see why.

Virginia and the deputy stepped out, and they both stood staring at a house Jody figured must be Virginia's. He climbed down from the truck bed and opened the tailgate so Worthy could jump down.

Then the four of them stood and stared at the house for the longest time, as if expecting it to make some kind of move.

It was old but comfy looking, with peeling white paint and bare winter vines covered in ice. When the wind blew, the ice on the vines made a strange sound rubbing against the ice on the shutters. The roof was thickly coated with ice, but Jody figured if it had held up this long, it would likely continue to hold.

All and all, the house seemed unscathed.

"You won't have electricity yet," Rodelle said. "So don't go burning the place down with a candle. You got a flashlight?"

"I do," she said. "Somewhere. It'll be light for a while, so I guess I'll have time to find it."

"Your heater work when the power's off?"

"No. It's gas, but it won't click on without power. But it's okay. I got that big old woodstove. We can make it cozy with just that. It's a big stove for such a little house. And I think the water heater works on just gas. Yeah, it must, 'cause it's got a pilot. So I can have that hot bath I've been thinking about for days."

Jody had been thinking about that hot bath, too. But he said nothing. Because it was probably too much to ask. It was enough she was taking him in out of the cold. Giving him someplace to be. The chance to be okay for the time being.

"How're you fixed for wood?" Rodelle asked.

"Good," she said. "Got a whole season's worth under a tarp in the back."

Jody felt a hand against his shoulder. A big hand, one that could only have belonged to the deputy. He gave Jody a little push.

"Go haul some wood for the lady," he said.

"Yes, sir," Jody said, and headed around to the back of the house.

"No, wait," Virginia said. "He sprained his wrist."

"It's fine," Jody said. He walked back in their direction, flexing it slightly. It hurt to flex it, but he didn't let on.

Rodelle took careful hold of Jody's arm and pushed his sleeve partway up. "Let me take a look at that," he said. "Well, it doesn't look too swollen, so hopefully it's not a bad sprain. Don't try to carry too much weight with it. Go easy. But you can bring in some wood, right? And salt down this walkway for her while you're at it. You got a bag of salt, Ginnie?"

"I do."

"Well, go on then, son."

"Yes, sir."

Jody took off toward the back of the house again.

He glanced around to see if Worthy was following, but the dog stood his ground close to Virginia, wagging his tail and watching Jody closely, as if wishing Jody wouldn't go away.

Jody saw them talking with their heads together. Virginia and the deputy. But he was too far away to know what they were discussing. He couldn't decide if he was sorry or relieved that he couldn't hear what they were saying about him.

Chapter Thirty-Two: Virginia

Jody came bouncing into the house before Virginia even got settled. And yes, bouncing was the right word. He seemed eager and enthusiastic, as though nothing emotionally difficult had ever happened to either one of them.

"Got a pickax?" he asked brightly.

"No. Why would I have a pickax?"

"A shovel, then. But not one of those wide, light aluminum shovels you use to clear snow from your driveway. Has to be the heavy kind, the kind you use for digging holes."

"Yeah, there's a shovel in the garage. But I'm not sure how you're planning to shovel ice. Or what shoveling has to do with hauling some firewood in here."

"That's because you haven't seen the firewood," he said. "You've got it under a tarp. Well. You probably knew that much already. But now the tarp is completely covered in a sheet of ice. And it's thick, too. And heavy. No way I can lift up the tarp, or even any little part of it, with all that weight on it. So I need something to hit the ice with. Break it up."

"Thank you," she said, and it seemed to surprise him.

"For what?"

"For being willing to do all this work to get us warm again."

He shrugged, then headed off in the direction of the garage.

Virginia put on a kettle of water for tea.

A minute or two into the task she heard the banging of the shovel against the sheet of ice he'd described. It made her wonder how it felt on that sprained wrist of his every time that shovel hit home. She lit the burner under the tea water, then crossed to the window to watch. Worthy tagged along behind her, his tail wagging against the backs of her knees.

Jody had his back to her, and she watched him raise the shovel over and over, smacking it down against the tarp, sending ice flying. He was using his right hand only.

Then, without warning, it was Buddy she was watching at work. Not that he hadn't been Buddy all along. But her brain made a clear shift. As if she'd gone back nineteen years to see this young man through the eyes of everything he was to her at the time.

She looked down at Worthy, who looked up into her eyes amiably. The way he did everything.

She knelt down and put her arms around the dog.

"Know what, boy? In all the confusion, I think I might have forgotten to tell you just how happy I am to have you back."

The dog kissed her nose, and she laughed.

She rose to her feet again and watched the young man stacking lengths of split wood into a little pile.

"Who'd have thought? Right, boy? Who would ever have imagined I'd be getting him back again?" Then it hit her. "Fern! I haven't told Fern! Oh, but I bet the phone lines are down."

She ran to the kitchen phone and grabbed up the receiver, expecting to hear silence. Instead a dial tone surprised her.

She punched Fern's number by heart.

Fern picked up on the first ring, and just started talking. She had clearly checked the caller ID, and she didn't bother with the formality of hello. "Well, you just about scared me into an early grave, Ginnie. Where the hell have you been?"

"Got stuck at the diner," she said. "It's a long story. I'd have called and told you I was okay, but the lines were down."

"They were down here in town, too," Fern said, "but the phone company made fixing them a priority. How did you—"

"Wait. Please," Virginia said. "I have something important to tell you."

"Who's stopping you?"

"He *is* Buddy. Turns out I was right. And he is."

A silence on the line.

Then, "You sure?"

"Positive."

"What about the name thing?"

"The grandfather changed the boy's last name to match his own when he took him in."

"Well, well," Fern said. "Small world. Guess you got what you wanted then, Ginnie. Finally. For a change, huh?"

"Not really. I mean, in a way I guess I did. But . . . why is it when you get what you want, it's never the way you thought it would be?"

"A question for the ages," Fern said, and it was only then that Virginia realized she had picked up that expression from Fern.

"You were right, Fern. He doesn't even remember me. And even if he did . . . I think that bond only went one way."

"Hate to say I told you so."

"No you don't. You love it."

"Not in a case like this I don't."

"I guess at least now I won't always have to ask myself how it might have been."

"You still don't know yet how it'll be," Fern said, adopting that tone she used when she felt she knew best. "The fat lady hasn't sung as far as I can see. All I was trying to tell you at the time is that he hadn't accepted you *yet*. And that little boys don't always do so great at accepting their daddies' new lady friends. But he's not a little boy anymore. Fine, so there's no bond yet. Make one."

Virginia wandered to the window with the phone and looked out again, wondering why he hadn't appeared with a stack of wood yet. He seemed to be picking and choosing carefully. Examining each stick. Virginia wasn't sure why. She always just took the five or six closest to where she was standing.

"I'm not so sure, Fern," she said. "It sounds logical. But you don't know this kid. He's kind of . . . remote. It's like he's just not put together to let people in."

"You don't know what he's put together to do in the long haul. You just know what he's put together to do right off the bat. Look. It's Buddy. How many years you been talking my ear off about Buddy? I thought he meant the world to you. For somebody who means the world to you, you sure seem set to give up on him easy."

Virginia breathed around a tightness in her chest. "But I tried everything I—"

She never had time to finish the thought. Because Jody turned back toward the house and trotted her way with the first stack of firewood.

"Call you later, Fern," she said. "I gotta go."

———

When Virginia arrived back in the living room after her bath, Jody had the fire going strong. It was almost uncomfortably warm. Or, anyway, at another time she might have thought so. But after those days huddled in front of a gas oven in her coat and scarf, there was really no such thing as too warm.

"Enjoy your bath?" he asked.

He was lying sprawled on his back on the couch, Worthy's head resting on his belly. He stroked the dog's ears as he spoke.

"While I was in it I did. But without the bathroom heater it was hard to force myself to get out into that cold room again. That being the farthest place from the woodstove and all. But I'm fine now."

She had gotten into her flannel pajamas, her heaviest winter robe, and her enormous fuzzy slippers. She settled in the stuffed wing chair across from him.

"Want your couch back?" he asked listlessly. As if partially asleep.

"You're fine where you are. You want to take a shower? It'll only take twenty minutes or so for the water to heat up again."

"By and by," he said, in that same dreamy tone.

Virginia envied his relaxation.

She watched the side of his face. She could do so unnoticed, since his eyes had drifted closed. It made her wonder how she could ever not have known who he was. Or even how she'd managed to talk herself out of the knowing she'd started with. Not only did he look like Buddy the boy, he looked like Aaron. It made her heart feel squishy, like it was twice its normal size and throbbing.

Talk to him, she thought. *Say something*. But no words came out. Well. No good ones.

"Remind me to call the locksmith in the morning," she said. "Get these locks changed, just in case."

Jody only grunted.

In time her eyes got droopy as well. Sleep had come hard on that cold linoleum diner floor. It had left her depleted.

Then he spoke, startling her. "I'm sorry I can't be all the things you wanted me to be," he said.

Virginia sighed and dug around for some words. Hopefully good ones.

"That's the problem with people," she said. "Not just you. All people. Not a one of us can be everything somebody else wants us to be. Trouble comes when we try to pretend we can. Or when people see it like a betrayal. You know. That somebody won't meet all their needs. My mom used to say it's because we weren't put here on earth to take care of each other. And that it's silly to get mad at someone for letting you down when they're just being who they are. She said it's like getting mad at your dog for not being a cat."

Then she waited, thinking she'd hear his thoughts on all that.

It took her several minutes of silence to realize he'd drifted off to sleep. She could tell by his breathing. That and the fact that his hand had stopped moving across the soft fur of Worthy's head.

———

Virginia woke with a start. She was in her own bed. She had no idea what time it was, but it was dark. But it was less dark than Virginia had expected. It was not pitch dark. It took her a second to realize that the streetlight at the corner was on, which meant the linemen must have restored the power.

But she didn't have time to think much about that. Because she had been wakened by a sound outside. Loud music. Heavy, dense, objectionable music. And a running motor.

She squinted at the clock. It was after 3:00 a.m., a terribly inconsiderate time for someone to be sitting outside her house with the engine running and the radio blasting. None of her neighbors, nor anyone her neighbors had associated with in the past, would do such a thing.

Besides, it sounded like the car was right in front of *her* house.

She got out of bed and crossed to the window to see.

What she saw was Lloyd's red truck idling loudly at the curb.

Swallowing against a lump that felt like her heart, she ran back to her bedside table and grabbed up the phone. She fumbled for the card Roger had given her. She'd left it by the phone in case of need, but now she couldn't find it in the mostly dark room. And the last thing she wanted to do was turn on a light. That would only serve to tip Lloyd to the fact that she was awake. That would only set the confrontation in motion. And Virginia had no doubt it was a confrontation Lloyd wanted. Otherwise he had no need to blast his radio loudly enough to wake her.

Her fingers hit the edge of the card . . . and knocked it off onto the rug.

She dropped to her hands and sore knees, stifling a cry of pain, more desperate and panicky now. She tried to stay calm and move her hands in a careful grid over the surface of the carpet.

When she finally felt the card—wrapped her hand around it— she held it to her chest for a brief second in gratitude.

Then she grabbed the flashlight—which she'd left by her bed on the assumption the power would be out all night—and picked up the phone again. She took them into the bathroom, where she huddled in the corner, crouched down in spite of her sore and swollen knees. She wanted to keep the beam of flashlight as far away from the small window over the shower as possible.

She punched in the numbers, vaguely aware that it was hard to breathe. She couldn't tell if it was a result of the cramped position— folded over her own gut—or her growing fear. Or both.

Roger's wife answered.

"Oh, Millie, I'm so sorry," she said. "It's Virginia McCarthy. Terrible hour to get you up out of bed, I know. But you have to tell Roger that Lloyd came back. I promised I'd let him know if I saw him. If there was any trouble. And I think he wants trouble."

She waited. No sound. No reply.

"Millie?"

"Ginnie?" she heard a second later. But it was Roger.

"Yeah, Roger."

"He's back?"

"Oh, yeah."

"Son of a bitch. What's he doing? He's not in your house, is he?"

"No! Thank God! He's idling his truck out at the curb, playing his radio real loud so I'll know he's out there."

"That sounds about right," Roger said, the words easing out of him like a disgusted sigh. "I'll be there in five minutes. Maybe four. Don't let him know you're awake. Don't go out there."

"I sure as hell wasn't going to go out there, Roger," she said on the breath of an almost laugh.

She was breathing again. She could feel it. And she hadn't changed her cramped position. So it must have been the fear. Now she could breathe, because Roger would be here in five minutes. Maybe four.

"I'm on my way," he said, and clicked the connection off.

Virginia held the phone to her chest for a brief moment of thankfulness, the way she had done with the card.

Then she turned off the flashlight and let herself out of the bathroom. She crossed quietly to the bedroom window again and peered through the curtains. Nothing had changed. Lloyd hadn't moved toward her door. He also hadn't driven away.

She felt her forehead crease as she thought about what options Roger might have at his disposal when he arrived. Did the fact that Lloyd was out on bail for a crime against her amount to any type of restraining order? And was Lloyd doing enough to break it? If not, can you charge a man for playing his radio too loudly at the curb?

Maybe all Roger could do was threaten him. He'd already done that, of course, and this new development was proof of how little good it had done.

She tried to force such thoughts out of her head again. There was nothing she could do but wait and see.

She laughed lightly—probably a release of tension—at Roger's suggestion that she not go outside. Like she would ever have been tempted to go outside.

The world went quiet.

Lloyd had turned off his engine, silencing both the truck and its radio.

Virginia heard the familiar sharp, metallic creak of his truck door opening. She saw light from the streetlamp glimmer off Lloyd's shiny bald head as he stood and moved toward her gate.

In that sudden state of waiting, of no breath, of feeling almost as though her heart didn't dare to keep beating, she saw Jody running down her heavily salted front walkway. He was dressed in only his jeans and his flannel shirt flapping open. He was carrying the shovel.

And he was running right into the heart of the problem.

Chapter Thirty-Three: Jody

It was Worthy's growling that woke him. It made his heart race, because Worthy had never growled at anything so far as he knew. Not in all the time Jody had known him.

Then he reminded himself he hadn't known the dog long.

Jody thought about the ice-coated vines, and the way the wind made them scratch and squeak against the equally ice-coated shutters. Maybe that was all the dog was hearing.

That and music. But dogs don't growl at music.

But a moment later he was awake enough to realize that the music was coming from outside the house. Something with a thumping bass. Something you'd listen to when you're angry, and you want to be even more angry. He'd heard it all along, but had not consciously registered it as a thing out of place. He was in a strange house, a new place. Maybe there was music at night.

But Worthy's growling changed his sleep-muddied thinking on that. The dog said it was a problem. So maybe it was.

He got up and walked to the window. The sight of the red truck seized in his chest. It almost paralyzed him. But then something happened that had never happened until very recently, and only once before. Something rose up in him and refused to be para-lyzed. If Virginia was in trouble, he couldn't afford to freeze.

No. It would have to be like the railroad bridge. Lloyd would have to be his new railroad bridge. Lloyd would have to be overcome.

Jody pulled his jeans on over his long underwear. Quickly slipped into his heavy flannel shirt, but didn't even take the time to button it.

He ran to the garage in the half dark, shirt flapping, Worthy trotting at his heels.

He opened the door into the garage quietly. He didn't want to tip Lloyd that anyone in the house was even awake.

He stood a moment, trying to force his eyes to adjust to the light. He could see the shovel leaning on the wall by the door, not a foot from his hand, but he only knew it was the shovel because he knew he had left it there. He really wanted a better weapon, but then he realized he didn't even know what that would be.

He wrapped his hand around the shovel's handle and ran to the front door.

He looked down at his bare feet. If he'd had slippers, he would already have put them on before ever leaving the guest bedroom. But he had only heavy socks and lace-up boots, and that would have taken too long.

That's when he realized the music had stopped. The truck's engine had fallen silent. He stood up on his tiptoes to peer out through the high window set into the door.

Lloyd was standing at the gate. Just standing. Staring.

"You wait here," he whispered to Worthy as he opened the front door. The dog tried to force his way through, but Jody pulled him back with a hand around his chest. "No! I mean it, Worthy. Wait here. He already tried to hurt you once. He's not getting his hands on you again. Not if I have anything to say about it."

Jody squeezed through a small space created by the slightly open front door, the shovel out ahead of him where it couldn't get caught or hung up. Then he pulled the door shut behind him before the dog could follow.

He ran down the front walk, aware of the sharp stabs of the salt pellets as his feet hit them, but not letting the pain stop him. At least he could run without slipping.

He stopped dead in front of the gate and looked at Lloyd, and Lloyd looked at him. He'd never stared Lloyd in the face before. He really hadn't known what the older man looked like except from a great distance. Now the streetlight shone from behind Lloyd, lighting him up in silhouette. Illuminating the great clouds of breath he blew. And Jody still couldn't see much. He couldn't see Lloyd's eyes or read his intentions.

What he could see all too well was the size of him. Like a mountain compared to Jody.

Then again, the railroad bridge had been bigger and stronger, too, he thought. He would just have to overpower the situation by being brave.

He could feel the pain of the cold on his frost-nipped toes, but he couldn't take the time to pay it much attention.

He held the shovel high. Held it with both hands, even though it hurt his wrist to bear the weight.

"If you come through this gate," he said, his voice surprisingly steady, "I'll stop you if I possibly can. I'll stop you if I have to die doing it. You've hurt them both enough. They deserve better than you, and I'm here to see they get it."

A long silence. Or at least a silence that felt long. It may have been only a second or two. Jody searched inside himself for his level of fear, but felt only a dark and quiet blankness. Like his insides had been switched to the "Off" position.

He saw Lloyd tilt his head, the way a dog will when faced with something he can't quite figure out.

"And who the hell are you?" Lloyd asked calmly.

"I'm her stepson."

"She doesn't have a stepson."

"She does now."

Lloyd opened the gate. Jody reflexively began to take a step back, but he stopped himself. He held his ground.

Lloyd took two more steps in and paused, close enough to Jody to reach out and touch his shoulder. And he did reach out. But what Lloyd's hand aimed for was the shovel. He grabbed the handle just below the shovel head and wrenched it out of Jody's hands. Jody tried to hold on, but his sprained left wrist wouldn't help enough.

Lloyd threw the shovel down on Virginia's frozen front yard.

"Now tell me again," Lloyd said, "how your tiny ass is going to keep me in line, or stop me from doing anything I choose to do."

Jody dove for the shovel.

He never got there.

Instead he was tackled by the huge Lloyd and pinned on the icy dirt, the crust of ice breaking as they hit it. He looked up at Lloyd, whose face was still framed and backlit. The clearest thing Jody could see was the great steam of his breath.

"You shouldn't go putting on a big show like that if you can't back it up," Lloyd said, his huge hands pinning Jody's shoulders to the ice. "That's what I call letting your mouth write a check your ass can't cover. Now, I don't know who in hell you are, but—"

Lloyd was never able to say more. Because in a sudden flash of fur and growling, Worthy had him by the forearm. And the dog must have sunk his teeth in hard, because Lloyd bellowed. He stumbled up and off Jody, dragging the dog along. Still wailing that deep cry of pain.

Jody sat up, catching his breath.

Lloyd and Worthy spun crazily in the front yard, Worthy still deeply attached to Lloyd's arm, and Lloyd still shouting out his pain.

Jody looked to the house to see how the dog had gotten out. To see if it had been his fault. He saw Virginia standing in the open doorway, in her bathrobe and slippers.

"No!" he called to her, and waved his hands wildly. "No, go back in!"

But it just all happened too fast.

Lloyd used his free hand to cut off the breath at Worthy's throat, and so got his arm back. He lunged at the dog in his rage, knocking Worthy off his feet and half landing on him, then centering his knees on the dog's side. He raised his fist to strike the dog. Jody could see blood running down Lloyd's arm in the light from the streetlamp. A lot of blood.

Jody covered the distance between them in an instant and caught the arm before it was too late. Of course, Lloyd struggled to take it back. But it was injured, that arm. It was deeply bitten. Probably down into the muscle. So Jody was able to prevail, at least for that moment.

Worthy struggled desperately under Lloyd's knees.

"He can't breathe!" Jody shouted, moving his grasp from Lloyd's arm to his throat. He wrapped his right forearm across the older man's throat, because he knew his weak left wrist would let him down. "Get off him! He can't breath!"

He levered harder on Lloyd's windpipe.

Lloyd pulled up, getting his feet under him and taking the bulk of his weight off his knees. Not enough for Worthy to struggle to his feet, but enough for the dog to gasp air again.

Then Lloyd lunged for the shovel. It was sudden, and timed just as Jody had loosened his grip on Lloyd's throat somewhat, so the movement broke Jody's grasp and sent him tumbling onto his side on the icy dirt.

When he struggled to his feet again, Lloyd had Worthy pinned down to the ice with the blade of the shovel pressing on the side of the dog's neck. Lloyd turned his face to Jody, and this time Jody could see him well in the light from the streetlamp.

"He can breathe now," Lloyd said, his voice rough and scratchy from having been briefly strangled. "Are you happy? Come at me one more time and I'll throw my weight down on this shovel and he'll never breathe again."

Jody said nothing. Did nothing.

"I should anyway," Lloyd said, his voice too even for a man contemplating such violence. "I should do it just because you bit me."

Lloyd turned his face down to the dog, who held very still under the blade of the shovel. He seemed to know better than to struggle. Maybe it hurt too much to struggle. Maybe he knew Lloyd meant business.

All Jody knew was that nothing moved. He didn't dare move. The dog didn't dare move. The whole world held still in hopes of preventing the unthinkable.

"Damn dog," Lloyd spat. "You never were anything but trouble. And then you go and do this." He nodded his head toward his arm, still pouring blood onto the leg of his jeans. "I should have done this back when I had the chance. None of this trouble ever would've happened if I'd gotten you out of the way proper."

"Lloyd," Virginia said.

Jody was startled by her voice, because he hadn't realized she was right out in the yard with them. Not three feet from Lloyd and the dog. And the shovel.

"Lloyd," she said again. Her voice sounded soft. Loving, even. "Lloyd, remember how good things were between us? Before you tried to hurt the dog? Don't do this, Lloyd. We can still get some of that back, you know? If you'll show me you're a man who wouldn't hurt him . . ."

Jody turned his face to her, his mouth gaping open. "*What?*" he shouted.

A long, static moment without words or movement.

Lloyd put down the shovel.

Worthy struggled to his feet, shaking himself off.

Lloyd took two steps in Virginia's direction. "Well, why'd you have me arrested then, Ginnie? If you felt like that?"

Roger Rodelle saved her from answering the question. He screeched to a stop behind Lloyd's red truck and threw his car door open. When he stood up in the street, he had his gun drawn. Out in front of him, held tightly in both hands.

In a moment of disjointed thinking, Jody wondered if Rodelle was scared. Then he realized it didn't matter. Just like it didn't matter if Jody had been scared crawling over the railroad bridge or facing down Lloyd with a shovel. He had done it. That's what mattered.

"You called the cops on me?" Lloyd asked, turning to face Virginia. "*Again?*"

Virginia never answered. She just waited for Rodelle to come through the gate, still aiming his service pistol at Lloyd.

"Ginnie," Rodelle said, "this man assault you?"

"No. But he assaulted Jody. And the dog."

"Good enough," Rodelle said. "On your knees, Lloyd. Hands behind your back."

Lloyd stood his ground a moment and gave Virginia one more long look. Virginia didn't meet his eyes.

"You're unbelievable," Lloyd said.

"*Now*, Lloyd!" Rodelle shouted.

Lloyd sank to his knees and allowed himself to be cuffed.

"Good job not going outside, you guys," Rodelle called over his shoulder.

Jody breathed for what felt like the first time in a long time. He ran to Worthy and felt gently around his neck. Brushed back the fur. But he saw no sign of injury. No blood. He eased his hands over Worthy's ribs. No matter how his hands moved, the dog showed no reaction of pain.

"Is he okay?" Virginia asked him.

"Seems okay."

"*You* okay?"

"Who, me? Yeah. I'm fine." Jody straightened and walked the few steps to her, the dog following at his heels. He stood in front of her. His face felt hard, like concrete setting up fast. "You were going to *take him back*? You *are* unbelievable!"

They were the harshest, angriest words Jody had ever said to anyone's face. An inner part of him flinched slightly, waiting for her reaction. So it surprised him, and knocked him completely off guard, when she laughed.

"Honey, I was never going to take him back."

"But you said—"

"What I needed to say to keep both you boys safe."

"Oh," Jody said, feeling out of words and unusually stupid.

They stood in silence for a few moments, watching Rodelle put Lloyd into the back of his car, her breath and his own coming out in clouds that met and intermingled in the beam of streetlight.

Virginia looked down at his feet. "Thought you knew better than to go out into the winter cold in your bare feet. Like your grampa."

"This was different," he said. He was aware of the strange but not unpleasant sensation of adrenaline draining away. "This was more important. What I had to do was more important."

"Than your *feet*?"

"Guess so."

"You want to tell me what's more important than your feet?"

"I wasn't letting anybody hurt you," he said. Then, when the unspoken reaction to those words felt unbearable, he talked over the moment. "That was smart, by the way. You know. What you

said to him. You used your head. I should've used my head. I just
went at him like a freight train. Not even paying attention to the
fact that he's twice my size. But you were smart about it."

"You get older," she said. "And you learn a few things."

Chapter Thirty-Four: Virginia

"Well, I just feel like I let you down seven ways to Christmas," Roger said.

It was mid-morning. He was sitting on the couch with his partner. But, as usual, he was the one doing all the talking.

Lloyd had been safely checked into the emergency room and then the county jail, and the deputies had come back in uniform to take a full statement.

"You shouldn't feel that way," she said. And she meant it. "You can't watch my house twenty-four hours a day. I know you can't. I'm nothing if not realistic, Roger. I know there are other things you have to tend to. It's just not reasonable to put all my safety on you like that. You can try your best to keep me safe, but you can't make any hundred percent guarantees. Any grown-up knows that."

On the word "grown-up," she looked at the boy. Jody. Well, the man. She knew she shouldn't think of him as a boy anymore. He looked distant. Asleep with his eyes open. But he didn't look shattered. He didn't look as though the events of the night had blown him apart. He had at first, but now something more solid seemed to have risen up in him. She couldn't be sure. She would have to wait and see. But it looked almost as though the night had pushed him a little closer to putting himself back together. She hoped she was right about that.

"I said I'd follow him," she heard Roger say. "It was my job to keep that promise. And he had a key to your house on him when we got him in for booking just now. That's what I feel the worst about. I went through all his stuff with a fine-tooth comb the first time I arrested him, just for that reason. That could have been a disaster. I just have no idea where he was hiding that sucker. But if Jody hadn't stopped him . . . nothing else would have, you know?"

"A key can hide nearly anywhere," she said, still looking at Jody. "In the pages of a book, or even in some papers. I just don't think you can blame yourself."

"Not sure who else to blame," the deputy said.

"How about Lloyd?"

She saw something flicker through Jody's eyes at the mention of Lloyd's name. As if it woke him from that half sleep. He looked up. Looked right at Virginia's face. Right into her eyes. Which, she realized, he never had before. Well, maybe on the railroad bridge. But not for long, even then. This time his gaze stuck there. They held each other's eyes for a second or two. Maybe three.

Then, much to her surprise, he smiled at her. It was just a little smile. But it looked genuine.

"Well," Roger said, "it was just a damn good thing Jody and the dog were here. Well," he said again. And stalled briefly. As if turning sharp corners in his mind. "Actually, I'm torn about that. Part of me wants to march old Jody here down the street on my shoulders like a hero. Part of me wants to give him a good thrashing for going outside in the first place. When you could've just waited for me to show up."

"I didn't even know she'd called you," Jody said quietly. "I didn't even know she was awake. I was just going to stand inside the door with the shovel. But then I saw he was at the gate . . ."

The deputy shook his head.

"One part brave and one part stupid," he said. "But I'm going to go against my better nature and give you credit for the brave. But think how bad I'd feel if something'd happened to you. Because I do still blame myself. Now I'm thinking it was my job to make sure he didn't get bail. Not sure how I could have done that. Can't really sway a judge much sometimes, but I sure as hell feel like I should have tried harder. But this time. This time he's staying in. I can tell you that just about for sure. Because when a guy gets out on bail and illegally enters the property of the party pressing charges, and threatens and assaults and strong-arms . . . well, that's all a judge should need to hear to deny bail. Now come on, Jody. We're taking you to the hospital."

"For what?" he asked, genuinely surprised.

"Looked at your feet lately?" Everyone in the room except Worthy looked down at Jody's bare feet. "Those toes don't look so good. Especially that pinkie toe on the right. Frostbite like that needs some medical attention. You might be on a fine line of whether all those toes can be saved. Now that can't all be from tonight, going out there in your bare feet like a fool. Had to have been a longer exposure than that."

A long silence. Jody stared at his own hands, as if waiting for the conversation to move along on its own. It didn't.

"Um. No, sir. I was out in the storm for a bit. But it's Virginia you should be getting checked over. She took some falls and . . ." Jody seemed to hit a hurdle he couldn't jump cleanly. He cleared his throat, figuratively backed up, then hit it again. "She did some things that hurt her knees. They're all bruised up and swollen."

Roger and his partner both raised their eyes to Virginia's. She looked away.

"And why was I not told about this before?" Roger asked.

"It's fine," she said. "It's just bruises. I don't need a hospital."

"You could've let me be the judge of that."

"But the roads were still all icy and you were taking your life into your hands just getting us home. The hospital would have been too much. Still is. For me. But Jody should get those toes looked at."

"Humor me," Rodelle said. "You're both going. Then he turned his attention to Jody, who was leaning forward in his chair, scratching behind Worthy's ears. "Just because I know this'll drive you crazy, son, when I tell this story around town, I'm going to leave out the reckless part, where you could've gotten yourself killed, and just tell the good part. The part where you threw yourself in between him and Ginnie. Then you can get a taste of the hero treatment. Get to be in the spotlight in a good way. Even though you're not a spotlight kind of guy. Don't argue with me. Just deal with it. Now put some shoes on and we'll go."

He rose to his feet, indicating it was time.

A sour look crossed the young man's face. As if the word "hero" were something rotten and smelly, like two-week-old kitchen garbage. "I'm not a hero," he said. "I just wasn't about to let that son of a bitch hurt *somebody else* I care about."

Virginia felt a little pang, sweet but stinging, in her lower belly, and in the space inside her chest. The room went silent, and she decided it would be the better part of valor to say nothing at all. Not even point it out.

After a few seconds of silence, Jody looked up, almost defensively. "What? What did I say?"

"Nothing," Virginia said.

"Besides," Jody said, "Virginia was the hero. She was smart. She used her brain. I just went barreling out there and got in over my head."

"Yeah," Rodelle said. "Well. Ginnie always could look after herself."

Virginia held still for another moment, both inside and out. Taking that in. Wondering whether she agreed with it. Wondering why she had never known that others, or at least this other, saw her that way.

"Really?" she asked the deputy.

"You don't agree? You bought yourself that diner and you run it, and make your own living, and didn't need anybody all those years. And when you finally did let somebody in and he let you down, you put him out on his ass, first time. None of that 'he loves me and he's sorry' crap I hear all the time in domestic disputes. You're a strong woman, Ginnie. Don't tell me you didn't know."

Virginia said nothing. Instead she just searched for whether she had known. She never got a clear answer. But one thing was sure. She knew now. She agreed. She could look after herself. She'd been doing so for years.

"And T-Rex," Roger said, talking over the awkwardness of the moment. "Did he come through with flying colors, or what? I'll never forget those lovely bites in Lloyd's arm. That took some stitches. I mean some dozens of stitches. I swear I didn't think that dog had it in him. Didn't think he was the type."

"I was surprised, too," Virginia said. "But his name is Worthy now."

"Oh," Roger said. "You're keeping that."

"Don't you think he earned it?"

While the deputy admitted that he did, Virginia looked into Jody's eyes again. This time the smile was a little stronger, a little more sure of itself, and came with a quick nod of the young man's head.

———

"I know this will sound weird," Virginia said. Then she stalled and failed to finish the thought.

She had spoken quietly, so the two deputies in the front would be less likely to hear. Or at least to think they were meant to hear.

She was riding in the back of the squad car with Jody, on their way to the hospital.

"Go ahead and tell me anyway," he said.

"I wish it was me you'd found out by the lake. I don't mean that literally. I just mean . . . oh, hell. What do I mean? I think I wish I'd never started with this."

"I think I know what you mean," he said. "But you shouldn't need anyone to tell you you're worth more. You should know that by now."

"I do," she said. "At least I'm pretty sure I do. But it's a little hard to tell because it's a new feeling. I think I didn't know until pretty recently."

He was looking out the window, Virginia noticed, watching the trees flash by. The weather had continued to grow warmer. Weirdly and suddenly warmer. Everything in the world had begun to drip. She could hear and feel the slushing of the car's tires cutting through melted ice.

She could feel how shaken she still was. More than she could ever have realized at the time.

"Know what I was thinking?" he asked her.

"I don't. No."

He turned to face her, but then shifted his gaze out the window again. "When he dropped Worthy out by the lake, the dog kept wagging his tail at him. And trying to lick his face. The whole time Lloyd was abandoning him, he just kept trying to be nice."

Virginia felt her face twist into a rueful smile. It was a sad mental picture.

"Never claimed he was the smartest dog in the world," she said.

"I don't think he's stupid," Jody said. "He was smart enough to know when I was in trouble. I think he just doesn't have a mean bone in his body. When it comes to *him*. No matter how somebody treats *him*, he's going to be nice. But if somebody mistreats *you or me . . .*"

"Yeah, I had no idea. But I'm not sure what that has to do with—"

"Even the dog knows we deserve better than that."

"I still don't see—"

"I just keep wondering why we can see the worth in everybody else except ourselves. Why we stand up for everybody we know except us."

"Well . . . that's . . ." But then she wasn't sure what it was. Confusing. Hard. True. Inevitable? She wasn't sure, but she hoped not.

"A question for the ages," he said.

She looked up to see Roger watching her in the rearview mirror. She had no idea how much he'd heard. But she couldn't really bring herself to believe it mattered much.

"Jody," he said.

"Yes, sir?"

"I want you to stay with her for a while."

She expected Jody to ask how long. Or make a face. Instead he just said, "Yes, sir." Then, as if upon giving the matter more thought, he added, "What choice do I have, anyway? I couldn't get back to the cabin now if I tried."

"Well, for a few days that'll be true. But I think you should stay with her more than a few days. She'll be scared at night. She'll need you."

Virginia met the deputy's eyes in the rearview mirror, challenging him without a word.

What kind of way was that to talk about her? she thought. She'd been living on her own, making her own living, taking care of herself, longer than Jody had been alive. He'd just said that himself. She didn't need anybody. She was a woman who could look after herself.

The deputy caught her eye in the mirror and winked.

Then Virginia understood. Then it was clear who needed what, and why he had said what he did.

"I guess that's true," Jody said. "Okay. I'll stay a while. You know. Just to make sure she's okay."

And then they pulled into the driveway of the hospital emergency room.

Chapter Thirty-Five: Jody

It was about an hour after bedtime, but Jody still hadn't managed to get any sleep. Or even to feel like he might be able to, given more time.

He got up, wrapping himself in the guest bed's big, fluffy comforter. He could do so without much pain, because his wrist had been properly splinted.

It was hard to walk in all that tightly wrapped padding, so he took small steps.

He walked to the open doorway of her room.

Worthy was sleeping with her tonight, he noted. He heard the tap of the dog's tail on her bedspread, and saw the motion of it in the dim light. There was moonlight to see them by, through the filmy curtains on her window.

"Virginia?" he asked in a loud whisper. "You awake?"

He heard the shifting of her weight under the covers.

"I am now," she said.

"Sorry to wake you up. But I didn't want to come into your room without letting you know who was here. After what happened, I figured that might scare you half to death."

She sat up in bed, and he could see her, mostly. His eyes were adjusting to the dim light, and he could see the shape of her, the wild messiness of her hair. Everything but the expression on her face and the look in her eyes.

"What's wrong, honey?" she asked him.

It was that motherly tone. The one he'd used to hate so much. The one that had always made him want to run away. Now he neither hated it nor loved it. It just seemed unremarkable. It just was.

"Nothing," he said. "Only . . . I thought you might feel safer if I slept on the floor in here with you."

"I'm fine, honey. Lloyd's in custody and I'm not scared."

"You sure?"

"Well, I was fast asleep until you said my name. That should say what needs saying."

"Oh," he said. It was impossible for him to deny his own disappointment, though he felt himself wanting to try. "Okay."

He turned to go back to his own room.

"Jody. Wait."

He waddled back to the open doorway and leaned on the jamb again. "What?"

"Is what you're trying to say maybe that *you* feel a little scared? And that maybe *you'd* feel a little better if you slept on the floor in here?"

"Yes, please," he said.

He waddled over to the rug under the window and stretched out as best he could, the comforter still wrapping him up like a mummy. He looked up through the window and could see the moon through the thin curtain. It was full, or nearly full. Or recently full.

"Thank you," he said.

"I don't blame you for being scared. Lord, honey, that man is two and a half times your size and weight. And here you were going out there to face him off and jumping right into it with him.

And with a sprained wrist to boot. I just don't know where you found all that courage."

"Adrenaline," he said.

"No," she said. "Courage."

He stared at the moon for a few moments in silence. "Well, maybe. Or maybe it was the fact that not letting him hurt you was more important to me than hurting you was to him."

He waited to see if she would answer, but she never did.

When she finally spoke, she veered off in a different direction.

"You deserve better too, you know."

"Better than what?" he asked, honestly not knowing what kind of compliment she meant this to be.

"Better than what life's dished out to you so far. Better than to be left all on your own over and over again."

"Nobody abandoned me *on purpose*, though. I mean, people die."

"I suppose. Still seems like a lot of heartache for one lifetime."

But Jody didn't really feel that he knew how much heartache was every person's fair share.

"Virginia? Can we talk?"

"Well, sure, honey. I thought we were talking right now."

"I meant more."

"Go ahead."

"Oh. No. I didn't mean right now. More like . . . in general. I feel like I don't really know how to talk to people. And so now I'm thinking it's because I don't get enough practice. My grampa was never much the talky type. I mean, he'd talk about what supplies we needed in town or what we should have for dinner. And he'd tell me stuff he heard on the TV news. But we didn't really talk about stuff that had happened in our lives and how we felt about it. And so now I don't know how to do that."

"I think you do fine with it. But, sure. You can practice on me."

"No. I don't do fine. On the inside, I can feel that I don't know how to do it. I can tell. It doesn't feel right. Other people do it and it's easy."

"I think you're overestimating how easy other people find it. I think if you could look inside somebody else and know how they feel, you might be surprised."

Jody had no idea what to say to that, so he made no reply.

He lay staring at the muted shape of the moon through the curtains, wishing it were possible to do such a thing. To look inside others. Then he could see for a fact if what she had told him was true. But like so much of life, he figured, you just had to take your best guess. You had to decide what you believed to be right and just run with that.

"Why do you think he put on a tie that night?" Virginia asked.

She was staring at a wooden box on her bedside table. Jody wondered if that was where she had put it. He hoped so. It was something he wouldn't have minded keeping. He didn't regret giving it away, but he might have. If she hadn't appreciated it enough.

"You probably don't remember," she added.

"Not really. Sorry."

"I was just thinking that when people dress up, they want to look nice for somebody. You know. Like he cared."

"I didn't know you ever doubted that he cared. He kissed you. You said so yourself."

"You're right. I know he liked me. I guess it just felt nice to get one more little piece of evidence about that after all these years."

Jody waited for her to say more. For a long time. But maybe there was nothing more to be said about that situation. Jody began to wonder if she'd fallen asleep.

"Virginia? You still awake?"

"Half," she said. "But go ahead."

"I know you don't really need me here. I know when the deputy said you did, he really meant I needed you, not the other way around. I'm not stupid. I know I'm kind of lost here."

"It's a little bit of both," she said.

And then it was morning, and Jody blinked into the light and wondered when and how he had even been able to sleep.

Chapter Thirty-Six: Virginia

"You want to be the one to go tell him?" Fern asked.

"Yeah. I think so. I think it should be me."

Virginia watched the backs of the big county workers as they lumbered out the diner's door, jingling the bells. Watched their big rubber boots slog through the melting slush as they ambled to their trucks.

Virginia couldn't shake the tightness in her belly.

"I wish they'd told us more about the cabin," she said quietly to Fern.

"Maybe they don't know. Maybe they didn't see it."

"But I asked if they'd seen it. And they wouldn't answer. I think if they hadn't seen it, they would just have said so."

"Well, guessing isn't doing us any good," Fern said. "Go tell him. When he's done with the dishes, we'll drive him out there."

"We?"

"I don't have to go if you don't want me to. I just thought you might want the moral support."

"Yeah. No, that would be nice, actually. Thanks. But I think I should wait till he's done with the dishes before I tell him. He'll want to go right away. It'll make him nervous, and then he'll just get more and more stressed out in the waiting."

"I'll finish up the dishes if you want."

"You know he'd never say yes to that. He takes his job too seriously."

"Well, you know him better than I do, Ginnie. You'll figure it out."

And with that Fern locked the diner's front door for the day and turned the sign to "Closed." Then she set about cleaning the tables.

Virginia stuck her head into the kitchen.

Jody was still at the sink, a starched white apron tied around his waist, his back to her. On the hook with the spare clean aprons she saw his wrist brace. He always took it off and hung it up at the start of his shift so he wouldn't get it wet. But he always seemed to manage without it. Though, if Virginia watched him work, which she often had over the past eleven days, she noticed he went to a lot of trouble to favor that unsupported injury. In spite of it, though, he was still the best dishwasher they'd ever had. It wasn't easy to find a worker willing to tackle such a menial task with commitment and gusto.

The stack of dirty dishes on his left was very short.

"You're almost done," she said.

He jumped and spun around, as if she'd fired off a gun behind his head. A big drip of soapsuds fell from his hand and landed on the kitchen linoleum near his shoe.

"Sorry," she said. "Didn't mean to scare you."

"It's okay," he said, and turned back to the sink and resumed his washing. "It's not your fault. I guess I'm still a little edgy in here. Because it's sort of a public place. Anybody can walk into the kitchen. But I'm getting used to it. I think. A little bit used to it, at least."

She walked the four steps to him and placed a hand on his shoulder. His muscles didn't tighten, and he didn't instinctively drop his shoulder as if to duck away from her touch. So that was progress.

"A bunch of guys from the county road crew were just in," she said. "Having lunch, mostly. But also to tell us some news." At that point she did feel his shoulder tighten. "Highway 22 is open again all the way out past the lake."

"What about my cabin? Is it okay?"

"We don't know. They didn't say."

"You didn't ask?"

"I did ask. They didn't seem to want to say. They said we should just go out and take a look for ourselves."

"Maybe they don't know. Maybe they didn't see it."

"Yeah. Maybe." But then Virginia felt bad. Because she knew she should tell him the truth, whether it was a happy truth or not. It was his cabin and his truth, and he deserved to hear it. "Actually . . . I asked that, too. And they wouldn't say if they saw it or if they didn't. They just said again that we should drive up there for ourselves."

His shoulder tightened further. Enough so that she removed her hand from it. Shoulders that tight didn't want soothing. At least, not if they belonged to Jody Schilling, they didn't.

"That sounds bad," he said, his voice a near whisper.

"Well . . . we don't know. We shouldn't think the worst before we know. Just go ahead and finish up the dishes, and then Fern and I will drive you out there."

"Fern's going?" he asked. He didn't stop washing to ask. In fact, if anything he worked much faster.

"Do you mind?"

"No. Not at all. I like Fern. I just wondered why she would want to tag along."

"For moral support," Virginia said.

He stopped washing dishes. Stopped all motion. His hands held perfectly still in the soapy water. He turned his head and looked directly into her eyes. "So it's not just me?"

"What's not just you?"

"This. Having to go out and see if my place is okay. That's not something that makes *only me* all stressy and blown apart? That would be a hard thing for *anybody*?"

"Yeah. Of course, honey."

He had asked these types of questions a lot over the past few days. Every time they talked—or "practiced," as he called it—his questions ran to what other people felt. In what ways they were like him and in what ways they were different. Mostly, it turned out, he was more or less like everybody else. Maybe with the volume turned up.

"Huh," he said, and washed the last dish. "Okay, I'm done. Let's go. Let's get this over with."

He shook his apron into the laundry hamper. Grabbed his wrist brace down off the hook.

As they walked through the dining area, Virginia saw him pause in front of the framed newspaper clipping. It was hanging on the wall near the door, the first thing customers saw on their way in. And Jody stopped and looked at it on every trip past. He had every day since Virginia had hung it there. But only recently had his stops become brief. At first he'd stopped long enough to read the text again, though he had read it a dozen times before it was even framed. The last couple of days he stopped maybe long enough to read the title of the piece, "Local Man Protects Diner Owner and Her Dog." Or maybe long enough to look at the photo of the three of them on the walkway in front of Virginia's house.

She waited, to give him his time.

"Oh," he said, looking back at her. "Sorry."

"Don't be sorry," she said. "If I were you, I'd want to see it again, too."

———

The road to the lake was almost completely thawed. Everything was. The world of ice had turned, in just a few days, to a world of half-frozen slush in the morning, then running rivers in streets and gullies and gutters in the afternoon sun.

In a couple of places, Virginia had to slow down to drive through impromptu streams across the road, some as high as her car's hubcaps.

"Such weird weather," she said, half to Fern in the passenger seat beside her, half to Jody sitting rigid and tall and silent in the backseat. "Less than a week ago we were frozen solid and now all of a sudden it's the spring thaw but three months early. Just weird."

"Must be something to that global warming thing," Fern said. "I was mostly set on reserving judgment. But I do believe this year has made me a believer."

Jody said nothing.

Virginia slowed down and rounded a couple more curves in the road. Then she decided to try to draw him out.

"What about you, honey?" she asked over her shoulder.

"Huh? What about me?"

"What're your thoughts on this weather? Think it's part of the whole global warming thing?"

"Oh," he said. "That." It was clear that his mind had been far away. And that it was neither a quick nor an easy task to haul it home again. "My grampa was very opinionated about that. He thought it was all just a big hoax."

"Okay . . ." Virginia said.

She waited for him to go on. He didn't.

"But the question was what *you* think about it," she said.

"Oh. Me. Well, that's interesting." But he didn't say what was interesting about it. At least, not until after a long, drawn-out pause. "Thing is, I'm not really very used to that."

"Used to what? People asking you what you think?"

"Right. That. My grampa had all these opinions. And I never really felt like I should have my own. Or at least I felt like I shouldn't *say* I had my own. I could have, I guess. It would have started a lot of big arguments, I'm sure. But I suppose I could have said when I disagreed with him on things. But I don't like it when people get angry. And it wouldn't have done much good anyway. Grampa always won stuff like that. Nobody could out-angry him. Or out-stubborn him. Or out-opinionate him. After a while I guess it's easier to stop trying."

"But you still didn't answer the question about what you think."

But before he could, Virginia's car swung around the last curve, and the cabin came into view. Virginia didn't realize it was already there to see. Not at first. It was Jody who saw it immediately.

"Oh, no," he said.

Then Virginia's heart sank when she looked where he was undoubtedly looking.

The trees all around the tiny cabin lay on their sides on the hill, shattered. Most of the ice on the branches had melted by day. The leftovers must have refrozen at night, but still the ice was dwindling. Even up here by the lake.

One long, slim pine had fallen with its trunk hitting the apex of the cabin's roof. The tree had broken in that spot, so that half the tree leaned on one side of the roof, half on the other. The roof had held up admirably well under the circumstances. In other words, the cabin was not squashed like a bug. But the roof was clearly caved and damaged in that spot.

Virginia hated to think what the rug underneath that section of roof must look like after all this thawing.

"Well, now, honey," she said. "It could be worse."

"Could be better, too," he said, his voice flat.

She turned right onto March Road and pulled into his thoroughly thawed driveway.

They all three stepped out of the car and stood looking up at the roof in the gleaming afternoon sun. Virginia could hear the sound of running water. Not from any one direction in particular. The melting ice was flowing in every direction. All around them.

"I forgot my keys," Jody said. "They're at your house. That was stupid."

"Well, honey, you didn't know today would be the day the roads got cleared."

"I'm going to climb up the hill behind the cabin so I can see better whether there's water getting through under that tree."

And he set off.

Virginia looked over at Fern.

"He's taking it pretty well," Fern said.

"I think so, too. You think it's livable?"

"I think it's fixable. But I don't think anybody should be living in the place in the meantime. Water'll get in through that broken spot in the roof. Heat'll get out. Not exactly what you might call cozy. Might not even fall within what the county officials call safe. My guess is they'll come out and tag it as unsuitable for habitation. You know. Until repairs are made."

"That can't be cheap," Virginia said. "I wonder if it's insured."

"Now there's a key question," Fern said.

Jody came trotting back down the hill to join them.

"How's it look from up there, honey?" Virginia asked him. She placed one hand on his shoulder as she spoke. The shoulder didn't feel tight.

"Not so good. There's an open spot. If I was standing in that living room, I'd be looking up at the trunk of a tree. With daylight all around it."

"It's fixable, though, honey. Everything is fixable."

"Can't be cheap," he said, mirroring Virginia's earlier statement on the subject almost exactly. Then again, what would anybody say at a time like that?

"I almost hate to ask this, honey, but did your grampa have insurance on the place?"

"Yeah. He did. But it has a high deductible. That's the only way he could afford insurance on his measly Social Security check."

"Still. That's better than not being insured. And you know you have my house in the meantime."

Virginia heard him sigh. But she couldn't read what kind of a sigh he'd meant it to be.

"What do I do about the fact that all my stuff is getting wet?"

Then they all stood silent for a moment, nobody seeming to have a good answer.

"We'll just have to recruit some help," Fern said firmly.

"What kind of help?" Jody asked.

"The kind where people pull together," Fern said. "It's a small town and people pull together. Think how many contractors and tree men and construction men we know from the diner. We just have to get some volunteers out here. They could bring a winch. Or a crane. Or even just a ladder and a good chain saw might do the trick. Some guys could get up there with a saw and cut that trunk into sections and throw the pieces down. And then maybe they could . . . I don't know. There has to be a way to seal a damaged roof. I mean, you're not the first person this ever happened to. I guess they take a tarp or some kind of plastic and nail or strap it down good. You know. Just to tide you over until the real repairs get done."

Silence while the three of them stared at the fallen tree on Jody's roof. As if it were possible to stare a tree down to the ground.

"It's going to be a long time before I save enough money to get that roof repaired," Jody said. But he sounded matter-of-fact. As if he'd just said, "It's going to be cloudy today." Not with the emotion Virginia might have expected. Not as though he had strong feelings about how long it would—or should—take.

"We'll help you, honey," Virginia said. "Me and Fern, sure, but everybody. Well, maybe not everybody will volunteer to help, but I'll bet you those who do will be enough. We'll put it out that you need help, and people will help you. People know you from the diner, and from that piece in the newspaper, and they all think well of you. They'll step up now, when they find out you need them to. And you can stay with me as long as you need to. As long as you like."

She looked over at his face. His eyes looked clear and untroubled, still fixed on the damaged roof. Then he frowned.

"I can't just stay with you forever," he said. It sounded like a question. A tentative, slightly frightened question.

"Why can't you?"

"Well, because . . . you know. You have a life. You're going to want to get back to your own life."

"There's space for you in it," she said.

But he only frowned again. "Now, maybe. But you'll meet another guy."

"I don't know about that. I'm sure in no hurry for that."

"But you will. Sooner or later you will."

"I recommend cats," Fern interjected.

"It doesn't matter," Virginia said. "It doesn't matter one way or another. I wanted to meet a guy because the house was empty and I was alone. Now it's not and I'm not. Maybe I'll date again and maybe I won't. But it doesn't change anything. Lots of women my age have grown children. Most of them, in fact."

"And I bet lots of the guys don't like it when the grown kids are living at home," Jody said. "What if he gets mad because I'm living at home and I don't even seem to have any plans for getting off on my own?"

A silence fell. Fern broke it.

"Then he can damn well get up on that roof and help you fix it," she said.

Jody sighed. Then he smiled. It was a subtle smile. But unmistakable to Virginia, who found the smallest expression of happiness wonderful if found on Jody's face.

"Well, I guess I should be glad for that," he said. "You were right: it could be worse. I could be in this alone. Or the cabin could have been hit by one of those giant trees, and then it would have been smashed to pieces. Leveled. I shouldn't have said what I said about how it could be better. Because everything can always be better. But this is not that bad. I have a nice place to live until it gets fixed. And it's fixable. Like you said."

Then he turned and walked back to Virginia's car. Let himself in and retook his place in the backseat.

Virginia exchanged a look with Fern.

"Pretty damned good attitude," Fern said.

"No kidding. I thought he'd be devastated."

"Don't look a gift horse in the mouth," Fern said. "Come on. Let's get back to town."

———

Jody was quiet on the way back down Highway 22. For at least half of that return trip.

Then he said, "I have to tell you both a secret."

"Okay," Virginia said.

"I was happy when I saw the cabin. Well. Shocked at first. And then a little bit unhappy, but mostly happy. I like it better at your house. It's bigger. And more light comes in. And it's warmer. And we mostly don't have to haul wood if we want to be warm, now that the power's back on. And it's not all empty and silent. You're there, and the phone rings, and Fern comes over, and people knock on the door. And it's more like being alive. I thought what I had before was like being alive. I guess because it was the only kind of being alive I knew. But now after a few days of being alive like this, I didn't want to go back to the way it was before. And I like my job. If I was going to go back and live in the cabin, then I don't know how I would have gotten to work every day. So when I scrambled up the hill and saw that big hole in the roof and knew I couldn't live in it the way it was . . . I felt kind of relieved."

"You could have lived with me even if the cabin was okay. I invited you to more than once."

"Yeah. I know *you* thought I still could. But I don't think *I* thought I still could. I don't like to bother people unless I don't have any other choice."

Virginia smiled to herself in the dark.

"We're going to work on that part of you," she said. "Help you get over it."

"Well, you can work on me all you want," he said. "But I doubt I'll get over it."

They drove in silence for a mile.

"Virginia?" Jody asked tentatively. "I think if scientists say global warming is a real thing, then it's a real thing."

"Nice to hear your opinions for a change," she said.

Epilogue

Three Months Later

Jody pulled the shovel out of the trunk of Virginia's car and carried it to the spot in the garden he had chosen, Worthy wagging along behind.

Virginia and Fern were off on the far edge of the cabin's property, looking down at the lake. As though they'd never seen it before. In time they wandered back over and stood watching him dig.

The weather had warmed into a nice early spring, with the ice mostly breaking up and melting in the lake, and no need for Jody to wear his gloves. In fact, after four or five shovelfuls, he stopped and pulled off his sweater.

"You sure this is where he'd want to be?" Fern asked, lighting a cigarette. "Not in the lake or the river?"

"No," Jody said. "Here. He didn't live in a lake or a river. He lived here. And he loved his garden. So he'd want to be where he was most comfortable. You know. Where he fit."

"You knew him best," Virginia said. "Besides. It's more legally right to put him on private property."

Jody dug the hole in silence for a time.

Then he said, "Virginia? Will you bring me the . . . you know. Will you bring me Grampa so I can see if the hole is big enough?"

"Of course, honey."

Jody leaned on the shovel and panted. Worthy rolled on his back in the dirt where the first blades of grass had poked their heads up for the season.

"It'll be nice to come up here in the summer," he said.

"Sure," Fern said, pulling another drag from her cigarette. "Nothing better than a vacation place by the lake. Especially now it's all fixed up proper."

"We can go swimming," he said. "And Grampa has a little rowboat down at one of the docks there. We used to go fishing. But I don't really like to fish. If I catch one, then I get to feeling bad for him, because he got caught. I start thinking he didn't deserve to end up on a hook. And then I always end up putting him back. But you could go fishing if you wanted."

"Me? I'm invited?"

"Of course you're invited, Fern. That's a silly question."

Virginia showed up then with the wooden box of ashes. Like the size of a cigar box, only heavier wood, and three or four times as high.

"I think it'll fit," she said. She looked down at the box in her hands. "Seems small for a whole person."

"There was less and less of him as time went by," Jody said.

He took the box from her. The hole was plenty deep enough. He reached down and set it on the bottom. Threw one shovelful of dirt over it. Stopped.

"I feel like I should say something," he said. "But I don't know what it should be." Silence for a time as Jody leaned on the shovel. "I don't want to do that thing people always do where they say what a wonderful man he was even though everybody knows it isn't true. But I don't want to insult him or anything. I don't quite know what to do about that."

"Neither Fern nor I ever met the man, honey, so we won't be any help to you, I'm afraid."

"I'm kind of thinking you and Fern are a better family than he was. But that sounds mean to say."

"That's sweet, honey. I didn't know you felt that way."

"Throw in Worthy and I know it for a fact." Jody chewed on his lip a moment. "I think maybe . . . I don't know. I have a question. Can you thank somebody for trying to do something . . . even if the truth is they didn't do it very well? But let's say they tried, probably tried their best. Can you thank them for trying?"

"Sure you can," Fern said.

"Okay, good. Because he really tried hard to make a new family for me. And after Gramma died, he tried to be my only family. He didn't do a good job at it, because it just wasn't in him. But it kept me going to here. To now. So I think I want to thank him for that."

"I could thank him for that, too," Virginia said, "even though I never met him. I could thank him for bringing you back here where I could meet you."

"In that case," Fern said, "you'd have to thank Lloyd for bringing you two together, too."

"No, I draw the line at that," Virginia said. "But that's a nice thought, Jody. And it feels like enough to me."

"It'll have to do," he said.

He shoveled the last of the dirt in silence.

Then he stood back and looked at the mound of loose soil.

"Looks like it wants to be tamped down some. But I can't bring myself to stomp on his grave."

"The weather'll settle it," Fern said. "In time. What about some kind of marker?"

"Like what?"

"Wood cross?"

"Oh, no. Grampa wasn't religious. He wouldn't like that at all."

"Big river stone with something painted on it?"

"I don't know," Jody said. "I think I know he's there and he knows he's there and that feels like enough. I think right now I just want to go home."

He whistled for the dog, who was standing with his front paws on the trunk of an evergreen tree, apparently hoping the squirrel he'd chased up into its branches would come down and volunteer to be eaten.

"Okay," Virginia said. "Fair enough. We'll go home."

The word sounded extra nice to Jody. Maybe it was the way she said it. It buzzed around in his stomach and made him feel warm.

That's when he realized the cabin had always felt like a cabin, and never completely like a home. He'd never been a suitable fit to Florida or vice versa. And if he'd had a good strong home with his father, he was long past remembering it now.

He felt lucky to finally have a place that fit that definition.

"Better at twenty-three than never, I guess," he said under his breath.

"What was that, honey?"

"Oh. Nothing. It was nothing. I was just saying I'm glad to be going home."

About the Author

Catherine Ryan Hyde is the bestselling author of twenty-seven published and forthcoming books. Some of her recent books include *The Language of Hoofbeats, Take Me with You, Where We Belong,* and *Don't Let Me Go.* Her short stories have been published in *Antioch Review, Michigan Quarterly Review, Virginia Quarterly Review, Ploughshares, Glimmer Train,* and the *Sun.* She has received numerous awards, including the Rainbow Award and the British Book Award.

Her bestselling 1999 novel *Pay It Forward* was adapted into a major motion picture and translated into twenty-three languages. Hyde is the founder of the Pay It Forward Foundation.

For more information, please visit catherineryanhyde.com.